THE
ELEVENTH
HOUR

ALSO BY SALMAN RUSHDIE

FICTION

Grimus
Midnight's Children
Shame
The Satanic Verses
Haroun and the Sea of Stories
East, West
The Moor's Last Sigh
The Ground Beneath Her Feet
Fury
Shalimar the Clown
The Enchantress of Florence
Luka and the Fire of Life
Two Years Eight Months and Twenty-Eight Nights
The Golden House
Quichotte
Victory City

NON-FICTION

The Jaguar Smile: A Nicaraguan Journey
Imaginary Homelands: Essays and Criticism 1981–1991
Step Across This Line: Collected Non-Fiction 1992–2002
Languages of Truth: Essays 2003–2020
Joseph Anton: A Memoir
Knife: Meditations After an Attempted Murder

PLAYS

Haroun and the Sea of Stories
(with Tim Supple and David Tushingham)
Midnight's Children
(with Tim Supple and Simon Reade)

SCREENPLAY

Midnight's Children

ANTHOLOGIES

The Vintage Book of Indian Writing, 1947–1997 (co-editor)
Best American Short Stories 2008 (co-editor)

THE ELEVENTH HOUR

SALMAN RUSHDIE

JONATHAN CAPE
LONDON

1 3 5 7 9 10 8 6 4 2

Jonathan Cape, an imprint of Vintage, is part of the
Penguin Random House group of companies

Vintage, Penguin Random House UK, One Embassy Gardens,
8 Viaduct Gardens, London SW11 7BW

penguin.co.uk/vintage
global.penguinrandomhouse.com

First published in Great Britain by Jonathan Cape in 2025
First published in the United States of America by Random House in 2025

Printed and bound in Great Britain by Clays Ltd, Elcograf S.p.A.

The authorised representative in the EEA is Penguin Random House Ireland,
Morrison Chambers, 32 Nassau Street, Dublin D02 YH68

A CIP catalogue record for this book is available from the British Library

HB ISBN 9781787336049
TPB ISBN 9781787336056

Penguin Random House is committed to a sustainable future
for our business, our readers and our planet. This book is made
from Forest Stewardship Council® certified paper.

This book is dedicated
to Steve and Annie Murphy
and
to Eliza,
of course

Contents

In the South

The day Junior fell down began like any other day: the explosion of heat rippling the air, the trumpeting sunlight, the traffic's tidal surges, the prayer chants in the distance, the cheap film music rising up from the floor below, the pelvic thrusts of an "item number" dancing across a neighbor's TV; a child's cry, a mother's rebuke, unexplained laughter, scarlet expectorations, bicycles, the newly plaited hair of schoolgirls, the smell of strong coffee, a green wing flashing in a tree. Senior and Junior, two very old men, opened their eyes in their bedrooms on the fourth floor of a sea-green building on a leafy lane, just out of sight of Elliot's Beach, where, that evening, the young would congregate, as they always did, to perform the rites of youth, not far from the village of the fisherfolk, who had no time for such frivolity. The poor were puritans by night and day. As for the old, they had rites of their own and did not need to wait for evening. With the sun stabbing at them through their window blinds, the two old men struggled to their feet and lurched out onto their adjacent verandas, emerging at the same moment, like characters in an ancient tale, trapped in fateful coincidences, unable to escape the consequences of chance.

Almost at once they began to speak. Their words were not new. These were ritual speeches, obeisances to the new day, offered in call-and-response format, like the rhythmic dialogues or "duels" of the virtuosi of Carnatic music during the annual December festival.

"Be thankful we are men of the south," said Junior, stretching and yawning. "Southerners are we, in the south of our city in the south of our country in the south of our continent. God be praised. We are warm, slow, and sensual guys, not like the cold fishes of the north."

Senior, scratching first his belly and then the back of his neck, contradicted him at once. "In the first place," he said, "the south is a fiction, existing only because men have agreed to call it that. Suppose men had imagined the earth the other way up! We would be the northerners then. The universe does not understand up and down; neither does a dog. To a dog there is no north and south. And in the second place, you're not that warm a character, and a woman would laugh to hear you call yourself sensual—but you are slow, that is beyond a doubt."

This was how they were: they fought, going at each other like ancient wrestlers whose left feet were tied together at the ankles. The rope that bound them so tightly was their name. By a curious chance—which they had come to think of as "destiny," or, as they more often called it, a "curse"—they shared a name, a long name like so many names of the south, a name neither of them cared to speak. By banishing the name, by reducing it to its initial letter, V., they made the rope invisible, which did not mean it did not exist. They echoed each other in other ways—their voices were high, they were of similarly wiry build and medium height, they were both nearsighted, and, after lifetimes of priding themselves on the quality of their teeth, they had both surrendered to the humiliating inevitability of dentures—but it was the unused name, that symmetrical V., the Name That Could Not Be Spoken, that had joined them together for decades.

The two old men did not share a birthday, however. One was

seventeen days older than the other. That must have been how "Senior" and "Junior" got started, even though the nicknames had been in use for so long that nobody could now remember who originally thought them up. V. Senior and Junior they had become, Junior V. and Senior V. forevermore, quarreling to the death. They were eighty-one years old. If old age was thought of as an evening, ending in midnight oblivion, they were well into the eleventh hour.

"You look terrible," Junior told Senior, as he did every morning. "You look like a man who is only waiting to die."

Senior—nodding gravely, and also speaking in accordance with their private tradition—responded, "That is better than looking, as you do, like a man who is still waiting to live."

Neither man slept well anymore. At night they lay on hard beds without pillows, and behind their closed eyelids their unsettled thoughts ran in opposite directions. Of the two men, Senior had lived by far the fuller life. He had been the youngest of ten brothers, all of whom had excelled in their chosen field—as athletes, scientists, teachers, soldiers, priests. He himself had begun his career as a college-champion long-distance runner, then risen to a senior position with the railway company, and for years he had traveled the railroads, covering tens of thousands of miles, to assure himself and the authorities that the proper safety levels were being maintained. He had married a kind woman and fathered six daughters and three sons, each of whom had proved fertile in his or her turn, providing him with a haul of thirty-three grandchildren. His nine brothers had sired a total of thirty-three more children, his nephews and nieces, who had inflicted upon him no fewer than one hundred and eleven further relatives. To many men this would have been proof of his good fortune, for a man blessed with two hundred and five family members was a rich man indeed, but abundance gave an ascetically inclined man like Senior a permanent low-level headache.

"If I had been sterile," he told Junior frequently, "how peaceful life would have been."

After his retirement Senior had been one of a group of ten friends who met every day to discuss politics, chess, poetry, and music at a local Besant Nagar coffeehouse, and several of his commentaries on these topics had been published in the excellent daily newspaper based in the city. Among his friends was the editor of that newspaper, as well as one of the editor's employees—a celebrated local figure, a bit of a firebrand and too much of a boozer, but the creator of wonderfully grotesque political cartoons. Then there was the city's finest astrologer, who had been trained as an astronomer but had come to believe that the true messages of the stars could not be received through a telescope; and a fellow who for many years had fired the starting pistol at the racetrack's well-attended meets; and so on. Senior had reveled in their company, telling his wife that it was a grand thing for a man to have friends from whom he could learn something new every day. But now everyone was dead. One by one his friends had all gone up in flames, and the coffeehouse that might have preserved their memory had been torn down too.

Of the ten brothers only he remained, and their wives, too, were long departed. Even his kindly wife was dead, and in his great old age he had remarried, finding himself, through a marriage broker, a widow with a wooden leg, a union of convenience for them both, with which they were both discontented. Instead of unhappy solitude they found themselves trapped in unhappy togetherness. He behaved toward her with an irritability that surprised his children and grandchildren. "Not having much choice at my age," he would say to her hurtfully, "I got you." She retaliated by ignoring his simplest demands, even requests for water, which no civilized person should ever refuse to fetch when asked to do so. Her name was Aarthi, but he never used it. Nor did he call her by a diminutive or an endearment. To him she was always "Woman" or "Wife."

He endured the multiple health problems of the very old, the daily penances of bowel and urethra, of back and knee, the milkiness climbing in his eyes, the breathing troubles, the nightmares, the slow failing of the soft machine. His days emptied out into tedious inaction. Once he had given lessons in mathematics, singing, and the Vedas to pass the time. But his students all had gone away. There remained the wife with the wooden leg, the blurry television set, and Junior. It was not, by a long chalk, enough. Each morning he regretted that he had not died in the night.

Of his two hundred and five younger family members quite a few had already gone to their fiery rest. He forgot exactly how many, and their names, inevitably, eluded him. Many of the survivors came to see him and treated him with gentleness and care. When he said he was ready to die, which was often, their faces took on hurt expressions and their bodies sagged or stiffened, depending on their natures, and they spoke to him reassuringly, encouragingly, and, of course, in injured tones, of the value of a life so full of love. But love had begun to annoy him, like everything else. His was a family of mosquitoes, he thought, a buzzing swarm, and love was their itchy bite.

"If only there was a coil one could light to keep one's relations away," he told Junior. "If only there was a net around one's cot that kept them out."

.   .   .

Junior's life had been a disappointment to him. He had not expected to be ordinary. He had been raised by doting parents who had instilled in him a sense of destiny and entitlement, but he had turned out to be an average sort of fellow, doomed by average academic achievement to a life of clerical work in the offices of the municipal water board. His above-average dreams, of long-distance road travel, rail travel, air travel, had long since been abandoned; yet he was not an unhappy man. The discovery of his affliction by the incurable disease of mediocrity might have cowed a less ebullient spirit, but he remained bright-eyed, with a ready smile for the world.

Still, in spite of his apparent enthusiasm for life, there was a certain deficiency in the energy department. He did not run but walked, and walked slowly—had done so even in the distant years of his youth. He abhorred exercise and had a way of poking gentle fun at those who took it. Nor did he interest himself in politics or the all-pervasive popular culture of the cinema and the music it spawned. In all significant particulars he had failed to be a participant in the parade of life. He had not married. The great events of eight decades had managed to occur without any effort on his part to help them along. He had stood by and watched as an empire fell and a nation rose, and avoided expressing an opinion on the matter. He was a man at a desk. Maintaining the flow of the municipality's water was a sufficient challenge for him. Yet he gave every appearance of being a man for whom living was still a joy. He had been an only child, and so there were few relatives to look out for him in his advanced years. Senior's immense family had adopted him long ago and brought him tiffin and attended to his needs.

The question of the dividing wall between Senior's and Junior's adjoining apartments was sometimes raised by the visiting hordes of Senior's kin: whether it should be taken down so that the two old men could share their lives more easily. On this matter, however, both Junior and Senior spoke with one voice.

"No!" said Junior.

"Over my dead body," Senior clarified.

"Which would make the whole exercise pointless, anyhow," said Junior, as if that settled things.

The wall remained in place.

Junior had one friend, D'Mello, a man twenty years younger than himself, an old colleague from his water board days. D'Mello had grown up in another city, Mumbai the legendary bitch-city, *urbs prima in Indis,* and had to be spoken to in English. Whenever D'Mello visited Junior, Senior sulked and refused to speak, even though, secretly, he was proud of his prowess in what he called "the world's number one tongue." He did not admit the reasons for his sulking, his dual resentments, firstly of the intrusion into the rhythm of his quarrelsome intimacy with Junior, and secondly of the advent into his days of so much liveliness, which reminded him of the chatterbox friends he had lost. Junior understood, and tried to hide from Senior how much he looked forward to D'Mello's comings, because the younger man bubbled with a kind of cosmopolitan brio that Junior found inspirational. D'Mello always arrived with stories, sometimes angry accounts of injustices against the poor in a Mumbai slum, sometimes funny anecdotes about the characters who took their ease at the Wayside Inn, the famous Mumbai café in the Kala Ghoda area, named after a no-longer-present equestrian statue, "the Black Horse district from which the black horse has been exiled."* D'Mello fell in love with movie stars (from a distance, of course) and provided gory details of the killing spree of a not-yet-arrested madman in the district of

*Since the time of these events, a black horse has returned, but without its colonialist rider.

Trombay. "The miscreant is still at large!" he cried gaily. His conversation was littered with wonderful names. *Worli Sea Face, Bandra, Hornby Vellard, Breach Candy, Pali Hill.* These places sounded altogether more exotic than the prosaic localities to which Junior was accustomed: Besant Nagar, Adyar, Mylapore.

D'Mello's most heartbreaking Mumbai story was his tale of the great poet of the city, who had surrendered to Alzheimer's disease. The poet still walked to his small magazine-infested office every day, without knowing why he went there. His feet knew the way and so he went and sat looking into space until it was time to go home again and his feet walked him back to his shabby residence through the evening crowds massing outside Churchgate station, the jasmine sellers, the hustling urchins, the roar of the BEST buses, the girls on their Vespas, the sniffing, hungry dogs.

When D'Mello was present and talking, Junior had the sense that he was living another, very different life, a life of action and color, that he was becoming, vicariously, the type of man he had never been, dynamic, passionate, engaged with the world. Senior, observing the light in Junior's eyes, inevitably became cross. One day when D'Mello was speaking of Mumbai and its people with his habitual, gesticulating fervor, Senior, breaking his rule of silence, snapped at him in English: "Why your body doesn't return there only since your head has already gone?" But D'Mello shook his head sadly. He no longer had a foothold in his city of origin. Only in his dreams and conversation was it still his home. "I will die here," he answered Senior, "in the south, among sour fruits like you."

Senior's wife, the lady with the wooden leg, increasingly took her revenge upon her unloving husband by filling their apartment with family members. She, too, came from a large family of hundreds of persons, and she began most particularly to invite her younger relations, the great-nephews and great-nieces, with their wives and husbands and especially their babies in tow. The presence in the small apartment of babies, toddlers, and high-speed pigtailed girls and slow plump boys in large numbers fulfilled her own matriarchal ambitions, and also, very satisfyingly, drove Senior wild. It was the babies-in-law that really got his goat. The babies-in-law rattled their rattles and giggled their giggles and screamed their baby screams. They slept, and then Senior had to be quiet, or they woke up, and then Senior could not hear himself think. They ate and defecated and puked, and the smell of excrement and vomit remained in the apartment, even when the babies-in-law had gone, mingling with a smell that Senior disliked even more: that of talcum powder.

"At the end of life," he complained to Junior, in whose apartment he often took refuge from the squalling hordes of his and his wife's blood kin, "nothing stinks worse than the smells of life's sweet beginning, of bibs and ribbons and warm bottled milk and formula, and farting, talcumed behinds."

Junior could not help replying, "Soon you also will be helpless and need someone to tend to your natural functions. Babydom is not only our past but our future too." The thunderous expression on Senior's face revealed that the words had hit their mark.

For, it's true, they were both fortunate men. They were neither wholly blind nor wholly deaf, and their minds had not betrayed them like the Mumbai poet's. The food they ate was soft and easily digestible, but it was not old buggers' mush. Above all they were still ambulatory, still able to climb slowly down their building's stairs to street level once a week, and then to shuffle along, helped by walking sticks and frequent little rest stops, to the local post office, where they cashed their pension slips. They did not need to do this. Many of the young who thronged Senior's apartment, driving him next door to quarrel with Junior, would readily have dashed down the street to cash the checks for the frail old gentlemen. But the gentlemen did not care to allow the young to dash for them. It was a point of pride to cash one's own pension slip—on this, if on nothing else, they agreed: to travel under one's own steam to the counter where, behind a metal grille, a postal services operative waited to dispense the weekly sum that was their return for a lifetime's service. "You can see the respect in the fellow's expression," Senior said loudly to Junior, who kept mum, because what he saw behind the grille was something more like boredom or contempt.

To Senior the pension trip was an act of validation; the weekly sum, small as it was, honored his deeds, transmuting into banknotes society's gratitude for his life. Junior thought of the weekly journey more as an act of defiance. "You care nothing for me," he once flatly said to the face behind the grille. "It means nothing to you to count out the cash. But when your turn comes to stand where I stand, then you will comprehend." One of the few privileges of very old age was that you were allowed to say exactly what you thought, even to strangers. Nobody told you to keep your mouth shut, and few people had the guts to answer back. "They think we will soon be dead," Junior thought, "so there's no point getting into a fight with us."

He understood the nature of the contempt in the eyes of the post office employee. It was the scorn of life for death.

On the day that Junior fell down, he and Senior set forth on their errand at their customary midmorning hour. It was late in the year. The local Christians, D'Mello included, had just finished celebrating their prophet's birth, and the consequent proximity of New Year's Eve, with its promise of a future—of, indeed, an interminable future in which a sequence of such Eves stretched out at their predetermined intervals toward infinity—was bothering Senior. "Either I will die in the next five days, meaning that there will be no new year for me," he told Junior, "or else a year will begin in which my end will surely come, which is hardly a thing to look forward to." Junior sighed. "Your gloom and doom," he moaned, "will be the death of me." This sentence struck them both as so funny that they laughed heartily, and then had to huff and puff for breath. They were descending their building's staircase at this point, so the laughter was not without danger. They clung to the banisters and panted. Junior was lower down than Senior, past the second-floor landing. This was how they customarily descended, some distance apart, so that if one of them should fall he would not drag the other down with him. They were too unsteady to trust each other. Trust, too, was a casualty of age.

In the front yard they paused briefly by the golden shower tree that stood there. They had watched it grow from a tiny shoot to its present sixty-foot grandeur. It grew quickly and though they did not say so, this rapid growth disturbed them, suggesting, as it did, the speed of the passing of the years. The Indian laburnum, that was another name for it, a name among many names; it was *konrai* in their own, southern language, *amaltas* in the tongue of the north, *Cassia fistula* in the language of flowers and trees. "It has stopped growing now," Junior said, approvingly, "having understood that eternity is better than progress. In the eye of God, Time is eternal. This, even animals and trees can comprehend. Only men have the illusion that Time moves." Senior snorted. "The tree has stopped," he said, "because that is in its nature, just as it is in ours. We too will stop soon enough."

He placed his gray trilby upon his head and moved through the gate into the lane. Junior was bareheaded and traditionally dressed in a white veshti and a long blue-checked shirt and sandals, but Senior liked to go to the post office in the guise of a European gentleman, wearing a suit and hat and twirling a silver-handled walking stick, like the man in the old song he liked, *who walked along the Bois de Boulogne with an independent air,* the Man Who Broke the Bank at Monte Caaar-lo.

The shady lane gave way to the brilliant sun-soaked street, where the noise of traffic drowned out the softer music of the sea. The beach was just four blocks away, but the city didn't care. Junior and Senior shuffled slowly past the homeopathy shop, the pharmacy where prescription drugs could easily be bought without troubling any doctor, the general store with its jars of nuts and chillies, its tins of clarified butter and imported cheese, and the sidewalk bookstall with its pirated editions of popular books brazenly on display, and set their sights on the traffic lights a hundred yards ahead. There they would have to cross the lawless main road, where a dozen forms of transport battled for space. After that a left turn, and another hundred yards of walking, and then they would be at the post office. A five-minute journey for the young, half an hour each way minimum for the two old men. The sun was behind them, and both men, inching slowly forward, were looking down at their shadows, which lay side by side upon the dusty pavement. "Like lovers," they both thought; but neither of them spoke, their habits of opposition being too ingrained to permit them to express so fond an idea.

Afterward Senior regretted that he had not spoken. "He was my shadow," he said to the woman with the wooden leg, "and I am his. Two shadows, each shadowing the other, to that we were reduced, that is so. The old move through the world of the young like shades, unseen, of no concern. But the shadows see each other and know who they are. So it was with us. We knew, let me say this, who we were. And now I am a shadow without a shadow to shadow. He who knew me knows nothing now and therefore I am not known. What else, woman, is death?"

"The day you stop talking," she replied. "The day these tom-fool notions stop dropping from your mouth. When your mouth itself has been eaten by the fire. That will be the day." It was the most she had said to him for over a year, and he understood from it that she hated him, and was sorry that Junior was the one who had fallen.

It happened because of the girls on the Vespa, the girls on their new Vespa making their way to college, pigtails horizontal behind them as giggling they rode toward murder. Their faces were vivid in Senior's mind, the long thin one driving the scooter and her chubbier friend behind her holding on *for dear life*. But life was not dear to such persons. Life was cheap, like a garment idly flung away after a single use, like their music, like their thoughts. This was how he judged them, and when he discovered afterward that they were not at all like his unjust characterization it was too late to change his mind. They were serious students, the thin one of electrical engineering and the other of architecture, and, far from being unaffected by the accident, they both went into dreadful, guilt-ridden shock, and for weeks afterward they would be seen almost every day standing silently with lowered heads across the lane from Junior's home, just standing there, heads bowed in expiation, waiting for forgiveness. But there was nobody to forgive them; the one who would have done so had died, and the one who could have done so would not. Haughty Senior looked down on them with disdain. What did they think a human life was? Could it be so cheaply bought off? No, it could not. Let them stand there for a thousand years, it would not be long enough.

The Vespa had wobbled, no doubt about that; its young driver was inexperienced and it had wobbled too close to where Junior stood, waiting to cross the road. Of late he had been complaining of a weakness in his ankles. He had said, "Sometimes when I get out of bed I do not think they will bear my weight." He had also said, "Sometimes when I go down the stairs I worry that an ankle will turn. I never used to worry about my ankles, but now I do." Senior had responded adversarially, as was customary. "Worry about your interior," he'd said. "Your kidneys or liver will fail long before your ankle does."

However, he had been wrong. The Vespa had come too close and Junior had leapt back. When he had landed on his left foot his ankle had indeed turned, and that had induced a second half leap, as Junior tried to save himself. So it had been a strange fall, more like a hop and a skip, but at the end there was the tumble, and Junior, toppling backward to the sidewalk, had bumped his head, not hard enough to be knocked out but, still, hard enough. Air left him in a great whoosh as he clattered down.

Senior was too busy shouting at the terrified girls on the Vespa, calling them assassins and worse things, to notice the moment when the thing happened that must happen to us all in the end, when the last little puff of vapor pops out of our mouths and dissolves into fetid air. "The spirit, whatever it is," Junior used to say. "I do not believe in an immortal soul, but I also do not believe we are only flesh and bone. I believe in a mortal soul, the noncorporeal essence of ourselves, lurking within our flesh like a parasite, flourishing when we flourish, and dying when we die." Senior was more formal in his religious beliefs. He read the ancient texts often, and the sound of Sanskrit was for him akin to the music of the spheres—the subtlety and profundity of those texts, which were capable of questioning whether even the creative entity itself understood its creation. Once he had discussed these texts with his students, but there had not been any students for a long time and he had been obliged to keep his own counsel on the grand matters of being. The ancient ambiguities gave him joy; Junior's lay-philosophical invention of a soul that died was banal by comparison.

So Senior thought and, ranting as he was, he missed the tell-tale little puff of air that might have persuaded him to think again. An instant later there was no Junior anymore, just a body on the sidewalk, a thing to be disposed of before the heat of the tropics did its malodorous worst. There was only one thing to be done. Senior reached into his friend's pocket and took out the pension slip. Then, sending the Vespa girls to his apartment to speak to his wife and relations to tell them the news, he set off on his mission alone. There would be time for death to be respected. In the traditions of the Palakkad Aiyars or Iyers, from whom both he and Junior were descended, the rites in honor of the dead lasted for thirteen days.

The next morning in the south of the planet, far away from Senior's hometown, but not far enough, there was a great earthquake under the ocean's surface and the mighty water, answering the agony of the land beneath it with an agony of its own, gathered itself up into a series of huge waves and hurled its pain across the globe. Two such waves traveled across the Indian Ocean and at a quarter to seven in the morning Senior felt his bed begin to shake. It was a violent and puzzling vibration because there had never been an earthquake in this city. Senior got up and went out onto his veranda. The veranda next door was empty, of course. Junior was gone. Junior was ashes now. The neighbors were all out in the lane, improperly dressed, hugging blankets around their shoulders. Everyone had a radio on. The earthquake's epicenter had been near the distant island of Sumatra. The tremors stopped and people went on with their day. Two and a quarter hours later the first giant wave arrived.

The coastal areas were smashed. Elliot's Beach, Marina Beach, the beachfront houses, the cars, the Vespas, the people. At ten o'clock in the morning the sea made a second such assault. The numbers of the dead grew. The lost dead, taken by the sea, the marooned dead, washed up on the remnants of the sands, the broken dead, everywhere, the dead. The waves did not get as far as Senior's building. Senior's lane was undamaged. Everybody lived.

Except Junior.

It was fortunate that the waves arrived at Elliot's Beach in the morning. The romantic young who laughed and flirted there in the evenings would all have been slain if the waves had come at night. So young friends and lovers survived. The fishermen were not so lucky. The nearby fishing village—its name was Nochikuppam—ceased to exist. A seaside temple survived, but the fishermen's huts and catamarans and many of the fisherfolk themselves were lost. After that day the fishermen who survived said they hated the sea and refused to return to it. For a long time it was hard to buy fish in the markets.

Senior did not like the Japanese word *tsunami* everyone used to name the waters of death. To him the waves were Death itself and needed no other name. Death had come to his city, had come a-harvesting and taken Junior and many strangers away. In the aftermath of the waves there grew up all around him, like a forest, the noises and actions that inevitably follow on calamity, the good behavior of the kind, the bad behavior of the desperate and the powerful, the surging aimless crowds. He was lost in the forest of the aftermath and saw nothing except the empty veranda next to his own and in the lane below the girls with the lowered heads. News came that D'Mello was among the lost. Perhaps he was not dead. Perhaps he had simply gone home, at last, to his storied city of Mumbai on the country's other coast, that city which was neither of the north nor of the south but a frontier ville, the greatest, most wondrous, and most dreadful of all such places, the megalopolis of the borderlands, the place of in-between. Or, on the other hand, perhaps D'Mello had drowned and Death, swallowing him, had denied his body the Christian dignity of a grave.

He, Senior, was the one who had asked for death. Yet Death had left him alive, had taken so many others, had taken even Junior and D'Mello, but left him untouched. The world was meaningless. There was no meaning to be found in it, he thought. The texts were empty and his eyes were blind. Perhaps he said some of this aloud. He may even have shouted out. The girls in the lane below were looking up at him and the green birds in the golden shower tree were disturbed. Then all of a sudden he imagined that across the way, on the empty adjacent veranda, he saw a shadow move. He had cried out, *Why not me?*, and in response a shadow had flickered where Junior used to stand.

Death and life were just adjacent verandas. Senior stood on one of them as he always had, and on the other, continuing their tradition of many years, was Junior, his shadow, his namesake, arguing.

The Musician
of Kahani

1

The story of the discordant musician and the billion-dollar baby began in a time of unsettling change. At first we didn't notice that change was in the air. The cars, the buses, the trams all wove their familiar paths through the city, and our lives, too, moved in unchanging patterns, our Sunday morning constitutionals around the Racecourse, our canasta evenings around one another's baize-topped card tables, our golf at the Willingdon Club. Then without any warning—or perhaps there were warnings we were too set in our ways to notice—the names began to change. And after the name changes, everything else began to be different too.

Our city's name was changed some years before the millennium came along to change time itself. Many older people, myself included, disapproved when the old place stopped being the old place and became the new place. It was wrong to tamper with history, we elders said, and rejecting the past was a dangerous thing to do. The old name had been a fine name, whereas the new name was alien to our ears. I decided to rename the place myself, just for myself, and began in my writing and conversation to call it "Kahani," or "Story," because it's where my stories came from. At times this felt almost reprehensible, as if I was elevating my personal untruth above the truth itself, as if a liar (me) was replacing truth and brazenly celebrating a lie.

However, I persisted, and instead of the colorless names of politicians that were replacing the old street names, I began in my imagination to change these names too, as I pleased, replacing the old colonial names with those of our beloved poets, storytellers, fictional characters of page and screen, or the names of films and books themselves. Nissim Ezekiel Marg, Sholay Chowk, Valmiki Drive (a.k.a. "The Bard's Necklace"), Amar Akbar Anthony Road (rapidly abbreviated to AAA Road), Vyasa Vellard, Tendulkar Terrace, Malgudi Circle sprang into being in my head, as also did—because this has always been a cosmopolitan city, facing outward to wider worlds—William Shakespeare Bunder, Dahl Market, Bond Bazaar, Petit Prince Parade, and Makioka Row, among a continually growing number of new Drives, Margs, and Chowks. So Kahani is here to stay, at least it is for me, and, after all, the city itself is and has always been a kind of wonder tale.

The twentieth century ended. It ended on all those streets and on many others too. It ended in the Breach Candy neighborhood of our city. And at midnight, the approved hour for miraculous births in our part of the world, a baby was born to a Breach Candy family, and a new thousand-year era began. The millennium baby was a girl, which would, regrettably, have disappointed some parents, but this baby's parents were overjoyed. Her father, Raheem Contractor, a mathematics professor at the city's university, was fifty years old and had frankly become uncertain of his ability to father a child of any sort. Her mother, Meena Contractor, was also numerically expert, although less "pure" and more pragmatic, less interested in abstract problems and more concerned with the application of her skills to the challenges of the modern world, such as the new field of information technology. She was . . . let us just say . . . younger than her husband. I am of the generation, perhaps the last such generation, that believes it impolite to discuss a lady's age. But, if you insist . . . twenty years younger. There was only a crescent moon that night, the night of the millennium—a third-night new moon, according to the almanacs—but it shone brightly nonetheless, and Raheem and Meena named their daughter after the prophetic moonlight. Chandni. Chandni Contractor. That's our girl.

Allow me to clear up one thing right away. This Chandni was not the billion-dollar baby that has been mentioned. No, no. She would grow up to be, one might say, not one but two significant characters. First she became the celebrated Musician of Kahani. And after that, as we shall see, she became That Baby's mother.

Breach Candy, that's a nice neighborhood. Hospital, swimming pool, fancy shops, Sophia College, Art Deco buildings, Scandal Point, gardens, sea view. The name itself, also. Nobody could agree on its origins, but all concurred on its niceness. So in our time of change it remained unaltered. The people living there, nice people. All kinds, all religions, Hindu Muslim Parsi Christian Jain and one-two Sikhs, getting along. Old-young, side by side. Well-to-do, for sure, well-off families, fashionable even, but not rich like the folks on the high ground, up on "those" parts of Malabar Hill or most of Altamount Road. Dear me, no. That's rich-rich-rich up there, big-big-rich, for which "rich" is too poor a word. Down here a single rich will more than suffice.

Meena Contractor had always wanted to live in Breach Candy, but on academic salaries and without family wealth, it was impossible. At first, after their marriage, the Contractors rented an apartment in a more modest part of town, near the Kahani Central railway station, and it wasn't so bad. But the heart wants what it wants, does it not. And sometimes the heart will find a way.

2

I t would, of course, have been highly improper of the professor to pursue his brightest student while she was still his student, so he waited until after her graduation to ask, with much diffidence, if she would consider dining with him at the Gaylord restaurant on Churchgate (old name, still used in common parlance), and immediately blushed and apologized and called himself a fool, and was then astonished when she said yes, she had always wanted to try the famous chicken Kiev served there. After that first evening, when Raheem was tongue-tied by love and Meena filled the silence with stories, the twenty-year age gap seemed irrelevant to them both, and Meena's father, who was the same age as the professor, proved to be surprisingly broad-minded about it. "I see that you are happy," he told his daughter, "and if that's what he does for you, then I am happy too." Her mother was more doubtful but didn't argue. (These parents lived in another city, the capital of the neighboring state to the north, also less attractively renamed according to the fashion of the times. They rarely visited Kahani, and may safely be dismissed from these pages.)

For the next eight years Raheem and Meena were indeed happy, except that the child they both wanted seemed to be in no rush to arrive.

Mr. Raheem Contractor was a man of few words, but he was eloquent in numbers. Indeed, from a young age, he had found that numbers had formed the basis of his philosophy of life. "Words are treacherous, dear wife," he told Meena, "but with numbers one is on solid ground. One cannot believe at least half of what men say, but two and two will always equal four." Mrs. Meena Contractor was in everyone's opinion a person of great forbearance. She had heard her husband's philosophy expressed on an almost daily basis throughout their marriage, yet she had not tired of it, or at least she had never expressed her displeasure at the repetitions. She took a fine silk cushion and brocaded it with the family motto. *Two plus two will always equal four.* "And one plus one is always two," she often answered her husband, "and two is always us."

Then a sadness began to grow in Raheem Contractor, and his wife was unable to assuage it. For much of his adult life he had given such spare time as his teaching work allowed to join the quest for a proof of Fermat's Last Theorem. More than three hundred years had passed since Pierre de Fermat proposed that "for any integer $n > 2$, the equation $a^n + b^n = c^n$ has no positive integer solutions" but left behind no worked-out proof. This assertion, incomprehensible to ordinary people, including the present author, whose age increasingly prevents him from grasping complex ideas, had vexed the minds of the finest mathematicians down the centuries.

Raheem had examined and rejected all the major attempts to untangle the thorny conundrum, delving into the intricacies of the Yang-Mills Equations, the Riemann Hypothesis, the P Versus NP Problem, the Hodge Conjecture, the Navier-Stokes Equations, the Poincaré Conjecture, and the Birch and Swinnerton-Dyer Conjecture, and found them all wanting. At last, after many long years, he had begun to understand that the answer lay within the Taniyama-Shimura Conjecture, sub-sequently known as the Modularity Theorem, and was on the verge of publishing his proof when he was beaten to the punch by a British scholar, who became famous and was showered with honors and awards, while Raheem Contractor remained anonymous in his university office. He was inconsolable, and his lifelong faith in numbers, and in his ability to use them as the building blocks of a good life, began to dissolve. He became vulnerable to other forms of belief.

In the time that followed, his loving wife brought him two pieces of good news that she hoped might brighten his spirits, but did not. The first had to do with money. The second, which came two years later, was that she was finally pregnant, and the future Chandni Contractor, the Musician of Kahani, was on her way.

First things first:

"A man came to the flat today," Meena told Raheem one evening in approximately 1998. "An American man. A big floppy-haired type with a red-and-blue checked shirt and round eyeglasses, wearing shorts. He looked like a schoolboy that somehow got enlarged and became a giant."

"What does a giant American schoolboy want with my wife?" Raheem asked, a little more suspiciously than neces-sary.

She cast her gaze down toward the floor because she did not want her husband to feel belittled or in some way attacked in his manhood by what she was about to tell him.

"He wanted," she finally said, "to offer me one hundred mil-lion dollars."

Raheem was shocked. "And what did you do to deserve that, or should I say what did he want you to do?" Some years earlier they had both seen the American movie in which the actress

Demi Moore is offered one million dollars for one night of sex. Surely *one hundred* million greenbacks would require far more indecency than that?

"He wanted me to sell him TALIB. My firstborn child. He flew here from California in a private jet just to buy it."

TALIB was Meena Contractor's pride and joy, a new technology program of the type that were just beginning to be known as "search engines." Most of these engines worked poorly, not finding anything of much use to the searcher. But TALIB worked. It was like a magic door that opened into a new universe of infinite possibility. She had only just launched a trial version, what she was learning to call a "beta" version, which she pronounced *béta,* which meant "son." She had given birth to TALIB, and it was quickly acquiring a reputation. And now here was this giant schoolboy, this moneybags in short pants, with American greed in his myopic eyes.

"Let me explain it to you in this way," the schoolboy said. "You have built something very good, and I want it, and I can acquire it in one of two ways. Either I give you one hundred million dollars today, and you and your family can be comfortable, more than comfortable, for the rest of your lives, or, if you refuse, then I put my best team of engineers to work, and in a short period of time they will have worked out everything we need to build your TALIB ourselves, and once that's done you don't get a fucking dime."

"Can I think about it," she said. "I need time."

"Take all the time you need," the schoolboy said. "But I have to leave in twenty minutes."

"So what did you 'think,'" Raheem Contractor asked, "without even telephoning me to discuss."

"I sold TALIB," she said. "I gave over all of it and now we are rich and we don't have to live here anymore and we can buy that place I like in Breach Candy and there's really nothing to discuss, and you can try, you can really try, to be happy."

"You called TALIB your *béta*," said Raheem.

"True," she said. "But I also do know the difference between a virtual offspring and a flesh-and-blood child."

3

I f you drive up Warden Road past Scandal Point, and you go around the little bend there, you'll see on the right a small run of shops. (If you pass the Breach Candy Swimming Baths on the left, you've gone too far.) When I was young, seven decades ago, there was a Band Box Laundry there, and a jeweler's shop, and in between them—do you see it?—a narrow, leafy lane running (slowly) up a small slope. Follow that road, follow it up that hill as it curves around to the left, trots along for a while, and then comes to a halt, a dead end, looking down on Warden Road and out to the Arabian Sea beyond, and at that endpoint four quaint gabled and turreted villas still stand, two on each side, like old aunties having tea and exchanging the latest gossip. Now you have entered the magic space of my childhood—and not only of my childhood but of my richest imaginings and happiest dreams. Wherever I find myself, and I have lived in many places in my long life, my heart very often finds itself on that walk up Westfield Compound Lane. Many of the stories I have told were born here. I think this will be the last such story. It's late in the evening, and almost time to sleep. The sun sets rapidly in the tropics. But before I say good night, I see the Contractors approaching the very house in which I grew up, the last villa on the right, at the very end of the lane, in what, long ago, was named the Westfield Estate. A name that has resisted alteration.

The house looks different these days. A second set of verandas has been added, and the pitch of the roof has been flattened out to allow an extra floor to be built. It is this top-floor apartment, which didn't exist when we lived in the house, and which boasts a long view of the Arabian Sea, that Meena Contractor has set her heart on. And now they have the money to buy it—*she* has the money—and buy it they do.

Did Meena's sudden access to serious money delight her husband? Or did it deepen his depression and further erode his sense of self?

What do you think?

The second thing was the baby girl, the future Musician. The millennium's gift.

She revealed her true nature almost immediately. "She doesn't laugh a lot," Raheem noted when she was still a baby. "Her default look is, I guess you might call it, sort of grave. And when she does look cheerful, she gives that strange little smile." Meena said that was okay with her. "I like it that she's already showing us who she is and who she's going to be."

The true revelation came when Chandni was four years old. In a corner of her parents' drawing room stood an old unused upright piano, which the house's previous owners had left behind when they moved out, and which her mother didn't have the heart to discard, almost as if she knew that its presence was a kind of prophecy. One day the little girl lifted the piano's lid, struggled up onto the stool, and simply began to play. Her astounded parents came into the room and stood and watched as people do before whose eyes a miracle is taking place. After some minutes the little girl stopped playing, turned toward them, and spoke.

"It's badly out of tune," she said.

They had it tuned. After that they would listen to her every day as she enchanted them with her playing. Meena told Raheem, "You know, sometimes, when she falls asleep, her fingers are still tinkling out a tune, and there are nights when I imagine I can hear the music in the air, which is impossible, of course."

They found her a piano teacher, Miss Harrison, a long, thin Anglo-Indian lady of a certain age, who came to the Contractor residence looking dubious about the job, but aware that she was being paid twice the going rate. She showed Chandni the correct way to hold her hands, but that was about all the child needed to learn, and in a short period of time she had outstripped Miss Harrison, who shook her head and marveled. "She should be teaching me," Miss Harrison said.

"Tell me something," Meena said. "I have heard that many gifted musicians come from families of musicians, or at least of people well versed in music, which my husband and I are not. He is utterly tuneless and you should avoid, if possible, hearing him sing, and I am not much better than he is—better, that is true, but not much."

"Yes," the piano teacher replied, "it is the case that many good musicians grow up in very musical home environments. But this gift comes directly from God."

"Yes, it is a gift. But if that's so, then must it be God who is the giver?"

"The well-known term is 'God-given' gifts, so called for good reason," Miss Harrison, a devout Christian, suggested.

Meena Contractor shook her head. "We are mathematicians," she said firmly. "And therefore, obviously, atheists."

"Does it follow?" Miss Harrison dared to ask. "Invariably?"

"Q.E.D.," said Meena Contractor. "Quite! Exacto! Definitivamente!"

Miss Harrison was impressed. "I see you're a linguist as well," she said. "A household of many talents, to be sure."

What Meena did not say to Miss Harrison was that while she herself was rock solid in her unbelief, her conviction that God or gods were unnecessary fictions who were no longer required to answer the question of our origins, and absolutely surplus to requirements when one considered the question of ethics . . . she wasn't so sure about Raheem. It was true that when she had been in his class at the university he had quoted Albert Einstein's famous letter to Eric Gutkind in which he had declared that "the word God is for me nothing but the expression and product of human weakness"—and when Raheem had quoted Einstein it was one of the moments at which Meena had thought that she might be in love with him—but it was also true that one day when she had been tidying his desk at home she had accidentally or not accidentally looked into what he called his commonplace book and found there another line attributed to Einstein, "The more I study science the more I believe in God," which had shocked her so much that she had confessed to him that she had seen it and he had said, "It doesn't mean what you think it means. It's not to be taken literally, but only as an expression of his humility before the majesty of the universe," and this had partly reassured her, but had left some scrap of doubt in a corner of her mind, a doubt that would surge to the forefront of her thinking when Raheem walked out of their marriage to follow a religious fraud.

They bought Chandni a Steinway grand even though it was too big for her; her arms needed to be longer, and her feet couldn't reach the pedals. She didn't care. She began to learn the great canon of Western classical music, symphonies, sonatas, the whole majestic tradition. Her musical memory was exceptional. From those early days she played solo recitals without needing sheet music, which she used only when playing alongside other musicians. As to the inadequate wingspan of her arms and the dangling of her feet, she grew strikingly tall at an early age; her arms elongated and so did her fingers, as if her body knew what was required of it, and as her feet stretched downward at the ends of her lengthening legs, the distance of the pedals stopped being a problem.

As she grew older her interest in other instruments grew as well, the instruments of her own land, the bansuri flute, the santoor or dulcimer, and, of course, the glorious sitar. Meena sought out, to be Chandni's mentors, the greatest living masters of these instruments, the transcendent flautist Hariprasad Chaurasia; the santoor maestro Shivkumar Sharma, who was often Chaurasia's collaborator; and, briefly, before his sad demise, even Ustad Ravi Shankar himself, who declared Chandni to be his fastest-learning pupil, "lightning fast," faster even than Beatle George. After Ravi Shankar left the world, Meena persuaded Imrat Khan, the brilliant younger brother of the immortal Ustad Vilayat Khan, to be Chandni's sitar master. The praise showered upon the young child by all these giants established her as a rising star before she was ten years old.

Her intense musical schedule meant that it was impossible for her to attend normal school hours. Meena Contractor decided to devote herself to homeschooling Chandni as well as managing her daughter's career, and rapidly discovered that the girl's brilliance extended beyond her mastery of music. Her academic abilities were far in advance of her years. She needed only to read a thing once to know it forever, and her powers of analysis and expression were likewise exceptional. She was a prodigy of prodigies, and any outsider would have believed that she was lucky to lead such a charmed life.

In reality, she was a lonely child. She was too intellectually advanced for children of her own age, and because she wasn't in school, it was hard for her to make friends; and she was too young for people at her level to want to hang out with her. Meena did her best, arranging encounters with the children of friends, which did not go well. The visitors wanted to play children's games, clapping games or pretend mothers or hospitals or (more energetically) seven tiles or kabaddi, but Chandni wanted to discuss the lyrical clarity of Beethoven's *Pastoral* symphony or extol the beauty of the raga Megh Malhar that is the music of the rain. It became clear that it would be impossible for Chandni to have birthday parties like other children, because there were no other children who would have wanted to attend. On her birthdays Raheem and Meena took her to listen to music, and she insisted that this was fine, and that she was perfectly happy.

She developed health issues. Her asthma was never very bad, but it became challenging for her to walk uphill, and finally she had to give up playing the bansuri, because she was a perfectionist and announced that she was not capable of playing wind instruments as they deserved to be played. Not even Chaurasia himself could persuade her to change her mind. She gave up the santoor too, to focus on piano and sitar, and this was when it became clear that her will was an irresistible force that could look like stubbornness and, were she to become possessed of the wrong kinds of ideas, could drive her down the wrong kind of road.

She acquired a strong allergy to fish. In our seaside city, fish dishes were everywhere, and people ate quantities of pomfret, which is *Brama brama,* and the fish we used to call Bombay duck, which was a variety of bummalo or lizardfish. When she was seven years old such foods became repellent to her, and a single mouthful could lead to extremely unpleasant consequences. She called it her "upside-down allergy," because it was more usual for people to be allergic to shellfish while able to eat the finny creatures without any difficulty. But for Chandni it was the other way around. Crabs, prawns, lobsters were all fine—a good Goan prawn curry was high on her list of favorite meals—but the Bombay duck was off-limits for good; and now that EpiPens were beginning to be readily available, she had to carry one with her at all times and keep a further supply at home.

None of this got in the way of her music. She was the pride and joy of her instructors. Even more remarkable was the fact that her prowess on the piano was so formidable that she soon needed no teacher. Miss Harrison admitted there was no more she could do for her star pupil and bowed out of the story. Chandni was her own *ustad,* and every year she was twice as good as she had been the year before. "More than twice as good," her mother marveled, comparing her daughter's development to the Richter scale for earthquakes. Each number on that scale was ten times the force of the number below, "and that's how she is. Every year ten times as good, even though she is playing on a different type of scale, of music, not of catastrophe."

But it was true that the seismic force of the daughter's talent was sometimes alarming to the mother. The "gift" felt in these moments like a hurricane sweeping through their lives. What was her role as a mother, she asked herself. How to foster the talent and at the same time protect and nurture the lonely child in which the talent lived, the talent that she found herself thinking of as a second self or even an alien creature inhabiting her child's body, becoming one with it through a deep symbiosis? Meena tried hard to educate herself in music, which had never been her world. She studied the texts, she listened to the recordings, she tried not to be a useless ignoramus, while knowing that in this world it was Chandni who was the adult and she, Meena, who was the child. But she was a good and attentive mother and tried to chase away the sadness in her daughter's eyes, to make her isolation feel less isolated. And she worried that sometimes she sensed, in her daughter's eyes, and in her playing too, a kind of shadow, a darkness.

There were nights, still, when she crept into Chandni's bedroom and watched her as she slept, and seeing Chandni's fingers moving in her sleep she went on imagining that she could hear ghost music playing and thought, "There is a power in my child that is unworldly, and power is a thing that can be used in two ways." Creation and destruction were two sides of the same coin, and even though Meena was godless, she knew what Lord Shiva signified to her Hindu friends, Shiva the possessor of both powers, of making and unmaking, the lord of that double dance. But Chandni had a kind and gentle nature, though also a focused and determined one, and Meena decided her daughter's gift was a thing to be admired, plain and simple, and there was no need to fear it, even though the power of her playing was sometimes shocking.

And her concerts! Our people are not reticent about expressing their appreciation in the presence of greatness. *"Wah!"* we cry out. "Wow!" And also *"Kya baat hai!,"* "What a thing!" And we do this during, not at the end of, the performance. Beethoven would not have approved, nor even the giggly showman Mozart (as portrayed in Forman's *Amadeus*). Those gents expected to be heard in reverential silence and applauded when they were done. Well, too bad, Ludwig van, Wolfgang A.! You're in India now. And here, during is the way. Here, the performer and the audience are as one. Each lifts the other higher. And the concert halls of Kahani, and then far beyond Kahani, had rarely experienced such mutual lifting as happened when Chandni played. Whether seated on the carpeted stage with her sitar or on her piano stool, she brought her listeners roaring to their feet and allowed herself, in response, the tiniest upturn in one corner of her mouth—almost, one might believe, a smile.

See her now, tall and thirteen, taking her bows before the wowed folks of many cities and towns, from Kahani to Shillong, Delhi to Goa, Pune to Bengaluru, and Jodhpur, and even Ziro, in Arunachal Pradesh. In Kahani's NCPA, the National Centre for the Performing Arts, she played both solo and along with the Symphony Orchestra of India, the SOI; in Kolkata she joined in the annual Dover Lane festival; and many times she could be heard at the Candlelight Concerts in Chennai and back in her hometown. In short, she was everywhere. Her star shone in the sky.

Not everything in her garden was rosy, however. The biggest problem, for her mother as well as herself, was the change in Raheem Contractor. In the words of his loving wife, Meena, "At an age when he was old enough to know better, the silly fellow has gone and got religion." From the tone of her voice it was clear to the listener that she thought of this as an infection. And that she was made unhappy by her failure to find a cure.

4

He had never had a brother, so he looked for one in many places. When he was a child—an only child—he had invented an imaginary brother, whom he had named Imago. Sometimes he thought of his shadow as Imago, but more often he envisaged a full-grown human sibling, maybe even his twin, running along beside him, playing French cricket with him, arguing with him, laughing and tumbling, being, in short, a boy. But from the beginning he sensed something almost demonic in Imago, and as they grew older this side of his imaginary brother grew more pronounced. He displayed not only a capacity for violence but an interest in it, an interest in menace and threat and how that might affect others, how it might make one powerful, dominant, impossible to disagree with. By the time Raheem arrived at puberty, he had begun to be frightened of Imago's increasingly menacing personality and understood that he needed to unmake him, to leave him behind, to erase the memory of him, but this was easier to decide than to do. Throughout his adolescence and beyond that, into adulthood, Imago lived on in the corners of his mind, until he was finally defeated by a combination of mathematics and love. Raheem's work expanded to fill the spaces where Imago used to prance, smiling his insane and dangerous smile, but he vanished from Raheem's dream life only when he met Meena, and then he dreamed of her instead.

In the world of pure mathematics, people were locked away inside their heads, watching the dance of numbers, so they didn't have a lot of time for friendship, much less brotherhood. He had become like that himself, which made him seem like a remote character to many of his contemporaries, and so he hadn't had many friends. The emotional individual hidden within him remained invisible to most people when he attained adulthood. Only Meena had intuited its presence and had fallen in love with it. But the absence of a brother went on gnawing at him. After the Fermat catastrophe, which, as he came to think of it, deprived him of the meaning of his life, his personality underwent a slow transformation. The emotional Raheem within him became darker and angrier. Meena understood that her great financial windfall, which had made possible their newly comfortable life, was a part of the reason for the change, that he felt injured in his masculinity by her wealth, and she began to fear that envy of their daughter's success might have something to do with it as well. He stopped going to Chandni's concerts. He retired from the university and received a full pension, but when compared to his wife's wealth it felt like peanuts. He sequestered himself in his study, and Meena no longer knew what he was thinking about in there. Sometimes he mentioned a new interest in mysticism. What had been a close and happy marriage became a distant and unhappy one. Meena found happiness in Chandni. Raheem didn't know where to find it anymore. And then he found his brother, not an imaginary one but a real man, who turned out to be living right next door. After that his search, post-Fermat, for a new meaning to his days went down a path that transformed not only his life but Meena's and Chandni's as well.

.   .   .

By now everyone in Kahani and beyond knows about V. Shankar (not related to Ravi Shankar), the creator and leader of the cult known as Gupt, or Raaz, or the Secret. But in those days when he and Raheem Contractor became close, he was still an academic, an intellectual and a lecturer with a deep interest in mysticism and the spiritual world, who first endeared himself to Raheem by expounding emphatically, over a glass of Johnnie Walker Red Label in his garden, his strong espousal of what he called "Anti-Religion," which he asserted was his core philosophy. "Fascist piffle!" he cried. "Not one, but all. I am an equal-opportunity adversary of all such systems. You name it, I oppose it. Spiritual awakening will never be achieved by following any of these hollow dogmas. The mind requires to shake itself free of them all. Then only can it think straight and begin, truly, to rise." Then he made what he believed to be a joke. "Let your karma run over your dogma!" he bellowed. And he laughed so hard that his Johnnie Walker splashed onto the white kurta curving over his ample belly.

Raheem and Meena were no longer confiding their innermost thoughts to each other, but after a series of evenings with Shankar, Raheem couldn't restrain himself. Meena listened to her husband talk about their neighbor's "Anti-Religion" and also his oratorical skills (Raheem had attended several of Shankar's lectures, which were drawing huge crowds and felt more like rallies than academic events). "The fellow can talk his way into people's hearts," he said. "And his Anti-Religion I totally agree with. This feels like the brother I never had, showing up at last."

Meena wasn't impressed. "Don't you see," she said. "He is only pushing all other faiths to one side in order to make room for himself. He can say he is on the side of Man, but I say he's aiming for the job of God."

"You understand nothing," Raheem scolded her. The chasm between them grew wider.

Chandni in her teenage years was a sad daily witness to the slow failure of her parents' marriage, and she began to dream of escape. She started imagining a Prince Charming who would materialize from nowhere to sweep her away into blissful happiness. Afterward, after everything that happened had happened, she understood that she should have been old enough, mature enough, to say goodbye to fairy tales, but she had been so busy extending her musical talent that the rest of her had remained more childish, more innocent, than might have been expected. And the fact is that she did think about Prince Charming. And such a prince did finally show up.

"What are the three fantasies," Shankar asked Raheem while they sipped whiskey in his garden, "that would cease to exist if we stopped believing in them?"

"Fairies?" Raheem ventured. "Like in *Peter Pan*? Clap hands if you believe?"

"Not only fairies," Shankar told him. "All supernatural beings. Up to and including gods."

"Okay, so that fits your philosophy," Raheem said, the whiskey making him a little argumentative. "Men made gods and not the other way around, that's what you say? And then men worshipped the things they made?"

"So, that is one foolish thing," Shankar said. "And then, there is money."

"Money doesn't exist?"

"It only has value because we say it does. What is gold? Just a yellow rock. What is a piece of paper with the face of M. K. Gandhi on it? Why is a rupee a rupee? If they took Gandhiji off the money and put Nathuram Godse on the banknote instead, would it lose its meaning?"

"I don't know, maybe?" Raheem said. "To put the assassin there instead of the assassinated? I don't like the sound of that."

"My point," Shankar said, "is that it's only worth twenty chips, one hundred chips, five hundred chips because we all agree to pretend that it is. And then we pay for a dinner or a house with a worthless piece of paper."

"And number three," Raheem said. "Let's have it."

"Number three is India," Shankar exclaimed. "Until August 15, 1947, there was no such country. The country that gained independence had never existed before as a single entity. Never in all of history."

"And these are the things from which you want to liberate us," Raheem marveled. "And this is an idea you came up with all by yourself."

"I'll settle for one out of three," Shankar confided. "No god worship will be enough for me. India and money, we can keep. Personally, I love India, and money also is okay—more than okay. We all need dreams, isn't it. And no, I didn't come up with it just out of my own head. I read something of the sort in a book I happened to pick up, which was maybe my running-over-dogma karma. Not every powerful idea has to be original."

So Shankar was in favor of money, and the nation got a thumbs-up, but God was out of favor. An interesting platform. And there was one more thing, because a solid platform should stand on four legs. The fourth leg was sex.

By the time his daughter had entered the middle years of her teens, Raheem, in the middle years of his sixties, had come to think of sex as a closed subject, and as his distance from his wife grew greater, he realized he didn't even know how the subject might be reopened, or even if he was still physically capable of performing his duty as a man. But his next-door neighbor, his "brother," had begun, in his public performances, to recommend sex as a gateway to the transcendent, and beyond that to the sublime; and as all his neighbors were tut-tuttingly becoming aware, he enthusiastically practiced what he preached. By this time he had dropped his professorial air and fulfilled Meena Contractor's prophecy by offering himself up as the one who could lead his followers to the light. "He doesn't use the term 'godman' to describe himself," Meena told Raheem contemptuously, "or not yet; but he's just the next in that line of frauds." Things between husband and wife had grown so strained that Meena's contempt for their neighbor served only to drive Raheem further in Shankar's direction. And then there were the women.

Shankar was becoming a problem for the residents of the Westfield Compound, or Westfield Estate; people called it by both names, but everyone who lived there valued its air of a peaceful haven where folks could enjoy their privacy and children could play safely in that trafficless hilltop cul-de-sac. Everything had always been quiet and tree-shaded and a happy contrast from the rattle and bang of bustling Warden Road, below. But as Shankar's celebrity grew, so did the crowds. Cars, taxis, scooters, bicycles, pedestrians swarmed up the little hill, jamming the lane, and the air was full of honks and bells and shouts. Fans, students, nosey parkers, and devotees manifested themselves in upsetting numbers, jostling and shoving around the entrance to Shankar's home. Shankar himself was unconcerned by the mayhem and opened his doors to all comers, acquiring a team of helpers who kept everyone in line to wait for their moment with the great man, when each visitor could ask one question and receive one answer, and benefit from the laying on of the great man's hand upon his or her bowed head. These helpers, all of them, were young women, undeniably attractive and equally undeniably in thrall to Shankar's charisma and rapidly growing power.

Raheem found the transformation of the neighborhood overwhelming and was keenly aware of the hostility of all the other residents, who had initiated appeals to the city authorities and the police. He decided to take it up with his "brother." "It has to stop—that's what they are saying, our neighbors," he told Shankar. "Maybe they have a point?"

Shankar waved a dismissive hand. "These people," he said. "So used to their privilege. But now the Common Man has arisen, and the Common Woman also. The neighbors see the love, and they themselves are unloved. You can feel the love, can't you, my brother? So much love. It's a beautiful thing."

His young women crowded around him, adoring him. "Maybe you need some love also, Raheem. There's enough love here for everyone. Let me share it with you."

Raheem felt his whole face reddening. "I am not fully understanding," he said, his voice faltering. "What is your suggestion?"

"Like Gandhiji," Shankar said, indicating the ladies, "I too am making my experiments with truth. Unlike Gandhiji, you see, I am prepared to share my co-experimenters with my friends."

Raheem didn't know where to look. "But surely," he said, "Bapuji was chaste in his relations with the ladies, and lay with them at night only to test the strength of his will."

This elicited one of Shankar's bellows of laughter. "So funny," he cried, wiping tears from his eyes. "Go on, Raheem *bhai*. Pull my other leg."

"I must go," Raheem said, not knowing what else to say. "I'll return at a quieter time."

"There will be no more quiet times," Shankar called after the mathematician's retreating form. "But there will be free love. Think about that. So much love coming this way that I can distribute it to all comers, for no extra charge, and still keep plenty for myself."

It wasn't long before Gurushankar (or "G.S.," as he soon started calling himself) moved out of the neighborhood. He was becoming a large-scale enterprise. Meditation had become big business, and he offered radical new techniques that many would-be meditators found attractive, especially as he associated them with his personal Free Sex Theory (FST). His wider philosophy was distilled into what he called the Possibilities of Mankind Movement, known colloquially as POMO. Among its chief tenets was the high approval given to material success. This endeared him to many materially successful persons worldwide, those who sought spiritual growth and the approval of those who possessed the secret of such growth but also thought, as G.S. did, that money was "more than okay." So money, happy to be given the spiritual thumbs-up, flooded into his accounts. Patrons, whom he welcomed, flocked to him.

"I'm going to the Moon," he told Raheem. "Far away from our so-friendly neighbors here upon this hostile Earth."

This Moon wasn't the Earth's satellite, however. It was a large facility he was building, an "experimental township" that was being promoted worldwide as a sort of utopia of "progressive harmony," located on the country's eastern, or Coromandel, coast. It was, one might argue, Moon-shaped, approximately circular, and could be thought of as a Moon-on-Earth if you could accept that the Moon had a peace zone at the center, featuring a temple and a town hall and a palace for the Man in the Moon himself, surrounded by a township that included yoga schools, singing-bowl meditation halls, sex-encounter private spaces, austere residences for disciples, vegetarian eateries, bicycle trails, and stores where one could buy many kinds of Gurushankar merch, merch you could eat, wearable merch, music and video merch, Man in the Moon china figurines, and pamphlets. You would also need to accept that the Moon was a place where the Man in the Moon owned a large garage that he was filling up with expensive motor cars. G.S. was a super car buff, and now that the cash was flowing freely he intended to indulge his love of luxury and speed to the full. He told Raheem that he had the number ninety-three in mind. Ninety-three Ferraris, which in his opinion were the greatest cars ever built.

"Why ninety-three?" Raheem asked.

"Because it's one more than ninety-two," the spiritual leader replied.

His villa was put up for sale, and quickly snapped up by an American disciple, a polo-playing real-estate billionairess named Bridget Hampton, who started out as his eager sex slave, became his business partner, and took the un-Indian name of Mommy—which, the cynical ones among us suspected, described the nature of their sexual relationship, even though she was younger than Shankar by more than a decade. Mommy paid twice the market price for the villa and announced to the world, or at least to any part of the world that was listening, "One day this place will be a global shrine." On the day when G.S. was moving out and heading south and east with Mommy, across the Deccan plateau to the opposite coast, he said to Raheem, "Come! You should come."

Raheem looked uneasy. "What would I do in a place like that," he mumbled.

"You could make soup," Gurushankar proposed. "Every day

we will have hundreds of mouths to feed, maybe even thousands. Making soup for the hungry masses would be a noble task for a retired gentleman like yourself."

"I'm a terrible cook," Raheem said.

"You'll learn," G.S. replied. "The spirit will move you, and you'll be fine."

First Shankar was Shankar and then he became Gurushankar and then G.S., and after his big move south he started calling himself "Man in the Moon," and from that he derived the name that stuck, M-i-th-moo, which became Mithmu. He loved becoming—being—Mithmu. It sounded ancient, Sanskritish, but it had a sort of alien, sci-fi undertone as well. Best of all, it sounded like the name of an immortal—it could have been Egyptian, Babylonian, Sumerian, or the name of a scion of the fabled Lunar dynasty of our own mythology—and though he was famously anti-god it sounded pleasingly godlike to his ears. Anti-godlike. Which felt like a special kind of divine. An undivine divine. Also, Mommy liked it. And although he didn't admit it, Shankar—Mithmu—did everything his Mommy said. As long as she let him buy his expensive cars.

After the newly renamed Mithmu and his formidable Mommy left Breach Candy for the Moon, Raheem found himself thinking once again about his imaginary childhood brother, Imago, who had frightened him so badly, and contrasting him with his second, non-brother brother. Unlike Imago, Mithmu had always treated him with kindness, respect, and something that could be called brotherly love. Mithmu could perhaps be described as the anti-Imago. Or to put it differently, Mithmu was the real Imago, the true manifestation of Raheem's idealized image of a brother, and the original dream Imago was the poorly imagined phony. Also, to state the obvious, Mithmu was real, whereas his predecessor had been a fiction. And real was a big improvement on fictional. Therefore, Raheem argued to himself, if Mithmu was now asking something of him, having given him the brother feeling he had always wanted, maybe it was time to pay attention, and give something back. This was the thought process that, once he had followed it down the path along which it was leading him, caused Raheem to forsake mathematics for soup, and to abandon his wife and daughter to go and live on the Moon.

What he failed to understand was that Mithmu was a real man who had turned himself into an imaginary one; so he was a fiction too.

5

Chandni found it hard to forgive her father for leaving even though, from time to time, living in the same apartment as her increasingly estranged parents had made her secretly, silently, beg them to separate. She could not understand why he had chosen to make himself look ridiculous—himself and, by extension, his family as well. *My father left me to make soup* was not a sentence she ever spoke, but it was in her head every day. And after his departure she refused ever to eat soup again. Meena agreed. "This household will be a soup-free zone," she declared. "Moon is *luna*, isn't it. So now he has become a *luna-tic*. Let him cook soup on the Moon for all the other loonies. We will go on living like respectable people here on planet Earth." The fatherless girl and the husbandless mother held each other in a protective embrace that would last for the rest of their lives.

Anger, pain, and grief deepened Chandni's musical gift. Her audiences spoke of being almost frightened by the sheer power of her playing. By the time she was eighteen she was able to unleash—on sitar or piano—a fury that felt as if it might destroy the world, though she could also command a sweetness rich enough to create the world anew. Only Meena Contractor, ever the perfectionist, believed she could sense one missing quality in her brilliant daughter's playing. "She has never been in love," Meena thought, "and any great artist needs to know what that's like—the real grand passion, overwhelming, tormenting, the tearing apart, the exaltation, the kind I never had myself."

The city I now call Kahani is not like the more conservative regions of our land. Here—among, let me say, the middle to better classes—there is little or no segregation of the sexes, so that young men and women have places to meet and the women can wear what they like, more or less, as long as the skirts are not too short. So the opportunities for falling in love are greater than they are elsewhere. We have fashion shows, horse races, mixed-use swimming pools, and beaches. We have picnics. Parties. We have nightclubs with disc jockeys and dancing, and jazz cafés with weekend brunch "jam sessions." And, of course, more traditionally, we have weddings. In wedding season at the nuptial ceremonies the mothers and aunties arrange marriages and many future unions come into being, not just those present-tense *I do*'s being attended by the marriageable young and the scheming old. We are, on the whole, sophisticated people, or at least enough of us are. Of the bitterly poor I do not speak. Life in the slums is different from the above and requires a different story. But on the local trains, the buses, in the office buildings, the bazaars, the streets, men and women, boys and girls on the whole get along just fine. And so when Meena asked Chandni, "Is there anyone?" and also "Wouldn't you like there to be someone?," these were not inappropriate questions to ask.

Chandni at eighteen was a poised and composed young woman who had learned to keep a lot of herself hidden inside herself, in which respect she was more like her father than she would have cared to admit. But when her mother asked her gently about the existence of a "someone," she allowed herself to reveal her fantasy that someday her prince would come. "But he hasn't turned up yet," she added, shrugging dismissively, even though secretly she did not feel at all dismissive about the subject.

"I see," Meena said. "You're what I'd call a theoretical romantic. Because there isn't, and as far as I know has never been, an actual person upon whom you bestow these feelings."

"I guess so," Chandni replied.

And then the prince appeared.

The prince was not a real prince, but that doesn't really matter. He lived, as princes must, in a palace overlooking the sea, in the exclusive Walkeshwar neighborhood of Malabar Hill—not the biggest, tallest palace in the city, which would merely have been vulgar, but the most beautiful, a thing in which one could take pride, a place of terraces and trees and mirrored halls and antique carpets and good music and fine food. He also lived in a magnificent beach villa at Juhu, filled with art by the leading artists of Kahani, and there were other residences elsewhere in the country, at a hill station and a lake, of which we will speak if the need arises. The prince's family owned steel mills, real estate, luxury hotel chains, textile works, shipyards, tea plantations, newspapers, television stations, and new technology manufactories in the south, and, perhaps regrettably, its corporations also built a range of state-of-the-art weapons systems for the national government. They were Zoroastrians, and among the prince's ancestors were eminent poets and philosophers, as well as captains of industry. They were also Anglophiles, so the prince had been given an "English-medium" education at the Cathedral and John Connon School, run "under the auspices of the Anglo-Scottish Education Society." It stood on what embarrassingly used to be called Outram Road after Sir James Outram, a colonizer who fought to suppress the Rebellion or Uprising of 1857, and it was an establishment also attended in another time by, among others, me. At Cathedral he was bad at Latin, chemistry, and the composition of limericks in English class. But his bat and ball conquered all, and by the time he left school he was already a star.

His sporting prowess had claimed him, so he had skipped college and attended, instead, the university of life. He was a stylish cricketer, an elegant batsman, and, as a spin bowler, a purveyor of mesmerizing googlies and chinamen. For the time being this was his focus, his prized place on the national cricket team, but regarding his long-term future he was undecided, perhaps because he, like Chandni, had never been in love. Love clarifies life. The prince's non-sporting life still required clarification.

His character was perhaps not yet fully formed. There were signs of willfulness, narcissism, and spoiled-brat behavior, not uncommon among the scions of the rich-rich-rich, but at this young age his natural charm and sporting stardom overrode all other considerations. So, Prince for sure, Charming up to a point. His name was Majnoo Ferdaus. The last name needs no explanation; everyone in Kahani knows who the Ferdauses are. Perhaps there was a note of warning in his given name, since Majnoo, Majnu, or Majnún is the hero of a famous love story to be found among the classics, and the name can mean "besotted" or "obsessed by love," which could be said to be good qualities, but it can also mean "possessed" or even "mad." Which is less good.

The rom-com movie *Jab We Met*—"jab" meaning "when," for the info of those who need the info—was already attaining cult classic status by Chandni's eighteenth birthday. In the Kareena Kapoor–Shahid Kapoor starrer, rich boy meets chatty girl on a train, he has broken up with his girlfriend and she wants to marry her boyfriend and various vicissitudes follow but in the end they notice that they love each other (and not the girlfriend or boyfriend) and bingo, happy ending! Later on (when Chandni was twenty), in the not so totally comedic rom-com *Anjaana Anjaani,* "Male and Female Stranger," the female and male strangers of the title—Priyanka Chopra and Ranbir Kapoor— try constantly to commit suicide in New York in different ways: by jumping off the George Washington Bridge, or being hit by a car, or drinking bleach, and so on. (Funny, huh?) But now they are not so much strangers and so just for a change instead of trying to leap to their deaths they go to Las Vegas! They fall in love! But then things go badly once more, and they try to kill themselves again! But then they kiss—phew! nick of time!— and bingo! Happy ending.

Such is love in the popular movies with which the whole country is *majnu.* Obsessed. Drama! We have to have it. (Also, songs.) So to tell a popular *kahani* in Kahani, I should come up with some stuff like the above. Twists, complications, danger, music! Reader, I am sorry to disappoint. The only one of the foregoing I can offer is music. And that, without words. Sorry.

The Ferdaus parents were universally known as "Jimmy and Dimmy." Jimmy was tall, thin, graying, a carefully spoken man, expressing himself softly (in a high tenor voice), with kindly eyes; and he ran his enormous empire without ever giving the impression of being busy, flustered, or in doubt. Dimmy was his perfect alternate self: the most glamorous grande dame in the city, extroverted, flamboyant, and given to talking nonstop in a low, cigarette-haunted voice. She stood—or perhaps *lounged*—at the center of Kahani's social life, was deeply in- volved in every kind of good cause, and was loved, envied, and gossiped about in whispers that were both adulatory and malicious, and that she, naturally, both encouraged and ignored. They were musically inclined billionaires, patrons of the best stuff, and they held regular soirées at their Walkeshwar mansion, inviting the cream of the musical fraternity-sorority to sing or play for the cream of society, and paying top rupee for the musicians' services. In musical circles it was considered a privilege to be invited to Ferdaus House to perform, and the money didn't hurt, either.

Majnoo was their only child. He wasn't particularly interested in classical music, Western or our own. He was a sports star. He liked nightclubs and disco beats and movie stars and fashion models, and he really liked parties. He didn't drink or smoke but oh, he could dance. If there were international dance Test matches, he would be captain of India. He didn't read books or care about the city's flourishing art scene. He liked fast cars even though the city's permanent traffic jams made it impossible to drive fast. When journalists asked him about his dreams, he usually answered, "Ninety-three Lamborghinis." Why ninety-three, the journalists asked.

"Because," he replied, "that's one more than ninety-two."

He paid little or no attention to his mother's charities and stopped by his father's offices only occasionally and briefly and usually because he wanted Jimmy Ferdaus's permission to buy something expensive. He would have been a disappointment to his parents had it not been for a few more positive qualities. He went nowhere near drugs. He was exceptionally well-mannered. He possessed the aforementioned easy, natural charm. He was, after all, one of the nation's sporting heroes. And he was absurdly, overwhelmingly, irresistibly gorgeous to behold.

On the evening that Chandni Contractor had been booked to perform at Ferdaus House for the first time, Majnoo, on his way out to meet some cricket-team friends, asked his mother, "So who's the entertainment tonight?" And when he heard the answer he evinced a flicker of interest. "Oh, yeah, her picture was in a magazine," he said. "She's really young, supposed to be really good, but is she more than averagely hot? I'll say nothing. Maybe it was the photographer's fault."

"She's better at what she does," his mother said, allowing annoyance into her voice, "than you are at what you do. And almost nobody on earth is equally good on the pianoforte and the sitar."

"That's like me," Majnoo said, to tease her. "I can bowl as well as bat. Double trouble." And before his mother could say something cutting in response, he threw up his hands and switched on the charm. "All right, all right, Mummyji. Maybe I'll stop by later for ten minutes and listen to the lady. And if you say so, maybe she is cool."

A less than auspicious prologue, one might say. And neither of these young persons was remotely ready to "settle down." Chandni was rapidly arriving at the pinnacle of her profession, and Majnoo was already at the pinnacle of his sport. Their lives were becoming international. The Test-level cricketing countries at that time—just to explain for persons from non-cricketing countries—were India, Pakistan, Bangladesh, Sri Lanka, Australia, New Zealand, South Africa, West Indies, Zimbabwe. Plus, just allowed into the exclusive group a year earlier, Afghanistan and Ireland. Oh, yes, and England. Birthplace of the game. Mustn't forget old Blighty. So, Majnoo was often on the road. Barbados, Cape Town, Colombo, and of course Lord's, a.k.a. "headquarters." And Chandni was receiving invitations from all over Europe and North America, and also Japan. Carnegie Hall, Wigmore Hall, Elbphilharmonie, Suntory Hall. So "settle down" was on neither of their young minds.

But then, surprisingly, bingo, romance! Their story was like a movie after all! Some urge he did not fully understand resulted in Majnoo showing up for the whole of Chandni's debut performance at Ferdaus House, and he found himself enthralled. And Chandni, the "theoretical romantic," fell for, how can we put it, a jock. A rich jock, but still. No art, no culture, only bat and ball and money. It was unexpected. It was as if Marilyn Monroe had fallen for Joe DiMaggio . . . oh, right. Maybe not so surprising, after all. Love lands where it lands and doesn't ask for explanations. Explanations come from the world of rationality, and love is unreasonable.

"I don't even know why I love him," Chandni told her mother. "We're like chalk and cheese, up and down, black and white. Can it be that I just have a stupid weakness for too much beauty, in whatever shape or form? Artistic or just plain bodily? Maybe that's why. Stupid but true."

And it was true. She loved him in the way one might love a tropical sunset, or a hummingbird, or a Chola bronze, or the long, lustrous hair of a cover girl. She appreciated him for his long-lashed eyes and turned a blind eye to his casual selfishness, or even indulged it, as young wives often do. She loved him because he could dance expertly and could hit a cricket ball a long way through the air, and because everyone else loved him—he was universally movie-star-level adored, so it seemed the natural thing to do.

And so, soon enough, a wedding. The wedding of the year, obviously, the splashiest, the one people would kill to be invited to. I should explain something here, about the way in which our country has changed. When old people like me were young, when the country was young too, it used to be said that when it was time for a wedding, Pakistanis dressed up and Indians dressed down. Pakistani weddings were ostentatious, sometimes ludicrously so, but Indian nuptials were modest. Here we preferred not to show off our wealth, knowing how many of us were poor or even destitute. In those days Gandhian values still had some meaning for us. Now, however, those days are gone. Pakistan, take a seat. The great wedding spectacles are across the Indo-Pak border. They are right here in Kahani.

A gossip columnist would be better than the present writer at listing the BOLDFACE NAMES who attended the celebrations, the SCREEN STARS, the MUSIC DIVAS, the INDUSTRIAL TITANS, so on, so forth. Such a person, with their finger on the pulse of what a person of that type might call KAHANI KOOL, would know that there were parties before the party, pre-things before the thing, taking place in KOOL locations around our great nation, in FATEHPUR SIKRI amid the ruins of the Mughal Empire and in HAMPI amid the ruins of the Vijayanagar Empire, as if to inform all who were there and all who were not there that those OUTDATED HAS-BEEN OLD EMPIRES had crumbled and fallen but the HOUSE OF FERDAUS was strong and ruling over empires of its own. In the gossip pages you could read about the SWEET HUMAN TOUCHES, how the snacks of the happy couple's favorite STREET FOOD VEN-DOR were served at Ferdaus House alongside the creations of THREE MAJOR WORLD CHEFS, and then the FIREWORKS WOW WOW WOW, turning night into day! And the week be-fore the wedding, the One-Day International match between the Indian Cricket Team and a WORLD XI played at famous old BRABOURNE STADIUM. All the greatest stars of the cricket world! And their WAGs! (This had to be explained to myself. Wives and Girlfriends, okay. I get it.) (Also a personal note of nostalgia. Happy to see the old Brabourne Stadium back in the headlines, long after it was discarded by the Powers That Be in favor of the new Wankhede built, humiliatingly, right next door.) But oh. We haven't finished! On the day of the wedding the WHOLE GODDAMN BERLIN PHILHARMONIC was flown in from Germany so that the bride could play with them! And then, only then . . .

THE WEDDING.

AWWW.

So beautiful. Everybody cried.

Ceremonies stretched over four days! First the AUSPICIOUS WEDDING ON THE NEW MOON NIGHT at Ferdaus Cultural Center, second the RELIGIOUS CEREMONIES THAT HONORED THE DEAD, third something else, never mind, and finally the BIG DEAL WEDDING PARTY! Guests in thousands! Big stars flown in to perform, excuse me for not recognizing names. Mister BUSTIN GEIGER? Miss BALLY IRISH? Somebody from for Pete's sake THE PANAMA CANAL singing music from THE PANAMA CANAL AREA? Why? Only goodness knows. (Okay, it was catchy, and everyone likes Panama hats.) And presiding over the whole affair, tireless, nonstop smiling, totally in charge, the queen herself, no!, the EMPRESS. DIMMY FERDAUS.

Bride and bridegroom take baths! Then white ceremonial dress! Then Procession of Gifts! (WOW, the GIFTS, oh my. More than one vintage Lamborghini, Miura! Espada! Et cetera.) And the traditions of the old ways, bride and groom SPRINKLING each other with RICE (good luck!), then an EGG circling the groom three times then SMASHED, then a COCONUT, then WATER GLASS, all thrown down, getting RID OF EVIL, you understand? And then from the priest the BLESSING.

"May the Creator, the omniscient Lord, grant you a

progeny of sons and grandsons, plenty of means to provide for yourselves"—*no problem there, methinks, apologies for
interjecting*—"heart-ravishing friendship, bodily strength, long
life, and an existence of one hundred and fifty years!" (*One century and a half! Those of us getting on in life now think, "I want a
blessing like that."*)

This whole Zoroastrian wedding thing, man. Great stuff! *Big*
respect.

Majnoo loved it all, reveled in the pomp and show. Chandni,
not one for such ostentatious display, would have hated it if she
had allowed herself so contrary an emotion. It was strange to
be, so to speak, only a member of the supporting cast at one's
own nuptials, to have merely a bit part in the grand *tamasha*. But
she was trying to be what Majnoo called a "team player," so she
put her personal preferences aside and accepted the hullabaloo.

. . . And after everything, the patriarch, Jimmy Ferdaus—
who had effaced himself almost completely throughout the celebrations, leaving the stage to his wife and the Happy Couple,
making of himself a sort of smiling ghost in the corner of the
frame—beckoned to his son and walked with him into the library, on whose shelves stood a thousand books, bought by the
yard from the best dealer in the city, and never opened by father
or son, and said, "Now, my boy, now that this bright global light
has shone down upon you, it is you who are the face and embodiment of the family—of, allow me to express it in my own
language, of the Brand."

This parental benediction went to the core of Majnoo's being.
It changed forever how he saw himself, and told him how, in the
future, he must behave. It is probable, as will be seen, that he did
not learn the right lessons from his father's words.

. . .

Contractor was almost always a Parsi (Zoroastrian) name, but, because of certain historical accidents and conversions that it is not necessary to explain here, Meena and Chandni were not members of the Parsi community. It was, however, easy for the wedding guests to assume that they were, and Chandni and Meena went along with it all without explaining, Chandni because at that moment she was willing to please her Majnoo and his formidable mother, and Meena because, unbeliever that she was, she could accept ritual as "mere" ritual and ascribed to it no deeper meaning than that. But in the light of everything that followed, it seems obvious that the end of the marriage began at its beginning. Playing with the Berlin Philharmonic was an honor indeed, and Chandni brought it off beautifully, but it would have had real meaning to her only if the orchestra had invited her because of its admiration for her playing, rather than accepting an invitation solely because of the amount of cash placed on the table. She saw, or imagined she saw, a scornful curl on the lips of the great conductor, Kirill Petrenko, when she sat down at the piano and did not dare to look in his direction when she finished, afraid that the sneer would still be on his face. In short, the overweening display of wealth was distasteful to mother and daughter alike.

And Meena Contractor had words for her daughter too. "We both know," she said, "that this is the world you have freely and willingly entered. This, now, is your life. You have become Chandni Ferdaus." And then, in a low murmur, she added, "Look out."

Raheem Contractor had a new life and a new name as well. Mithmu's Moon had become immensely successful and powerful. Mithmu himself was traveling the world, and movie stars and capitalist barons alike were falling under his spell. Free Sex Theory was a smash hit. And at the very heart of the Moon-world was the arcane ideology that Mithmu had named the Secret, also known as Raaz or Gupt. In this age of renaming, his flock of devotees took the surnames of Raazi or Gupté—"believers." If they wished to, they also took new first names for themselves, and so Raheem Contractor the soup chef became Arif Raazi, Arif because it meant "learned" or "knowledge-able," and, as he told Meena when she called him on his mobile to tell him about his daughter's engagement, he had "chosen late in life to forsake one sort of knowing for another." Trying to hide her exasperation, Meena asked him what this "new knowing" was teaching him, and he replied, "It's forbidden to speak of it." At that moment she became fearful for him, under-standing that he had finally sacrificed the last scraps of his ratio-nality for the false certainties of hero worship, and in spite of the deep wound of abandonment she began to think about how he might be rescued from the spider's web in which he had been trapped. "Two webs," she thought, worriedly. "One for Chandni and one for him, and both of them woven out of cash."

He said he couldn't come to the wedding. He had responsi-bilities at the soup station on the Moon and he couldn't just walk away to go to a party.

"Fuck you, Raheem," she said.

"Call me Arif," he told her. "I'm Arif now."

"Maybe that's right," she said before she hung up. "You really aren't Raheem anymore."

6

The new life. Liveried staff, gold dinner plates, priceless art on the walls, handmade furniture, a personal dressing room for Chandni almost as big as the Westfield Estate apartment. "Everything you want in life is here for you," Majnoo told his bride. "And if you can dream up something that isn't here, I will bring it to you."

She made one demand. The Steinway grand had to move from Breach Candy to Malabar Hill: not so far, but not so easy. "Why move it?" Majnoo asked her. "We have a great piano at our place already, and another at the Juhu house." She shook her head. "But you haven't got mine," she said. "I audition pianos, and only mine passed the audition."

He shook his head, frowning as if he had suddenly been spoken to in an unknown language. "We failed your test?"

"A piano is like someone you marry," she said. "You live together every day. The relationship has to work."

Marriage changes things in a relationship. Either things get better, or they get worse. What things don't do is remain the same. In the case of Chandni and her piano, the marriage grew richer and deeper as they got to know each other. In the case of her human *shaadi*, the path was less smooth.

The first thing was the noise. Chandni was in the habit of practicing on each of her favored instruments for several hours a day. The sound penetrated every corner of Ferdaus House, and even though her playing was exceptional, the members of the household soon enough found that it was getting on their nerves. "Doesn't she ever stop?" Dimmy Ferdaus demanded of her son. "Doesn't she want to go to the movies, or shopping, or I don't know what?"

Majnoo brought the question to Chandni. "You're a genius, obviously, darling," he said, "but you're also driving everyone nuts with your racket."

"My racket," Chandni said, "is not only what I do. It's who I am."

Majnoo went back to his mother. "She says the noise is her identity," he said.

"Tell her her top number one identity now is, she's your wife."

Majnoo could not bring himself to ask Chandni to stop playing. But he didn't know how to defy his mother. The stress of the situation affected his cricket game. People noticed his loss of form. There were rumors that the selectors were getting ready to drop him. And meanwhile, Chandni's star continued to rise. She was "the Musician of Kahani" and in ever greater demand. Majnoo discovered that he was starting not to like it. Where was the wifely behavior he had every reason to expect? The modesty, the adoration, the laughing at his jokes, the undimmed enjoyment of his oft-repeated stories, the massaging of his feet? "Buzzing off to a different city or even different country every week," he complained to Dimmy. "Playing with God only knows what other egomaniac music people. I've heard what these Western conductors and soloists are like. Even our own tabla players. Lustful bastards, the lot of them."

"Let her go," Dimmy advised. "At least in her absences we get a welcome break from her nonstop practicing."

Let us try to dig a little deeper into this young man's story, this Majnoo Ferdaus whose choices and actions would unleash such a tumult, such a disaster for all. Let us grapple with him sympathetically for the moment even though, as our story proceeds, it will become harder to feel sympathy for him.

He was a firstborn male child (like myself), after whom came . . . nobody (unlike myself). So he was a precious jewel, the future of the bloodline, his parents' only hope. He was not only the heir but the one upon whom fell the responsibility of producing his own heir. (Chandni was an only child as well, but fortunately for her, she was not the child of people who thought in dynastic terms. However, she had entered the lair of dynasts now.)

As to his further education after he left the Cathedral School: thanks to his good looks and sporting talent, he learned a great deal from the women of the cricketing nations (some helplessly swooning, others going into doomed flings with him with open eyes, and all of them smarter than he was, all of them setting aside his deficiencies of brain for the sake of his other qualities), and taught them nothing in return except the art of having—however briefly—a pretty good time. In short, until he met Chandni Contractor he had led a life that was charmed as well as charming, of excellence in his chosen sport and frivolity everywhere else; which was why both his parents had been surprised, perhaps even shocked, when he'd declared his serious intention to marry the musician girl. Jimmy and Dimmy had conferred privately in Jimmy's cigar room to decide whether or not to give the romance their blessing and celebrate it properly.

"The question is," Dimmy said, "what does she see in him? She's obviously brilliant, and he is obviously not. I thought, maybe, it's money, but I see that that doesn't interest her so much. So it must be sex. In which case, it won't last. In our own case, fortunately, it was never that."

"It may not last," Jimmy agreed carefully. "We also know our boy. He plays the field even when he's off the cricket pitch."

Dimmy threw up her hands in what looked like, but was not, a lighthearted fashion. "Never mind, Jamshed," she said. "She will be a very good first wife for him."

Majnoo lived in his own apartment at the top of the family home, which meant that Chandni had to accept the loss of privacy that comes from living with one's in-laws. In the months after the wedding she noticed that the eyes of the whole household were focused on her, following her around, and not just the household's eyes but those of its friends and relatives too. The attention had nothing to do with music. It had more to do with her menstrual cycle, on which topic Dimmy Ferdaus was inquisitive and direct. "Are you regular? Is it late? Did you miss one?" And the answers, to Chandni's deep embarrassment, were quickly circulated to all who were taking an interest. It became clear that the only way to put a stop to this was to produce a baby promptly, and, if possible, a boy.

"But I'm too young to have a child," she said to Majnoo. "We're both too young. Let's wait a little? Let's have some more youth? Also, our careers . . ."

"There are so many persons here to look after a baby," Majnoo said. "Our two mothers, my grandmother, also aunts, cousins. No shortage. Plus, you can have all the ayahs you desire, so it won't interrupt anything. But a baby! Just think! So nice! And what a celebration we will have! Bigger than the wedding, even. A Festival of Birth to welcome the little one into the world. No expense spared! It will be so good."

Chandni understood three things. First, that her husband's true passion and skill, greater even than his sporting prowess, was *having a good time*, and he was an artist in that field. Second, that such ostentation was considered by his family to be good for the Brand. And third, that she had no choice.

No sooner had the pregnancy been confirmed than Majnoo, with Dimmy's full support, began to plan the carnival of its gestation. Meena Contractor came to the big Walkeshwar mansion to plead with the Ferdauses for privacy. "At least allow three months to pass," she said. "It's normal to keep a pregnancy under wraps until after the first trimester, just in case, just to be sure everything's okay."

"Nonsense," Dimmy Ferdaus airily replied. "They are both healthy young people and the newborn will be the same, no question. The next generation has announced its presence to us! Now we must extend that announcement to the world. We must celebrate immediately, and we will. Relax, Contractor Begum!" And here a faint curl of menace arrived in the corners of her smile. "Our kids are hitched now! So Chandni signed up to be part of our gang, not just yours! This is all part of that—how to say it?—that Contract."

7

R aheem—we will continue to call him Raheem to avoid forcing the non-lunatic reader to rename him—was finding life on the Moon difficult. The news of his daughter's pregnancy, his coming grandfatherhood, was tugging at him, asking him hard questions: Who exactly was Granddad Raheem? Did he, would he even exist? And if he did exist, if he was going to exist, if he wanted to exist, what sort of elder would he be, and what would he have to say to the newcomer? Would he have any teaching to hand down? And what might that be? Mathematics or soup? His old wisdom, however flawed and inadequate and disappointed that wisdom was, or the Secret, the thing that could not be spoken of? The old Raheem was beginning to be reborn within him, as if he was pregnant as well as Chandni, pregnant with himself. So now there were two Raheems in a single body, fighting against each other, Raheem-Raheem versus Arif-Raheem. Raheem-Raheem, waking up as if from a long sleep, was groggily aware that what he had done was, by any normal standards, "wrong." Maybe even "selfish." Because of his growing disillusion and depression on the one hand, and his seduction by the charismatic and fraternal figure of his reality-altering neighbor on the other, he had walked out of not only his own life but two other people's lives as well, people who, to use the old language, "loved him." And now a third person was on the way.

Was it time to feel guilty, Raheem-Raheem asked. Was it time to repent, to beg forgiveness, to return? When these questions were asked, Arif-Raheem fought back. The path of the ascetic was not shameful but noble. There was nothing to apologize for or regret. Even Siddhartha Gautama, the Buddha himself, had stepped away from worldly things, picked up a begging bowl, and set out down his mendicant path in search of enlightenment. There was nobility in humbling oneself, in shedding one's professor-self, one's Breach Candy reality, to become a servant of the community and—yes!—a daily chopper of vegetables, a boiler of water, a user of seasonings, a maker of soup. To find the light, to rise up into the brightness, it was necessary to shed burdens, even if doing so brought pain. Pain would fade. The eternal truths as interpreted by Mithmu, their teacher and guide, were worth the sacrifice.

Yes, but, the Raheem-Raheem voice murmured a little more loudly, the world according to Mithmu was proving to be the opposite of ascetic. Self-denial was not on the menu, and the truth was that it never had been. The Moon was not for the poor. Mithmu had become a sort of saint of the global rich.

The Ferrari count at the Moon's garages was rising. Wealthy musicians handed over their Rolexes. There were rumors of a great vault beneath the temple at the center of the Moon, a safe place for quantities of cash and jewels donated by willing devotees. There were credible rumors that Mithmu had followed the lead of Haile Selassie in Ethiopia long ago. The emperor had hidden millions of U.S. dollars under the expensive carpets in his palace in Addis Ababa. Mithmu's Moon palace boasted many large, expensive Persian rugs. Nobody was allowed to look under them. Mommy did not permit such impertinences.

Mommy liked banknotes. A number of leading currencies were acceptable, but U.S. dollars were preferred. Mommy disliked tax authorities, and in the year of Chandni's pregnancy the tax authorities decided they disliked her too. An investigation into the financial structure of the Moon began. Mommy bribed the investigators who showed up at the Moon and they went away and declared themselves happy, stating that they had discovered no irregularities and were satisfied that all was aboveboard. (They did not look "below board," under the carpets, for example.) Some faceless killjoy in a bleak office somewhere high up in the tax system was not convinced. The first investigators were reprimanded for sloppy work and more investigators were sent. This second team also declared itself satisfied, having been generously rewarded by Mommy for its happiness. And for a while everything was calm.

Mithmu went to Raheem's soup station to congratulate him on his coming grandfatherhood. "But what's this?" he demanded, looking at Raheem's face. "I see sad-sackness looking at me. How to wipe that glummery off of your kisser?"

"The baby is coming, but it's all the way over there," Raheem replied. "And I am so far, down here."

"In that case," Mithmu told him, "we'll just have to bring the baby down here."

More renaming: Mowbray's Road in the Mylapore neighborhood of Madras was renamed TTK Road in the also-renamed city, Chennai. TTK was the former finance minister of India, the late Tiruvellore Thattai Krishnamachari, whose name was far too long to bother with, and so was universally shortened to its initials. This happened to South Indian politicians with amusing regularity. (See also the two movie stars turned chief ministers, MGR and NTR, a.k.a. Maruthur Gopalan Ramachandran and Nandamuri Taraka Rama Rao, but that's enough about them.) Anyway: TTK took a lifelong interest in music and had a deep connection with the Madras Music Academy, so as well as the road on which the academy stood—at "New No. 168 (Old No. 306)"—the main concert hall at the academy was named after him too. And it was to this TTK Auditorium that Chandni Contractor Ferdaus—or should we begin to call her CCF?—was, at short notice, invited to play.

The distance from the Moon to the TTK Auditorium was approximately one hundred miles, so it didn't occur to Chandni that there was any connection between the two. It was explained to her apologetically that an unexpected vacancy had occurred owing to a sudden illness and the Music Academy would be eternally grateful if she would be so good as to step into the breach. The fee offered was unusually large, and in those early days of her pregnancy it offered her a respite from her husband's family's big (and, to her way of thinking, objectionable and premature) celebratory plans. She accepted the invitation.

Her father was waiting for her at the hotel when she arrived.

I touch your feet. I bend down, I kneel before you. I ask for forgiveness. You bear my grandchild, and that is everything.

I'm not even sure who you are anymore. Do you even remember being a husband, a father, a mathematician, anything? Your golf handicap or the rules of canasta? Or are you one hundred percent lost to yourself? So deeply inside the foolishness that you think it wisdom. I don't know what you have become.

I wanted to see you. You have become something extraordinary. Musician, maker of magic. I wanted to know you. And the life you carry.

You got Mr. Shankar to pay the Music Academy to bring me, didn't you. I don't like that. I don't play for the Man in the Moon. I won't play here. You never came to hear me anyway. What changed? The baby?

The baby changes everything.

You can't even hear how offensive that is to me. I will not play for you. If I play for you, the music will curse you.

What do you want. I'll try to do whatever it is.

There's a woman at home whose heart you broke. She lives alone. She can't understand. I can't understand. You don't just step back into our lives. Time has passed. You have a lot of work to do.

Can I hear you? Will you play something for me?

I told you. If I play to you now, the music will curse you. There is so much anger. Don't you know that?

Can there be peace?

I'm not the first person you have to ask that question. I'm the second person. The first person has to answer first. Go and touch her feet, bend down, kneel. You're in the wrong place. I'm in the wrong place. We should both go. This was a mistake.

Give me a chance.

I'm not the person who can give you anything. You want something? Talk to her. I don't know if she can listen to you anymore. I don't know if she can hear.

Play the concert. So many people want to hear you.

Don't come. Not you, not your Moon man, not that American woman. If they come, they will be cursed too. My music can do that, I promise you. It has that power.

So you are a sorceress.

Yes. Maybe you should be afraid of me.

When she returned to Ferdaus House, the wheels of publicity were already turning. Dimmy Ferdaus had written out the text of the "happy announcement," which Majnoo had released like a white dove into the brilliant sky. Chandni herself was in the sky, flying back, when the white dove of good news took flight, and when she landed, the airport's arrivals hall was blazing with photographers' flashes, and the screaming voices of reporters, mostly women, echoed all around her. *Look left Chandni look right look straight ahead let's have an over the shoulder let's have a smile a bigger smile you must be so happy it must be the happiest day for you let's see it on your face up here Chandni see my waving hand up here down here also I'm down here on the floor smile smile laugh we need you laughing give us more we need more let's have it all up here down here right now. What is it Chandni boy or girl, girl or boy, you must know, readers are dying to know, you can tell us, no need for secrecy, boy or girl or girl or boy. Give us your good quote about how happy you feel, ecstatic, no? You must be. Say ecstatic. Say overjoyed can't wait best day of my life gives new meaning to my existence, say I can't believe it, I'm going to be a mummy! How does your mother feel, Meena madam, Chandni she'll be a grandma! Must be so amazing for her, na? Totally amazing. Say totally amazing Chandni we need your good quote. Exclusive interview Chandni? Biggest magazine in the country, cover guaranteed, inside ten–twelve pages best photographer best fashions best stylists makeup hair, we are ready to go, we can donate money to your preferred charities, just say yes. And oh, hope we find you in good health, all going well, please confirm? Look at you, glowing, the joy can be seen on your cheeks, so many congratulations! Congratulations in the heartiest! Don't go Chandni look left look right look down look up and smile smile be happy you must be happy let us see everybody needs to see.*

And shoving and pushing and jostling and crowding. The level of the frenzy arcing ever upward toward insanity. Her security team overpowered. It took time to clear a path to the waiting car. Until then she was engulfed, shaken, a small boat in a storm.

She came into Ferdaus House trembling uncontrollably. Majnoo was waiting for her, grinning his cat-got-the-cream grin, and killing him felt like a serious option at that moment. "Everybody's so excited," he said. "It's going to be so good."

"Don't talk to me," she said. "I'm going to be sick."

The nightmare of the billion-dollar baby began that day, her pregnancy in its first confirmed weeks already made public without so much as a by-your-leave, blazoned across the front pages of the newspapers and the television networks and the radio channels her husband's family owned, and discussed in horrifying detail in the new online forums where anonymous individuals with anonymous lives insulted one another and denigrated people they did not know but disagreed with or envied or misunderstood or knew nothing about or were prejudiced against or looked down on or hated for reasons they themselves did not properly understand and could not have explained. She retreated to her room, the room Dimmy Ferdaus called a boudoir, a word Chandni disliked and refused to use, and she shut herself away from the world for a day and a night and another day, and when she emerged she discovered that the program for the entire term of her pregnancy was already set in stone.

The threat of a curse that she had hurled at Raheem Contractor was not merely rhetorical. In those days she had begun to discover that her music really had acquired powers of enchantment, and that these were steadily growing stronger. When she was at the piano, these powers were less pronounced because the music was written down and asked only to be interpreted, and even though she was capable of profound interpretation, there was less room in the music for herself. However, when she was seated on a beautiful rug with her sitar's long neck in her hand and a raga beginning to flow from her finger-tips, she understood that because this music allowed her so much room for improvisation, it was capable of carrying into the hearts of the audience not only a great composer's intentions but her own. At the Music Academy she had been so badly disturbed by her encounter with her father that her disturbance had infused her performance, and after the end of the sitar recital that formed the second half of her program, the audience had left the TTK Auditorium mystified by the floods of angry tears pouring from their eyes.

What could she do with such a gift, a second power growing out of the first? How big might it become? She asked herself these questions all the time but did not know the answers. As the saga of the billion-dollar baby unfolded, she began to understand what those answers might be.

"No expense is being spared," Dimmy Ferdaus told Chandni when her daughter-in-law emerged from seclusion. "This family is making its best effort for you and the life you bear within you. I hope you will appreciate, and not be an ungrateful little so-and-so."

Majnoo handed Chandni a thick folder. She turned to the first page.

Welcome, Baby!
Event No. 1

The renowned American singer [*insert name of singer when finalized*] will perform a range of classic hits, including "Be My Baby," "Baby Love," "Everybody Wants to Be My Baby," "Ooo Baby Baby," "Baby" (Bieber version), "My Baby" (Temptations version), "Santa Baby," and "Baby I Don't Care."

After that there were many more pages. She closed the folder, shaking her head in what might have looked like wonderment.

"You have no idea who-all we are talking to," Majnoo told Chandni, peppering his speech with such terms of endearment as she had never heard coming out of his mouth before. "Biggest, biggest stars. Whoo-eee. Immortals, sweetie baby. And not just one concert. One every month until the Big Birth and then a whole fucking Woodstock Coachella Glasto type wowzaroo. Oval Maidan, Brabourne Stadium, Wankhede Stadium, using them all. You will *love.*

"And the guest list! This time we are not only reaching for the top, not even the top-top, we are going so over the top it's out of *sight,* baby doll. Royalty, honey pie, European et cetera, our own also obviously, but only the hottest young ones. And okay maybe some cool aunties. But not a lot. And everyone famous you ever heard of. Don't you worry. They will all come. Planes being supplied. All travel needs met at super-luxury level. Financial inducements being subtly offered. Million-dollar swag bags. Security systems at full availability. If escorts slash translators required, we have those on tap.

"I haven't even mentioned the banquets, the wines, the locations at heart of Incredible India. Can you believe for the final celebration one month after the expected birth date we have the Taj? No, not our beloved but overused Bombay grand hotel, darling . . . the Taj itself. Agra, baby. Taj *Mahal.* World's greatest monument to love, isn't it, but instead of being a tomb, *boring,* we will turn the whole shebang into a festival of beginning, arrival. India's Baby. Your baby. Our baby. The Taj Mahal Baby will be at the heart of the Ferdaus brand. Don't even ask what we had to fork out for *that,* who-all we had to promise what-all, a lot of persons requiring let us say placating, *big* operation.

Clearly to hold the date you will have a voluntary C-section so we can confirm the full-moon night without worrying about delays. Full moon shining down on us! *Chandni,* the moonlight, for our own Moonlight Mama! The *chandni* for Chandni! Forget about Supermoon—we will have Babymoon! Ferdausmoon! Super*duper*moon for the Ferdaus baby."

"A voluntary C-section," Chandni tonelessly repeated. "A voluntary choice that you have chosen for me without asking."

"*Arré,* just a slip, darling! Nothing bad meant by it. Too much muchness on my to-do sheet! So many balls in the air! Still working on so-many too-many details, darling," Majnoo said, "but we wanted you to have the overview immediately. The big picture. Exclamation marks every day from now until Birthday and beyond. You have to do nothing! Only stay pregnant, show up, and enjoy. What do you say?"

"She says thank you," Dimmy Ferdaus interjected. "What else is there for little piano girl to say? Only a barbarian would not fall on her knees with gratitude. No mother-to-be was ever spoiled like this in the history of the world. Little sitar girl would have to be seriously out of tune if not impressed. Impressed, and moved. Totally moved."

Majnoo again asked his wife for her opinion, with just a trace of uncertainty behind his big, confident smile. "Chandni? You like?"

She tried to smile back. "Of course it's astonishing," she said. "But I'm worried. Suppose the pregnancy isn't easy. Suppose I don't feel well when you have arranged all this *tamasha*? And the C-section, I don't know."

"Don't worry about any of that," Dimmy Ferdaus said, with a commanding sharpness in her voice. "The C-section matter is settled. Put it out of your mind. And if you have to miss events and rest because of the unborn baby's health, everyone will understand, and we will go forward to celebrate you and Baby Ferdaus in your absence."

"The show must go on," Majnoo added. "You are a performer, so you know."

"Yes," Chandni said quietly. "Your show must go on."

8

The dismantling of the Moon began when the third team of tax investigators arrived. This time they came in two tiers, arriving separately on different days: an official, aboveboard team with all the proper accreditation, and an undercover team posing as new disciples. Each team was also given the task of keeping an eye on the other team, which was intended to make underhanded shenanigans harder to conceal. "We were honest men," one of the overt team told the media after the gigantic fraud was revealed, but that may have been a half-truth. Perhaps they were honest because they had to be. Let us, however, give them the benefit of the doubt, because they did, did they not, visit and reveal what quickly came to be called the Dark Side of the Moon. A Chinese spacecraft had only recently made the first-ever landing on the actual Moon's unseen hemisphere, so the hidden "dark side" was at the front of many minds. As it turned out, Mithmu's lair on the Coromandel Coast also contained much of interest that had hitherto lain concealed.

Mithmu's associate and lover Mommy confronted the overt team when it arrived and accused its members of harassment. "Three times in quick succession, it's too much," she declared.

The team leader responded sternly. "I have two words for you, madame," he said. "Alphonse Capone."

"Tax evasion, eleven years in prison, major financial penalties, died broke," his associate added, redundantly, because Mommy, being American, had understood the threat without requiring the long-form version. "We are not gangsters here," she said. "We tend to the things of the spirit, not the things of the world."

"Apart from the ninety-three Ferrari motor vehicles, we hear, and for which we would like to see full documentation ASAP," the team leader rejoined. "And many extreme sexual practices, very probably illegal and rumored to be disgusting. You are fortunate we are not the sex police."

"Acts between consenting adults are of no concern to the law," Mommy said, stone-faced, immovable, not about to be bullied.

"This is true," said the lead investigator, "unless, theoretically speaking, one of the parties is not adult, and-slash-or not consenting, and another party, let us say the instigating party, the boss party, is possibly suffering from an undeclared transmissible disease, viz., theoretically speaking, syphilis."

"Somebody has been lying to you," Mommy said.

The lead investigator shrugged dismissively. "I repeat," he said, "I am the taxman only."

The parade of confiscated supercars out of the Moon was the first sign to the neighborhood, the news media, and the outside world that, to paraphrase what the lead investigator said to a television reporter, the jig was up. In faraway Modena, a Ferrari spokesman rejected all accusations of wrongdoing. "None of these models were acquired directly from us," the spokesman declared. "In every case intermediaries were used and the end owner remained anonymous. Until today no Ferrari officer was aware of this large agglomeration of our products in southern India." The statement was accepted, by and large, without unfavorable comment. The questions of how and where the vehicles were serviced, how spare parts were acquired, et cetera, went unasked. Nobody was after Ferrari. The target was the Man in the Moon.

There was a thing the investigators did not mention in public because they agreed it would make people think them insane, although all of them heard it, the covert team as well as the overt team. That thing was music, classical sitar music, the raga Megh Malhar, filling their ears, even though no sitarist could be seen. And the music in some way . . . again, impossible to express without being thought crazy . . . *guided them.* It grew louder when they were close to what they were searching for and weaker when they were farther away. With the help of the inexplicable music, they found the millions upon millions hidden under the palace rugs and the gold ingots in the secret basement and the watches and jewels buried under the stepping stones near the water fountains and all the treasures in secret panels in the sex rooms and the singing-bowl meditation room and everywhere else. And once they had found it all, the heavens opened and a heavy rain began to fall, as if the magical rain raga were congratulating them on their work.

Only the open-air soup kitchen was clean. Raheem with his ladle stood wide-eyed in shock while the truth about the Moon operation was revealed, and then even wider-eyed with wonder when the rain began to flood the Moon, soaking all of it, falling inside the buildings as well as outside them, except on that exact place where he stood, ladle in hand. Not a single drop fell into his steaming pans of bone soup, and he himself remained bonedry.

When the rain stopped, the covert investigators revealed themselves and joined forces with the overt team, entering the palace to arrest Mithmu and Mommy for large-scale tax fraud.

But Mithmu had gone. There was no more Moon and therefore no more Man in it. Nor was G.S. or Gurushankar ever seen again, and even plain old V. Shankar as he had been in his professorial beginnings was nowhere to be found. A revised count of the seized Ferraris revealed that one was missing, and that car, too, was never seen again. Many people believed that the old fraud, after being so publicly shamed, must have driven into the sea and drowned. Others claimed to have seen him in Bali in the company of an old benefactor or alone on the island nation of Tuvalu, which was sinking into the ocean and would take him with it when it went. And of course there were some true believers among the bedraggled, departing Moonfolk who were convinced that the State was the true criminal and Mithmu in disgusted innocence had abandoned this world and risen to a higher plane.

Mommy did not run but stood proudly erect in the palace's throne room to receive her captors. "In a way, Madam Bridget Hampton, you are a collector of taxes also," the lead investigator told her as she was led away into captivity and out of our story. "This secret undeclared fortune of yours was freely given to you by deluded fools, so we may call it a tax on stupidity."

Raheem heard sitar music too, but unlike the taxmen he knew where it was coming from, who was playing it, and what it meant. This was not the rain raga but a song of renewal, a dawn raga; he was not expert enough to identify it, though maybe it was the raga Lalit or else the raga Bhairavi or another one, but its beauty called him to arise gently and begin a new day. He felt like a man waking up from a dream. Yes, you were stupid too, the music sang to him, you are proof that an intelligent man can be a fool, can be led astray, off the path his life should have taken and onto the road of folly, that a man who thought himself to be kind and decent can be led into cruelty and indecency, you are proof that within you there is a creature who wanted to be led and told what to think and how to be, and all your scholarship disappeared down the drain when you met your seducer, and so there you stand with a ladle in your hand, in a place of crookery, with the meaninglessness revealed of all you thought had meaning, and nobody wants your soup anymore, and your life is meaningless too. Then the music changed and became kinder and called to him: In spite of everything you have done, come, come, and maybe there can be forgiveness, and maybe there can be love, maybe the path you deserted can be found again. Come, put down that spoon, and walk.

Raheem Contractor let go of the soup ladle, picked up a mendicant's begging bowl and a wooden staff to help him when he felt weak, put a straw hat on his head against the fury of the Deccan sun, and walked off the Moon to begin his long journey on foot across the country from coast to coast, a redemption walk of more than nine hundred miles.

9

It was a tough pregnancy. She was sick for most of it, and there were fears for the child's well-being. Chandni had to cancel all her bookings and lead something close to an invalid's life. The child was found to be male, but the Ferdauses wanted to keep that a secret until after the birth, when the father could hold his son triumphantly up above his head, proving that the dynasty's survival was assured. And in spite of Chandni's poor health, the billion-dollar celebrations of the forthcoming Happy Event continued unabated. She was placed under pressure to attend all the events and did so, briefly, retiring as soon as possible, feeling dizzy, nauseous, and faint. Teams of doctors attended her. Her own health seemed unimportant to these medicos. She was merely the vehicle for the one whose health was of paramount importance. Meena was with her every day, growing angrier by the hour.

Chandni lay in bed with her eyes closed, but her fingers were moving. "I used to imagine I could hear music when you played air piano or air sitar like that," Meena told her daughter while putting cold compresses on the young woman's brow. "I was just beginning then," Chandni replied. "Now I've found out how much I can do."

Meena asked her what she meant. Chandni squeezed her mother's hand. "He's coming home," she said. "Now you have to decide if you want him."

Meena's face reddened and her hand went up to her mouth. "You sent the music to summon him," she said. "This also you can do."

"But only you know if you can take him back," her daughter replied. "Music can't help with that."

"You know," Meena said, almost to herself, "in all this time, hardly anyone has asked me how I feel. My brilliant husband falls for a stupid fraud. My brilliant daughter falls for a stupid playboy. I am left alone in our home without the two people who were my whole world. But everyone says, 'Oh, Meena Contractor, she's tough, she can't be broken, she'll be fine.' But guess what, I don't think I'm fine. I think I am broken. And yes, you're right, there are things that magic can't repair."

From the Moon he came to Tindivanam and from there to Thellar. Then to Mazhaiyur, Arani, Adukkamparai, the Little Flower Convent. He ate what people put in his bowl and he slept on the warm earth. He took the ferry across the Palar River. Names and places began to blur together. The days stretched into weeks. Chittathoor, Guddiyattam, the Perumal Temple, the Babu Mahal Palace, Ashok Nagar. Then the long, long walk beside the interminable Palamaner road. At the Om Shakti Temple he rested. In the Synagunda forest he was afraid of animals. At a Siliguri café the kind owner fed him well. Then came Charitha, then the Siddi Vinayaka temple in Bearupalli village, and so, interminably, on and on. The land felt infinite. The journey was endless. He passed the Muslim seminary of Darul Uloom without pausing. He did not stop at the Mother Teresa school, either. By the time he reached the Jeevadhatha old-age home, he felt one hundred years old.

There were things that magic couldn't repair. In the greatest scene in the greatest film ever made in India, *Pather Panchali*, or

"The Song of the Little Road," the story of a poor family living in a little Bengali village, Harihar, the father, returns home from the city, where he has found work and made a little money, and he opens his bag and holds up the gifts he has bought for his daughter, Durga, not knowing that she has died in his absence. Then his wife, Sarbajaya, tells him, and as she speaks his face contorts into a scream of grief. Ravi Shankar's music surges, and it's the music that best tells us how they feel. Music has that magic, but it can't undo a death.

I'm thinking about *Pather Panchali* because I have to tell now about another terrible day. Here it is, as plainly as I can tell it. Meena is with Chandni in her daughter's room in the Ferdaus mansion. It is nighttime and the household has retired. Chandni is feeling unwell, as has become normal, but tonight she has another concern. The baby isn't kicking, she tells her mother. It doesn't seem to be moving at all.

There is a team of top-notch ob-gyns on twenty-four-hour call, and their equipment is already installed in Chandni's bedroom. Meena makes the phone call, and soon enough the doctor has arrived and wheels the ultrasound machine into position, spreads the water-soluble gel over Chandni's distended stomach, picks up the handheld transducer, and performs the test. Then he performs it a second time, and then a third.

Finally he sets the transducer down. He is a young man, so perhaps he hasn't had to do this very often, but he keeps his voice steady.

"I'm sorry," he says, "but there is no heartbeat."

It's Meena, calm, collected Meena Contractor, who is the first one to scream.

The things that impinge on his awareness, that register in spite of his exhaustion, are becoming a random, whimsical bunch. A Hanuman gym center. Yes, that's what he needs now, a little workout. A temple to rest at, where he is given food. Anjaneyaswami, that was the name. Then a long way of nothing. There are names that strike him as amusing just because of their sounds. Edigapalle. Amilepalli family fields. Madanapalle, where are located an industrial oil store and a rubber-stamp works. Lord Siva temple: more welcome alms. Then more names, alien to his eyes and ears. Mana Gromor Angallu. Tummanam Gunta. At Burakaylakota he passes a shoe factory and is moved by the generosity of the workers, who give him fresh sandals and a spare pair as well. Mandlipalli Kalli Palli Allugundu Kutagulla Yerradoddi. Then a string of public gardens where he can dawdle and even sleep under trees and stars. Lion P. Mansoor Ali Khan Gardens, Ashok Reddy Garden, Ramala Garden, Somala Narashimappa Garden. A bridge across the Chitravathi River. Onward, onward. The Sri Krishnadevaraya University campus. Generosity of students toward a tired old man. Another footwear factory, but no luck this time. Pilligundla. Jelli Palli. Waterfalls. He bathes at the base of the falls. The Daroji bear sanctuary. He is afraid. The Dyamavva temple. He rests.

"The baby must be carried to full term," Dimmy Ferdaus said firmly. "There isn't very long to go. The C-section is already scheduled, as you will be well aware." She and Majnoo had joined Meena and Chandni in the young woman's bedchamber.

"That's ridiculous," Meena Contractor replied. "On the contrary, we must bring Chandni immediately to the Breach Candy Hospital so that this sad event can be dealt with properly."

The young doctor, still in the room, began to agree. Dimmy raised a silencing hand. "Shoo," she said. "You can go. This is now a family conference. No outsiders allowed." Such was her air of authority that the inexperienced youth exited the room with his head hung low.

"Surely," Meena said, "it was wrong to dismiss the medical expert. The health of the mother is the paramount issue now."

"The paramount issue, Mrs. Contractor," Dimmy retorted, deliberately avoiding Meena's given name, "is the triple-venue superconcert next weekend. *Far* too late to cancel. Talent is already in town, more arriving on every incoming flight. You understand we have expended major funds."

"And so your intention is to risk my daughter's life for the sake of your brand identity. Come on, Chandni, we're leaving now."

"I'm afraid that can't be permitted," Dimmy Ferdaus said. "My son's wife will receive absolute tip-top care until the C-section, which will be after the superconcert. The nation will be plunged into mourning when the announcement is made. Our media outlets will ensure that. Then the event at the Taj will be even more moving. The whole world will mourn alongside us. It will be extremely beautiful."

"I see that you are insane," Meena said.

"Given your attitude, we can't permit you to leave, either," Dimmy said. "We will therefore place you in a super-comfy guest suite. You will kindly surrender your mobile."

"Chandni," Majnoo pleaded weakly. "It's for some days only. Please concur." Chandni understood that he was his mother's son first, a champion of the Ferdaus brand—a "team player"—second, and a husband third. Third at best. Maybe other things came ahead of her as well. The cricket team. His dancing skills. His haircut. Maybe she was really low down on the list and had failed to understand that. Something in her heart hardened. Some dark new resolve formed.

She gestured to her mother, and Meena bent down and placed her ear against her daughter's lips.

"What did she say?" Majnoo wanted to know.

"You wouldn't understand," Meena answered. "Mother-daughter stuff."

Chandni had whispered just three words to Meena.

Best eaten cold.

The Western Ghats. Forested hills, hard going for a tired man, but cooler temperatures. Beauty-spot hill stations, beloved retreats for the dwellers in the city by the sea. Mahabaleshwar, Lonavala. Then the descent to the shore, the long ferry ride, the Gateway of India. Home.

He walked slowly up the hill to his old home, his home no more, his once and he hoped future home, and when he got there, there was nobody home. What this meant was that only Mary the Mangalorean cook was home and Mohan the Gujarati bearer and Kamal the Goan houseboy, or *hamal,* and the toothless old lady sweeper whose name he had forgotten was there doing her sweeping rounds of the neighborhood, and Arvind the gardener, who worked for all the apartments, was watering the flowers downstairs in the garden. He understood that the term *nobody home* was a relic of an old elitist self. Of course many people were home, and he had learned, now, about the dignity of labor. But he was the one who had left and filled this home with grief, and the people who were there greeted him with caution, even with suspicion. His appearance disarmed them a little. He was dusty from the road and his beard was ragged and his clothes needed washing and his hair was matted with dirt and the sandals on his feet needed to be thrown away. He was a man who had walked nine hundred miles to be forgiven, and the first gesture of forgiveness came from Cook Mary, who said he needed a good meal and fed him. And then he was allowed to shower in his old bathroom, and to his surprise Meena had kept his clothes in the old almirah where they had always been, so he had clean things to put on. And his shaving things were in the bathroom cabinet still. It was as though he had never left. But the people who were there were feeling disloyal even as they helped him, he could see the guilt in their eyes, and maybe the reason they overcame their reservations was that they were worried. Mrs. Meena, they explained, had gone over to Walkeshwar to be with Chandni Bibi, but that was many days past and now neither of them were picking up their mobiles and when Mohan called the grand house he was told by the voice that answered that nobody could come to the phone.

"Then I will go there," Raheem said, and clean-shaven in his clean clothes and still wearing his now-frayed straw hat he walked down the little Westfield Compound hill, along Warden Road, up along Gowalia Tank Road to Kemps Corner, and thence up Malabar Hill to Walkeshwar, where, when he presented himself at the gates of the Ferdaus property and asked to be taken to see his wife and daughter, he was first told by a Pathan security guard, impolitely, "Wait on," and then after a long time of waiting the same security guard returned to say, "Those ladies do not desire to meet with you at this time."

It was a humiliating rebuke, but there was a voice in Raheem's head that said, *You know these two women better than you know anyone else, and so you know that this is not their voice speaking, which means that someone else is speaking for them and the harsh rejecting desire being expressed is not theirs.*

"In that case," he told the security guard, "I will sit down here on the sidewalk and fast, and wait until they express a different desire."

"It is impossible for you to remain there," the security guard scolded Raheem as he squatted down in the dust. "This is a big man's house, a big family's residence."

"And this is the public street," Raheem said, "and it belongs to no man or *khandaan,* however big."

He sat there all day. After several hours the security guard softened and brought him water to drink. He was grateful for that. At night the gate opened and a limousine emerged carrying Jimmy, Dimmy, and Majnoo Ferdaus, who were on their way to the huge triple concerts at the Oval Maidan and the Brabourne and Wankhede Stadiums. Extra security guards barred the way to prevent Raheem from entering when the limousine exited. The limousine paused beside the squatting man, and Dimmy Ferdaus lowered her window. "You're just embarrassing yourself, Raheem," she said. "Nobody cares, okay? Do yourself a favor and just fuck off."

But there are things even the rich-rich-rich cannot control. On the night of the three concerts Chandni's waters broke, early, and so instead of the planned C-section at Breach Candy Hospital the delivery took place at the Ferdaus mansion with the assigned home team of doctors in attendance. A stillbirth is a terrible thing, and the body of the unnamed baby boy was removed from Chandni's presence and she was left with her mother to encounter the flood of emotion from which there was no escape. And when the doctors became aware of the man fasting at the gate and the treatment of the two Contractor women by the Ferdaus family, they refused to be parties to what was going on and ordered the mansion staff to admit Chandni's father immediately and return the ladies' possessions, and in the absence of any Ferdaus family member to command otherwise, it proved impossible for the staff to resist the doctors' orders and Raheem was allowed into the mansion and brought up to Chandni's room to join her and Meena in their grief and horror . . . and beneath that sadness was the arrival of something that was not sad, but was a happiness deferred.

Reconciliation.

The three Ferdauses, parents and son, had been informed by mobile of the developments, but they were guests of honor at the three concerts, one Ferdaus at each of the three, and they did not leave their seats or give any indication that anything was amiss. They texted one another and agreed that an early announcement would have to be made and after that Chandni and Meena could no longer be held against their will, but that was a matter for the morning. They surmised that a separation was inevitable, and that Majnoo would return to bachelor status soon, but that also was a matter for the future, and Dimmy already had a short list of possible second wives. This night was not for any of that. It was for music, world music, not Chandni Contractor's kind of old-school stuff but the music of billionaire musicians playing billionaire music for their billionaire hosts. Music that was rich-rich-rich. The billionaires sat back in their seats and applauded.

When the three Ferdauses returned home, however, they were informed that the three Contractors had departed and would not be returning. The celebration of the billion-dollar baby was at an end. The dead child was ready to be taken to the nearby *dakhma*, or Tower of Silence, to be consumed by the traditional birds.

Rumors spread rapidly that the death of the child in the womb had been known to the family before the night of the concerts, and the general public was appalled at the Ferdaus dynasty's decision to conceal the news and continue to "celebrate" when in fact they should have been mourning their loss. Although the Ferdaus media did their best to present the sad news sympathetically—the family had briefly suppressed its personal tragedy so as not to destroy the happiness of the gathered, excited crowds, et cetera, et cetera—the general response continued to be strongly negative. The event at the Taj Mahal was canceled, but that made no difference. Although the Ferdaus empire went into damage-limitation mode, severe reputational damage had been done.

This was not how things ended. When Chandni regained her health and strength, the situation became much worse.

The present decay of ethical society around the world is a matter of some concern. Words such as "good" and "bad" or "right" and "wrong" are losing their effect, emptying of meaning, and failing, anymore, to shape society. Other words, such as "power," "weakness," et cetera, are replacing them. Also, "knowledge" is being replaced by "ignorance," "memory" is being replaced by "forgetting," and nothing, no shameful action, however atrocious, remains in the public mind for long. These are days in which "shamelessness" is king. In such a time, even a great scandal like the story of the billion-dollar dead baby is not, by itself, potent enough to derail a great capitalist enterprise. Jimmy Ferdaus, the silent leader, the still center of the turning wheel, remained calm. The storm would pass, and his corporations would weather it and go on. It was not his way to issue family orders, but his wife and son understood what was required of them. They, too, fell silent, and withdrew from the public eye.

What Jimmy failed to take into account was the rising power of another modern-day dynamic. When that dynamic can be combined with supernatural powers, its ability to damage families, industries, even nations becomes formidable. Perhaps even irresistible.

The name of that dynamic is *revenge.*
Best eaten cold.

The day came when Chandni's fingers began to move once more in their particular fashion. She was back in her own room in her own family's residence in Breach Candy. She had not thought, since her return, of sitting at her piano or picking up her sitar—both of which had quietly been returned to her—but this time when her fingers moved Meena was in no doubt that she heard music. First Meena heard it, then Raheem. It was music of a kind they had never heard before, and the instruments on which it was being played were unknown to them. It rose above their home like a pillar of smoke, like a column of fire, like the weapon of an invading alien species, and then it rushed across the city and the country to do its deadly work. At the Ferdaus shipyard, the state-of-the-art destroyer being built for the national navy mysteriously exploded in its dry dock and was ruined beyond hope of repair. At the Ferdaus steel mills, the labor force walked out without warning and began an indefinite strike. At the Ferdaus hotel chains, the reservations clerks experienced an unprecedented flood of cancellations. Three skyscrapers being built in the city by Ferdaus construction entities were discovered to be structurally unstable and were scheduled for early demolition. A fire in the southern tea plantations wiped out the Ferdaus tea crop. The mainframe computers in the south, where many of the world's biggest megacorporations lodged their data, overnight lost the business of the three largest information-technology industries on earth. The Ferdaus print media experienced a catastrophic avalanche of canceled subscriptions, and the Ferdaus television and cable stations experienced a parallel plague of canceled advertising.

At the city's stock exchange, the price of Ferdaus Industries plummeted so steeply that trading in the stock had to be frozen. And wherever the destruction was occurring people swore that they heard unearthly music, music of a kind that had never been heard before, and there was no way of knowing who was playing it, or where it was coming from, or on what devices it was being made. It was music that frightened everyone who heard it. The old could not remain standing while it played, and the young found that their hair had turned white.

More than one person, at the shipyards, at the TV stations, at the stock exchange, in the streets, used the same phrase to describe the terrifying music: "It sounded like the end of the world."

In the early evening the Ferdaus mansion was visited by two tax investigators, who insisted on seeing the patriarch himself. They advised Jimmy Ferdaus that undercover teams had been working inside Ferdaus Industries' many enterprises and had now delivered their report, as a consequence of which the Ferdaus Group as a whole and Jimmy Ferdaus as an individual were to be indicted for large-scale bribery, corruption, and income-tax fraud, and the high court would be asked for long jail terms for all concerned.

"I have just two words for you," said the more senior of the two investigators. "Those words are 'Alphonse Capone.'"

"Tax evasion, eleven years . . ." the junior investigator began, but Jimmy Ferdaus raised a silencing hand.

"Please," he said. "Kindly spare me the explanation."

On the second day the music continued across the city and the destruction of the Ferdaus Group went on apace. In addition, Dimmy Ferdaus was told by her physician that a cancer had spread rapidly through her body, was inoperable, and there was no hope of recovery. On the third day Majnoo Ferdaus was playing at Wankhede Stadium, facing slow left-arm spin bowling, when the ball improbably—impossibly—accelerated after leaving the bowler's hand. Like many batsmen, Majnoo did not wear a helmet when facing slow bowling, so he was unprotected when the ball, reaching a speed of over one hundred miles an hour, struck him on the side of the head, broke his skull, and ended his career. And in the days that followed an unnamed plague began to infect people in the hundreds, the thousands, the tens of thousands, and Meena Contractor burst into her daughter's room and grabbed her hands to prevent the fingers from moving, crying, "Enough. You have more than crossed the line. How many people do you want to kill?"

"This sickness is not my doing," Chandni calmly said, and insisted it was the truth, even when Jimmy Ferdaus fell sick with the plague and died of it before he could be sentenced for his crimes.

Time passed. The plague receded and Meena accepted that it probably wasn't brought into the world by her daughter's devil music. However, the collapse of Ferdaus Industries and the whole of the Ferdaus Group was a thing in which Chandni did have a hand. What she started was completed by others. After the days of the music, the sharks of the rich-rich-rich descended upon the broken corporations, tore them apart, and swallowed them. And on the country's far coast the Moon, too, had been torn apart, seized by developers, demolished, and remade, and the music had been there as well. So Chandni the Musician of Kahani can be said to be one of the very rare artists whose work directly impacted and shaped the world in which she lived.

· · ·

And now I am taking one last walk up the little lane off Warden Road leading to the four villas of the Westfield Estate at its end, the gabled villas named after the royal palaces of Britain, Sandringham Villa, Bal Moral, Glamis Villa, and Windsor Villa, which was once my home and is now the residence of my characters, Raheem and Meena and Chandni, all together again and—should I say—happy? Or at least working things out, and on the way back to happiness?

I'm walking slowly. There are children playing around me and I know they aren't really here, they are the ghost children of my childhood, Beverly the Australian girl on her bicycle, Michael and David the blond English boys, my South Indian friend whom we called Ramani for short because his real name (Balasubramaniam Venkataraghavana) was too long, the friends who visited from elsewhere in the city, Fudli and Darab, Anju and Neelam, and the next-door chums, Arif (not Raheem-Arif! This was Next-Door-Arif!) and his sister Nusrat. And there's also and always my sister Sameen. And Saleem, don't forget him, Saleem Big-Nose, he isn't real but he's here too. They chase one another around and kick balls and laugh and shout. Here I am visiting my yesterdays one last time and they are visiting me. I will not come this way again. And at the end of the lane, while the children play, I look up at the end of my story.

There they sit, the three Contractors, on their late afternoon veranda as the day cools toward evening. Chandni doesn't play the sitar anymore. Her parents were frightened of what it had the power to unleash, and she agreed to set it aside. She still performs professionally on the piano with considerable success, and because symphonies and sonatas are all written down, there's no room for devil magic there, except such magic as the music already contains. But these changes were not enough. Meena and Raheem had seen what music their daughter could make without any instruments at all. "We love you," Meena told her, "but we are also a little afraid of you."

Chandni swore an oath of forbearance. "Never again," she promised, and her parents, who knew her for the truthful person she had always been, accepted it. Or almost accepted it. Or agreed with each other that they had no choice but to accept it. To accept it and hope for the best.

And that is how they live now. I look up at them as I prepare to take my leave, and there they are on the veranda. Chandni is calm, but in Raheem and Meena's eyes I see a double light— a light of love, but also just a glimmer of fear. And Chandni, who doesn't laugh a lot, whose default expression is sort of grave, is smiling her strange little smile.

Late

The College was almost six hundred years old. It had been founded by a king who was mad for most of his life. After his death he began performing miracles, blinding an enemy from beyond the grave and raising a plague victim from the dead, or so people came to believe. Such occurrences, if true, may serve as a sort of foreshadowing of the unusual events that occurred more recently, approximately fifty-five years ago, and that will be set down without judgment in this belated account. They are events that cannot easily be accommodated within a rigorously rational description of the world.

1

When the Honorary Fellow S. M. Arthur woke up in his darkened College bedroom he was dead, but at first that didn't seem to change anything. All was familiar: his curved-back "boat bed," the cough drops and the assortment of morning medications, all in their place on the bedside table beside a small black notebook, the "dream diary" in which he wrote down the sentences that sometimes came into his sleeping mind instead of images. He certainly didn't feel dead; in fact, he felt unusually healthy, well rested, and eager for the day. The side effects of his various medications had disappeared, the sluggishness he was used to was absent, his eyes felt good. He reached for his small bedside alarm clock to see what time it was—it was the day when the clocks went back, a Sunday in October—and now he had his first surprise. The clock hands were stuck at midnight. It was obviously not midnight. He had not forgotten to wind it, as he did every night before retiring; but it was not ticking. And then a second strangeness became apparent, even in the gloom of the early morning bedroom. The clock was in his hand, that was incontrovertible—here it was, he was holding it—but it was somehow also still standing untouched on the bedside table. It had apparently multiplied. He had no explanation for this, and sat up in bed, scratching his head.

"Well, I'll be damned," S. M. said aloud. (Let's just call him S. M. for the time being. His full name will be revealed at the proper time.)

He got out of bed in his blue pajamas to go to the bathroom. He felt surprisingly light on his feet, which he saw as a good sign. Maybe he had lost a pound or two. When he entered the bathroom he didn't bother to turn the light on. He knew where everything was. He didn't bother to lift the toilet seat, and waited. Nothing happened, nothing began, and finally he gave up, scratched his head for a second time, and went back into the bedroom, where another man, a stranger, was sleeping in his bed, also wearing blue pajamas. S. M.'s heart began to pound, or at least he felt as if that was what was happening, and then a confusion gripped his mind, because the body in the bed—the stranger—was himself.

Duplicates everywhere, he thought. *The clock first and now me, too.* The gravity of his situation still eluded him. He had not envisaged this turn of events. He was sixty-one years old and had been expecting several more years, twilight years, golden years, whatever people said these days. There were meals to eat, galleries to visit, music to listen to, films to see, books to read, and occasionally other human beings to meet, although of late he had become a man for whom art was more interesting than people. Had something untoward happened? Had he—here he felt himself shudder even though there was no body to do the shuddering—been murdered? If so, then by whom? The darkened room showed no traces of violence. Still, it had to be considered.

After what might have been a long while—his grasp of time had begun to feel inexact—the cleaning lady entered the room, and then the inevitable machinery of death went into operation, and it became clear to him that his life was over. The lights went on and the noise in the bedroom increased as people crowded in, the professionals of death. Official voices, peremptory and neutral, rose and fell. The Provost of the College, Lord Emmemm himself, entered as regally as he always did, floating forward as if conveyed on a small airborne rug, the invisible bejeweled crown glittering as usual on his shining head, the imaginary orb and scepter of kingship in his hands. "Tragic," he intoned, with an imposing shake of the head, and then he floated away and left the work of death to those best suited to do it. S. M. found this work intolerable and went into his study to think.

Now that he was detached from his body, his mind was doing all the work: in fact, he realized, he had become his mind. However, in spite of the evidence of his own eyes—the sight of his own body lying dead in bed—he continued to see himself as having his usual physical form. That is, the disembodied mind he had become had created for itself the illusion of a housing entity, his body, which no longer contained it, and as a result he was able to continue using a vocabulary whose verbs had been separated from their physical meanings, just as he had been separated from his physical self.

He tried to clear his thoughts. This being dead was not at all what he had been led to believe, and he needed to understand what exactly it entailed. He had always had an orderly mind, so perhaps he could begin with some lists. Things he would never do. He would never visit the Pyramids or Greece or his mother's grave. Things he would never do again: sex would be at the top of the list for many people, but in his case it hadn't been a subject for a long time, so it didn't count. He should put "eat Chinese food" up there instead. He would really miss Chinese food. He would also never again swim, or sunbathe, or occupy a seat in an airplane, or perhaps even a car. He had been unseated.

This was no time for levity, he reproved himself. He attempted to raise the tone of his analysis. It seemed clear from what had happened that the old argument about the relationship between the body and the mind had been conclusively settled, and they were shown to be separate entities, the one housed within, but capable of surviving, the other. Descartes had made a distinction between the mind and the brain. The mind was not matter but could influence matter. The mind worked the brain the way a rider worked his horse. To which could now be added a second proposition: when unhorsed, the rider could still work. Guess what, René? *Mostly right*. Finally, he had never been drawn to Buddhism (or any other spiritual practice), but the old fellow Gautama's idea of the mind turned out to be interesting. According to Gautama, it, the mind, was made up of five elements: feelings (yes, he still had those), perceptions (unless everything presently happening to him was a delusion, he was still able to perceive), will (to be honest, he wasn't sure how much volition he still had at his disposal, or how free it might be), sensory consciousness (definitely problematic; he was conscious, yes, and appeared to have some senses at his disposal, vision and hearing, to be precise, but touch, taste, and smell seemed to have bid him farewell), and physical form (well, that was a definite no). Still, four out of five, at least partly relevant. Not bad for a two-and-a-half-thousand-year-old man.

He needed to clarify, if possible, one important question: What was the exact nature of the space into which death had propelled him? If this was an "afterlife," was this all there was to it? This solitary wandering, unseen, through the untouchable untasteable unsmellable world of "life"? What about heaven, hell, the whole rewards-and-punishments narrative? What about the bardo, reincarnation, et cetera? What about God? So far—and he conceded that it hadn't been very long;

although, again, his grasp of time, of duration, had loosened considerably—but still, so far, there was no indication that any of that otherworldly apparatus actually existed. Nor was there any guidance on how long this type of death might last. Was it a kind of lonely immortality to which he had been forever consigned? Or was it finite, ending in a second death, a death that brought oblivion—or perhaps allowed one admission into that long-imagined *inferno e paradiso* eternity? And was what was happening to him the fate of all the dead, or were there different deaths for different people? And if so . . . why?

There was a commotion in the bedroom. *They have come for the body,* he understood, and was struck by the note of detachment. *His body* had already become *the body,* in the time that had elapsed, which he now understood must be longer than it seemed. *It's so strange,* he told himself. *All my life I was famous for my punctuality, even for showing up earlier than required, and now that time has slipped my grasp, I'm going to be—well, I am—forever Late. The Late S. M. Arthur.*

This struck him as funny and he began to laugh, too hard, almost a hysterical laugh. *Control yourself,* he thought. *You're a dead man. Dead men don't have much to laugh about.*

He felt strongly that he needed to leave his rooms, to get away at least temporarily from the situation in which he found himself. He was not sure how this could be achieved. He didn't want to wander the grounds of the College in his blue pajamas. If he was a "ghost" now, whatever that was, he did not want to become a laughingstock as well, a phantom in nightclothes. The likelihood, though, was that he would be invisible; after all, nobody who had entered his rooms that morning had noticed him standing there. All this was very new and hard to make judgments about. But even if he was now invisible, he preferred to be properly dressed.

It was easier than he had feared. The "duplication principle"—the alarm clock in his hand as well as on the bedside table, his body in the bed as well as its phantom version within which his selfhood now found itself—worked on his wardrobe too. He was able to take ghost undergarments and socks from the drawers in which their originals lay—and continued to lie, undisturbed—and then to put on his favorite outer garments too. His knob-headed walking stick yielded up an ectoplasmic variation as well. Thus attired, he moved toward the door, which he found he could pass through as if it were not "sporting its oak" but lay open for all persons to come and go. Here was his staircase, Staircase A, and he made his way down it without knowing where he was headed. He was at once in his old familiar surroundings and also a stranger in a strange land. There was a whole new way of things to understand and learn.

2

The College stood among other colleges on the banks of a thin river in a flat landscape, and its illustrious chapel rose above manicured lawns like an impossibility: stone transformed into music. Every morning and afternoon the chapel burst into song, and while the old stones sang of God, the surrounding world briefly felt pure and even holy. Honorary Fellow S. M. Arthur was far from being a religious man but that word, "holy," seemed unavoidable, and in any case he was no longer able to say what sort of vocabulary might be appropriate to his new reality. Was he about to meet some sort of Supreme Being or Beings? There was no indication of any such possibility, but on the other hand there was no indication of its impossibility. What there was, he found as he came out into the open air of the Front Quadrangle, was a fog.

It was thick and greenish, an old-fashioned fog of the sort that people of S. M. Arthur's generation had once called "peasoupers." The College buildings could not be seen, although here and there a window's yellow light made its way through the opaque air. The Gatehouse and the chapel were both blotted out, so that the Sunday choir's voices sounded even more angelically disembodied than usual. Unseasonable weather, he thought. He should have worn an overcoat. But he didn't feel cold. Maybe the dead were no longer sensitive to such concerns:

heat, cold, wind, pollution, climate issues, earthquakes, and so forth. The dead no longer occupied the natural world. They were in the unnatural world, the supernatural sphere. What the concerns and laws of this new world might be, he had yet to discover. He had only just arrived in it, and there was no guide, no Virgil, to show him the way.

All hope abandon, it occurred to him to think. The song filling the air seemed to agree.

"Fading is the worldling's pleasure," the choir sang. "All his boasted pomp and show."

There were figures moving through the fog, brief imprecise silhouettes that appeared and then vanished. Were these the living or the dead? His erstwhile colleagues or the phantoms of those long gone, half visible, caught in this foggy Limbo? He felt suddenly afraid and turned and went back indoors. The undergraduate bar and common room was on the ground floor of Staircase A. Here were its double doors of golden maple. He passed through them and entered.

The College was small, and for most of its history all of the students had been young men; neither did its Fellows number any women among their ranks. Regrettably, there were those who maliciously gossiped that the College contained "too many homosexuals," even though the single-sex rule also applied to most of the other colleges along the thin river. However, in the year of S. M. Arthur's death there had been a change, and women had finally been allowed in. There were women Fellows now as well as undergraduates. The eighteen-year-old Indian scholar I will for the moment identify only as R. was a member of the first intake of female students, and she was the person who first saw the phantom of the late author.

She said afterward that she felt on that first sighting as Horatio and Marcellus must have felt on the ramparts of Elsinore when confronted by the ghost of Hamlet's father. But this was no royal specter. It was a figure in a flat tweed cap, wearing a matching tweed jacket and brown corduroy trousers, sitting in a small booth and pretending to sip a half-pint of lemonade shandy; and its manner, on realizing that it had been seen, was surprised—yes, certainly that—but also friendly and welcoming. She sat down in the booth, on the other side of the little table, and could not speak. The ghost didn't speak either. But the silence between them was neither frightening nor uncomfortable. It was, as she told people later, really quite pleasant. "I thought it—he—was glad to be seen," she said. "He seemed relieved."

Finally he spoke. His words sounded like distant smoke, or what such smoke would sound like if it had a voice. "As I look at you," he said, "I find myself believing that you hail from that faraway country which I love more than any place on earth." She had no idea who he was. News of the death of the eminent gentleman at approximately midnight the previous night had not yet spread among the students. Those were times, fifty-something years ago, when news—lacking today's mechanisms of rapid transmission—took longer to get around. Although she had read his celebrated book, she failed to recognize him from his jacket photograph, in which he was much younger and more formally—even absurdly formally—dressed.

She knew, as all students at the College knew, the legend of the Honorary Fellow. He was a member of that rare breed of literary geniuses who published only one single book but had been propelled by that book up to the stars. After its publication, at the height of his fame, he had been awarded the Honorary Fellowship. This was normally nothing more than a piece of paper presented at a convivial banquet, and did not carry with it the right of residence on College premises. But soon after the award was made, the young gentleman had presented himself at the porters' lodge in the Gatehouse and asked to be shown to his rooms. As he was, at that moment, one of the two most celebrated authors in the land, the College acquiesced, and gave him a spacious set on the *piano nobile* of Staircase A. He moved in at once and lived there for the rest of his life (with the exception of the war years) and never published another book. When a brave soul asked him the reason for his long silence, Honorary Fellow S. M. Arthur replied, "I always wrote out of deep unhappiness, and ever since I came to the College I have been happy, so writing has no longer felt necessary."

It was one of the longest silences in literary history. When his singleton novel was published he was just twenty-five years old. The silence lasted thirty-six years, before, during and after the world war. At the time of his death there were two more wars raging, in Indochina and Bengal, so his passing received less attention than one might have expected.

When she heard the news, R. felt foolish for not having identified the Honorary Fellow at once. For it was true that his novel had been set in her country, and his affection for that capacious, multifarious land was well known. Maybe that was why he was visible to her. They shared a common love.

On the subject of happiness: when he was a student at the College himself, S. M. Arthur had fallen in love with someone from the "beloved country," as he afterward began to call it: Khan Sahib, an art historian, aristocrat, aesthete, and lover of fine wine and polo ponies. In those days it would have been illegal for them to be lovers in either of their countries, but Khan Sahib's culture, beauty, and grace overrode all S. M.'s concerns about the law. Sadly, when S. M. declared his feelings, when he finally and terrifyingly said the words "I love you," Khan answered only, "I know." The aristocrat was not interested in illegal love, his preference being for the legal kind, but he had a gift for friendship, and S. M. happily (or perhaps unhappily) settled for that.

This friendship was the gateway to another love: the love of the nobleman's country, its culture, its music, its sacred texts, its art, its history. A journey to the newly beloved land became essential and Khan Sahib opened all doors for him. That first journey plunged S. M. into a frenzy of conflicting emotions. In those days S. M. Arthur's own country improbably still ruled over the other country, even though the ruler was a small island off the shore of Europe and the ruled was a great subcontinent. S. M. found that alongside his new, great affection for the colonized country he was filled with a deep loathing for his own country's presence there, and a profound sympathy for the independence struggle that was gathering strength. Also, he met Mr. Shah, a chartered accountant, a second someone who was, this time, of the same disposition as himself, and a love story began.

S. M. Arthur boarded a boat and went back home for a time, to complete his studies; but he longed to return. After he graduated, Khan Sahib found him a job as personal secretary to a rich uncle, a textile magnate living in an antique courtyard in the oldest part of the capital city, and S. M. spent two years there, visited often by Mr. Shah, and these were happy times. The love story eventually ended, as real-life love stories often do; that is, it dwindled, lost energy, and finally just stopped. Mr. Shah went his way into whatever unrecorded future lay in store for chartered accountants; S. M. Arthur returned home and wrote his great book. It had not yet become fashionable at home for young men to express hostility to empire or admiration for the "little man in a loincloth" who led the freedom movement, and for a writer of S. M.'s illegal longings this was decidedly risky, but the work was acclaimed even though it went against the grain of the prevailing attitudes, and then came the Honorary Fellowship, which gave him a dignified status and afforded some protection against those forces that might have moved against him.

A decade later, after the world war, the beloved country won its freedom, but by then the two men who had been S. M. Arthur's great loves, Khan Sahib and Mr. Shah, the unrequited aristocrat and the requited commoner, were both dead of unnamed diseases. S. M. never traveled east again, and never published another word. His declaration that he stopped writing out of happiness must be revealed, by the present author, to be a flimsy veil placed over the truth. The truth was a deep secret. It will be revealed in these pages.

In his later years S. M. Arthur hardly ever left the purlieus of the College. He dined in the Great Hall, he played croquet in the Fellows' Garden, and in the summer he could sometimes be seen lounging on the Backs, watching the river go by. And now he was dead and still on College property, enveloped in a greenish fog.

His name was still above the door of his rooms, painted in neat white capital letters on a black ground. But now there were lurid strips of yellow tape across the entrance that bore, in large black letters, the legend DO NOT CROSS. It was like a crime scene in a TV show. In his new state, such prohibitions no longer applied, and he entered.

Then he was alone again with his death. He contemplated the idea of the future, and returned to the finite/infinite dichotomy. If his condition was finite, then perhaps he would dissolve slowly into the fog and become a part of it. The living did not see the fog. In the opinion of the living, the autumnal air was crisp and clear. The fog was a cloud made up of the dead, millions of them, no longer conscious, no longer anything, and only he, as a dead man about to become a part of it, was aware of its existence. As a living person he had believed that death was an ending followed by nothing, but he could not have guessed that the descent into the Nothing would be the opposite of immediate. That he would be a lump of sugar dissolving slowly in water.

He examined his "body," the illusion he now inhabited, to see if particles were streaming out of his fingertips, if the edges of his ghost garments were losing definition. Perhaps his consciousness would dissipate slowly too, and he would succumb to a posthumous version of dementia or Alzheimer's disease. Could the dead be diseased? He knew nothing. He didn't even know how to begin knowing. He was lost.

What about the girl, he thought. *Was that not a good sign. A good sign of what?* He had no idea. But it had felt good. *Felt, feelings,* these words had irritated him in life, because people generally associated them with the heart. Feelings happened in the heart; thought happened in the brain. That was idiocy. It all happened in the brain. Or, he now needed to make the distinction, in the mind. So, in the mind, his encounter with the student had felt good. Where did that lead? Could he expect that in his finite or infinite death he could continue to engage with some portion of the living world? The living world's word for this was *haunting.* The living world was scared of being *haunted* by *ghosts.* Haunted houses were scary places. The subject of exorcism arose. Could an atheist ghost be exorcised by a priest? He truly hoped not. And the student from the beloved country had not been afraid. She had been calm. That was definitely a good sign. Of what, that would become clear in time. Or not.

But what if this was infinite? If this simply was infinity? What were the rules of that? He remembered an old film, *Lost Horizon*. Starring Ronald Colman, directed by Frank Capra. (He had been, in life, something of a film buff, able to discourse fluently on American cinema—Capra, Hawks, Preston Sturges, Sirk— and world cinema too. Buñuel, Pagnol, Bergman, panoramic Jancsó, and of course the immortal Satyajit Ray.) He had seen *Lost Horizon* when it was new and his own book was new too and enjoying its global success. He had never forgotten it: the plane crash in the Himalayas and the survivors' arrival in the enchanted valley of Shangri-La, where nobody grew old. But if they left Shangri-La the years fell upon them like an avalanche and they crumbled into nothingness.

Was the College his Shangri-La?

He felt a surge of excitement for the first time since his death. Had Frank Capra and James Hilton, the author of the book on which the film was based, stumbled upon the secret of life eternal? If that was true, then as long as he remained on College property, he could live—or at least continue, even though deceased—forever. This idea was attractive to him. He was by nature solitary, so loneliness would not be a problem. He would not need to eat or drink or bathe or piss and he would not feel the heat of the day or the cold of the night. He would never be unwell. His mental powers would remain sharp. He could listen to the choir, wander in the library, play ghost croquet when in the mood, and he could think, think through all eternity, and with that much time maybe he could even come up with an original thought.

He was sitting in his favorite leather armchair. On the walls were paintings by contemporary Indian artists. Khan had introduced him to this body of work and he considered many of the artists to be of high quality but they were astonishingly cheap to buy because of the nose-in-air, colonialist attitude of the lords of the art market. As a result S. M. Arthur had acquired quite a collection. Husain, Raza, Souza, Gaitonde, Subramanian, Amrita Sher-Gil, Jamini Roy, and the two Tagores, Abanindranath and great Rabindranath. Also some of the younger artists. They loomed around him now in the unlit room (the undertakers had drawn the curtains shut) and he thought of them as friends, even as family. There was no actual family to mourn him. Nor were there any true friends. His parents were gone and he was estranged from his sister, who had emigrated long ago to Canada, and who disapproved of his sexual proclivities and refused to read his scandalous anti-colonialist book. She was an equal-opportunity bigot, also disapproving of the dark-skinned peoples of the world, as well as Jews, Poles, and so on. She had found the Indian independence movement "ridiculous" and spoke with scorn of the nation that had come into being in the month of her twentieth birthday.

He was comfortable with the estrangement. There were moments when he considered reaching out to her, but he forbore to do so. She was a woman possessed of an inexhaustible bad temper, and he could not bear the idea of letting her rage back into his life. As to friends, he had the Fellows of the College. He had met them most days at dinner at the high table. There was always good wine to be drunk and much convivial conversation and he learned, from these colleagues, a great deal about economic theory, medieval European history, Marxism, the nature of the universe, the harmful social effects of the nuclear family, and the art of Peter Paul Rubens and Francisco Goya and Hieronymus Bosch. Away from the high table, however, everyone went his (and now also her) own way. These were not friendships as commonly understood. They were non-intimate connections. And now that he was disconnected, he understood that his erstwhile colleagues would express regret, but they would not—they did not—really care. Death came to all parties. You doffed your hat to it and moved on. The work of scholarship flowed on without interruption.

He was sad, but not excessively so. This was not a new situation. He was accustomed to it. What was new was his arrival in Shangri-La. That was deeply pleasing. If this was death, then it was something he could live with.

3

I *t must be lonely, being dead,* the young Indian scholar R.
thought. She herself was lonely, far from home, out of
contact with the ones she loved. Because of the war in the
east, the army of her country had requisitioned all long-distance
telephone lines, telegrams could not be sent, and aerograms
were taking six weeks to arrive. She was a full-scholarship student and it was plain that many of the other women in this first
intake came from wealthier homes and that was intimidating.
Also, this was the time of the "counterculture," and she found
that even more intimidating. The idea of "free love" was
horrifying—she could see that boys would like it but to her it
seemed shameful, like giving up one's honor. And the idea of
smoking *bhang* or *charas*—which here were "pot" or "hash" or
"grass"—or, worse still, *afeem,* which was opium, was repulsive;
she had seen dope-dazed men walking the streets at home and
had no desire to be like those addicts. She had never tasted alcohol; and while the pounding music of the period excited her
senses—she admitted that it did—she was also afraid of that
excitement, of where it might lead her, what it might seduce
her into doing. In those early weeks the library was the only
place where she felt at home. Her hometown was far away.
Books were her homeland now.

This was another thing she had in common with the dead

man. They both, for different reasons, were citizens of the country of the mind.

She thought about him a lot after that encounter in the students' common room. More exactly, she wondered at her reaction to seeing him. She had never seen a ghost before and yet she'd been neither surprised nor afraid. What did he have to say to her? The ghost of Hamlet's father wanted his son to avenge his murder. Banquo's ghost was the product of Macbeth's wickedness and came to accuse him. Charles Dickens's ghosts were meant to force Scrooge away from his cruel Scroogery and toward a kindlier humanity. Oscar Wilde's Canterville ghost was a joke, or even worse—the butt of a joke. In her own folklore ghosts were almost always dangerous and wanted to hurt you, drive you mad, or even kill you. None of these ghost stories seemed to apply to the writer in the flat tweed cap. Maybe he would never reappear. But she should probably read his book again.

It was impossible at first to imagine talking about her encounter with any of the young women crowding the corridors of the College's new women's building. She feared she would immediately become, in their eyes, the exotic brown girl who saw spirits. The crazy exotic brown girl. Not the kind of person you'd invite home for the weekend. There were some Africans in the building, a couple of Jamaicans, one Thai student, and two Japanese. Maybe in time she might be able to confide in one or two of them. It was the English girls she was most nervous of.

The classic Japanese film *Ugetsu Monogatari* was playing at the art-house cinema near the market square. That had a female ghost in a leading role. And, also at the art-house cinema, there was the Polish film *The Saragossa Manuscript,* featuring more alluring ghost women. So ghosts were all around. She was beginning to see that it was a moment in which mysticism had a great appeal for young people here. People asked her about Transcendental Meditation—treating her as if she must be an expert because it had originated in her country—and were surprised by her absolute lack of interest in rishis, maharishis, gurus, mahagurus, and other such "godmen." But a belief in magic and mystery was definitely in the air. No doubt the hallucinogens helped foster that belief. So . . . maybe she could eventually talk. But not yet. Not anytime soon.

The Honorary Fellow did not quickly reappear. She became busy with her studies. She was a history scholar and it was time to take a deep dive off the shores of the present into the ocean of the past. She was a pragmatic, matter-of-fact character and told herself severely, *If the ghost comes again, you'll deal with it—him—then. In the meanwhile, pay attention to the history of the medieval Papacy, the Holy Roman Empire, and also, balanced against that, the rise of humanism during the Italian Renaissance.*

She was not religious, but the historical struggle between Church and State, between God and the World, enthralled her. She fell in love with the vocabulary and imagery of it all. The past swirled within her. The Humiliation at Canossa, the Diet of Worms, the *Eigenkirche* conflict. The struggle of ideas engrossed her more than the actual battles, although military engagements, and also the weaponry of the faith, anathemas, excommunication, et cetera, had their own pleasures. She studied the argument that the Church possessed divine authority, *auctoritas,* while the monarch only enjoyed temporal power, *potestas.* And the counterargument about property: the Church might own the churches but the State claimed ownership of the land they stood upon. She found pleasing the idea of the invisible Church that stood above the visible one. Luther's Ninety-Five Theses nailed to the church door in Wittenberg. The war between this world and the world beyond. In Italy the two united because of the sheer worldliness of the Papacy and the power of the Papal States. The control of the Papacy by the great families. The Medici popes. The Borgia popes. The della Rovere popes. And the fear of the new humanistic ideas. Pico della Mirandola's *Nine Hundred Theses* condemned and burned. Giordano Bruno burned at the stake—not just his new ideas about the possibility of life on other planets and the probability that the Earth was not the center of what he proposed was an infinite universe but his fifty-two-year-old body too.

Until she saw the ghost she had conceived of the Church-State battle as a war between fiction and fact. The divine realm was fiction. The world was real. That seemed self-evident. But now, some confusion. She needed to understand the nature of the phantom phenomenon she had witnessed. Was it just some sort of leftover echo of life—an aberration that did not fundamentally undermine her views—or might it be proof of the reality of life after death? She needed to see it again. She had so many questions to ask.

The war in Indochina continued and was much on the minds of her fellow students. But the war in Bengal, which she alone cared about, ended. The enemy surrendered, and a new country, Bangladesh, was born. On the same day—an auspicious coincidence, surely?—an opportunity arose that, R. hoped, might lead to the additional spectral encounters she so fervently desired. It was announced by Lord Emmemm at a meeting in the Great Hall that Honorary Fellow S. M. Arthur had left all his worldly possessions to the College, in perpetuity, including his art collection and the copyright of, and all future income from, his classic novel. In return the College authorities had decided that the Honorary Fellow's rooms would not be reallocated. Rather, they would be preserved exactly as he had left them, as a kind of museum, a shrine to his genius, and they would be open to the public for three hours, one afternoon a week. The task of supervising these public sessions would fall to a willing undergraduate, and applications were invited. No sooner had the words left Lord Emmemm's lips than R. leapt to her feet with her arm upraised. The Provost of the College nodded imperiously.

"Ah, a member of the sexual revolution," Lord Emmemm cried, meaning, she supposed, the arrival of women in a space reserved for men for almost six centuries. "See me tomorrow," he commanded, and turned away.

To enter the Provost's Lodge was to come into a sacred space in which it would not have been surprising to discover a burning bush or a pair of stone tablets that had been engraved with commandments by a pillar of fire. A somber butler ushered her toward what in her faraway land would have been called the Diwan-e-Khas, the Hall of Private Audience. Here, in the presence of many leather-bound books and a large Florentine celestial globe, she waited. She was an independent-minded and resourceful young lady, but in spite of her strength of character the thought occurred to her, when the Provost came into the room, that she should bow her head or curtsy, although it would be going too far to kneel. His great domed head made him look like a sort of human cathedral, and she wondered if in the depths of this residence there might actually be a cathedra, the throne of the College whose overlord he was. What he resembled most powerfully, she thought, was one of the Medici or Borgia popes she had been learning about: cultured, monarchical rather than saintly, and probably ruthless. In his presence one did well to lower one's voice. He wore a three-piece red suit of a flamboyant hue, the scarlet of cardinals' robes, which—no doubt deliberately—heightened his air of an ecclesiastical grandee. There was a chapel on the far side of the Front Lawn, that was true. But the Vatican was here.

"You're Christian, they tell me," Lord Emmemm said.

"Not really, my lord," she answered. "Although my family is, and as a child I used to be taken on Sundays to the Anglican Cathedral of St. Thomas in Bombay, sir. Doubting Thomas."

"So that's where he ended up. Excellent. 'Not really' is the best way to be Christian, anyway. And a member of the church of Doubt. Excellent also. You'll do well here."

"Thank you, Provost."

"And so how in fact are you doing? Getting used to being a girl in a boys' club?"

"I think it's more a case of the boys' club getting used to us," she replied, surprising herself by the defiant note in her voice.

"Couldn't have a better custodian of the Honorary Fellow's effects," Lord Emmemm said. "His ghost would approve of you."

This caught her off guard. Had Lord Emmemm seen what she had seen? "His ghost, sir?" she said, too quickly, without thinking. "He appeared to you also?"

"My dear," Lord Emmemm said, "these ancient stones house many ghosts."

"Oh, yes, sir, I see," she said. "Yes, I'm sure they do."

Lord Emmemm frowned. "Did you say *also*?"

"Excuse me, Lord Emmemm," she said. "I must have misspoken."

The Provost nodded. "Difficult language, English. I must say you speak it very well."

. . .

She was captivated by the Indian art on the walls of the Honorary Fellow's rooms. There was a painting on one wall in which four women, who all looked like the same woman, were shown in the condition of mourning—in white saris with their hair cut short. They sat on upright chairs atop a richly patterned carpet, a design of leafy plants twining on a gold background, and amid the plants, miniaturized, were things that presumably had belonged to the dead man: a tiny car, a mini-armchair, a little bed. The dead man was there too, as small as a child's toy, lying in white clothes among the twining plants like a discarded doll. How sad could the mourners really be, R. wondered, if the one who had passed away was so insignificant? She began to see the work as a sign of the Honorary Fellow's celebrated modesty. A story told about him in the College was that when the novelist Evelyn Waugh died, Honorary Fellow S. M. Arthur had pronounced during a high table dinner, "That was a great English novelist. Not like me." That would have sounded like false modesty coming from someone else, but from him it felt genuine. So if she imagined that the dead man in the painting was him, then it, he, was saying that he wouldn't be greatly mourned, and didn't merit much mourning anyway.

She began to see the art collection as a guide to the man. There was a painting showing, against a flat red ground, a man recumbent beneath a stylized tree, from whose upper trunk there dangled a bright blue electricity cable with a plug at the end. This was the Buddha, a small text at the base of the work declared, and the tree was the bodhi tree beneath which the great sage had gained enlightenment; but, as was plain to see, the tree was not plugged in, so enlightenment had not, or not yet, occurred. Perhaps acquiring this painting had been the

Honorary Fellow's way of telling himself that he, too, lacked genuine wisdom. The image did not contain any representation of a socket or power outlet for the plug, so enlightenment looked impossible to achieve. Honorary Fellow S. M. Arthur was telling himself that he would never be wise.

And there was a painting of a window cleaner holding up a hose with water spurting from its bright pink tip. When she learned more about the artist she was not surprised to find that his sexual inclinations matched those of the Honorary Fellow, and that he was obliged by the legal necessities of the time to paint his true nature, so to speak, in code. She had made it her business to read what had been written about the Honorary Fellow and his work, and in more than one essay she saw, expressed guardedly—also in code—the suggestion that his inability to put his true nature openly and honestly on the page was the real reason for his long silence. But here was that true nature on a wall of his home. He himself was the window cleaner.

Finally she gazed upon a work that felt like a comment about the afterlife. In the lower part of the canvas the artist had depicted an urban scene, painted in dark grays and blacks—an unlovely, dirty city. But rising from its midst was a golden rope, and as it rose up the skies cleared and became a brilliant blue, and at the top of the painting there were white fluffy clouds and just a hint, a glittering hint, of the gates of paradise.

Well, she hoped that for him, that ascent toward glory, but she also hoped that before he made that final journey she might see him again, and talk.

4

On Tuesday afternoons, when his rooms were open to visitors, the visitors' book remained empty and unsigned. He had been silent too long. His novel was remembered, but he had been forgotten. He found that he minded, that it stung. This was unexpected. He had been accustomed to solitude in life, had in fact sought it out, had retreated from his renown when young and strong into this ivory tower of infirm old men, and had died among them; so why should that chosen solitude be hurtful in death? It appeared that death was a more sentimental, narcissistic condition than life. It wanted—*needed*—attention. It was strange to find that proposition distasteful and still be affected by death's neediness. He was no longer himself. What he was was unclear. But not himself as he had known himself, as he had believed himself to be. As if the mind, when freed from the body, became alien *to itself.* As if selfhood resided in the union of flesh and thought.

He chose to avoid his rooms during Tuesday's visiting hours, in spite of the presence there of the student who could see him. He chose for the moment not to be seen; he needed to regain his equilibrium, if a dead man could even perform such a feat. What use was poise to the dead? What use was confidence? And yet he wanted those things.

There was almost nothing for him to do. He couldn't turn

the pages of a book or turn on the television or drink a glass of Burgundy. He had lost his power over the things of the world. He supposed that this was the trouble with poltergeists: they wanted to continue their relationship with material things, but they couldn't, and the best they could manage was a phantasmal clumsiness. They broke things.

If worldly things could not be used, what then were the things of the dead?

The days had lost their rhythm, were no longer given form by waking, sleeping, and eating. He wandered the College grounds timelessly, in the unyielding fog. The fog was not lifting. If anything it seemed thicker than before. It was a fog that ate time. Hours, minutes, weeks lost their meaning. It was hard for him to abandon the concept of punctuality, timeliness, by which he had always lived. Time meant nothing now, except for Tuesdays between one o'clock and four o'clock in the afternoon, when his rooms were open to visitors, who didn't show up.

He decided to test his Shangri-La theory. If his supposition was correct, then it would be dangerous to step outside the boundaries of the College, he warned himself, but he needed to know the truth. *Dangerous? Are you an idiot?* He treated his own warning with scorn. What could possibly be dangerous to him now? He was already dead.

He knew exactly where he was in spite of the fog. Here, right next to Staircase A, was the stone wall, with its arched windows, that separated the College premises from the public street. Here was the Gatehouse at the wall's midpoint. The wall ended and, at right angles to it, the long south flank of the chapel began. Here, after the small side chapels, was the chapel door. He turned right along the building's west wall, with the great stained-glass window above him, somewhere up there, invisible; and ahead of him, also invisible, was the side gate to the

College. He reached out and felt the iron rods of the gate. It was open. Did he dare to go through?

He took the tweed cap off his head. It had been "created" in the same way he had. Just as he had risen out of his body to become whatever he was now, so also his cap had been lifted out of its material self and somehow retained its cap-ness. It followed that they were made of the same stuff, that they were the same species of illusion, and so the cap would serve very well as a test piece. Before he could change his mind he flung it through the open gate. And before the fog could swallow it up there was a loud, terrifying sizzling noise and S. M. Arthur plainly saw the tweed cap being blown to bits.

The destruction of his cap filled S. M. with fear. No longer did the "Shangri-La effect"—which was now proven to be real—feel delightful. Now he saw himself as a broken entity trapped in a kind of prison. It might look like the College but, for him at least, the reality was very different. He no longer lived, could do almost nothing, had no further purpose, and his only options were either to remain in this condition indefinitely or else to follow his cap beyond the boundary and be violently destroyed.

This was not an immortal paradise. It was the anteroom to hell.

5

She held in her hands the Honorary Fellow's never-published work. She had been asked by the College to go through his papers, so that, once she had organized the material, members of the literature faculty might examine it to see what was there, and what might be done with it. At first R. felt like a trespasser, an intruder entering a secret zone not intended for any eyes but the author's own. Her hands shook as she read. But soon that initial reluctance was replaced by a kind of readerly sadness, because what she found was a long series of failures: beginnings without middles or endings, ideas sketched out that remained unwritten, and at least two projects—filling two bulging box files, one green, one red—on which the Honorary Fellow had labored mightily, writing many versions running to hundreds of pages, without ever finding the way to a finished book. What was plain even after a cursory look at the papers was that S. M. had never abandoned his art, although he had stopped publishing. He had gone on, refusing to accept that the art might have abandoned him.

There were unfinished things that were almost good.

A meditation on his father's hands that, if completed, would have been a portrait of that gentleman, a hard-nosed merchant who died young. *Gentleman* was the wrong word for him. The old man's hands were not genteel. He had climbed the class ladder, and his son, S. M., had become the first member of the family to go to college. The father's hands were workingman's hands. S. M. Arthur's father, like Kafka's father, had been a brute. Maybe that similarity had prevented S. M. from finishing his work. Brutish fathers had already been "taken" by the literary insurance officer from Prague.

A story about a young man who became frightened of airplanes (written in the English way, *aeroplanes*) and refused to travel in them, but then discovered that he himself was able to fly.

An apocalyptic vision (that is, a fragment of one) in which Eden appeared at the end of time, rather than the beginning: "The Garden at the End of the World." Adam and Eve stood naked in the garden and watched the death of the universe.

A comic story called "William Shakespeare," about a man whose name actually was William Shakespeare, a fact that made him hate his parents. He worked as a sales executive in a company that manufactured foam mattresses. (This started promisingly but went nowhere.)

A story she wished had been finished, in which the Honorary Fellow revealed that he had been thinking about mortality for some time. It was called "The Country of Shrinking Borders." The hero lived in a land that was mysteriously growing a little smaller every day. The idea seemed to be that in the end the borders would arrive at the edges of his own body, and beyond that there would be nothing; but the author was unclear about the dénouement, and the text tailed off and stopped.

At the top of the papers in the red box file was a personal letter from Evelyn Waugh, writing from his home, Combe Florey House in Somerset. He was only seven years the Honorary Fellow's senior, but he sounded like an elder statesman addressing a young Turk. "You travelled a long way to find your excellent novel," it read, in part. "Don't you think you might find its companion a little nearer to home? You have given us your 'matter of India.' Grant us, perhaps, your <u>Matter of Britain</u>?" (The last three words were underlined twice.) The Indian student, R., knew the famous story of Pushkin giving Gogol the idea for *Dead Souls,* and here in her hands was an English version of that gift. "The Matter of Britain" was the name given to the constellation of tales surrounding the figure of King Arthur. The homonymous Honorary Fellow S. M. Arthur had battled for many years to do as Waugh had requested. He tried with increasing agitation to turn the Round Table and the Grail quest into metaphors of contemporary Britain during the Second World War. In his own opinion (and in R.'s as well, as she read) he had not succeeded. The attempts and work notes in the red box file revealed his despair.

The green box file, titled "Lateness," contained more recent, less developed texts. She found herself copying some sentences into her own notebook.

Timeliness = being of one's time vs. lateness = outsiderness, apartness. "Anachronism."

Mozart = insider. Beethoven = outsider. Mozart is church, Beethoven unchurch. M not a misfit, B angry/because deaf/challenges norms.

Prospero "I'll break my staff." Age as renunciation.

One can die at peace with the world, with everything resolved, or go angry, tearing everything up. Rage, rage against the dying &c.

Death—refracted—as irony.

Otherland. Land of the Other / Land in which one is Othered. Motherland without the M. Its opposite.

Lateness = acceptance of one's flaws/fallibility, unpomp-
ous, but w/ the confidence of experience.

When young, pretend to be wise. When old, pretend to
be energetic.

And one mystery, written in capital letters, with underlinings
and exclamations:

EMMEMM. FREEDOM VERSUS GOODNESS???

NONSENSE NONSENSE.

NOT CREDIBLE.

NONSENSE!!!

There was one last box file, a black one. This one had a lock,
and there was no key. It was a simple lock and it would not be
hard to force it but she couldn't in good conscience do something like that. She would have to talk to Lord Emmemm.

R. had almost despaired of seeing the Honorary Fellow again
when there he was, sitting in his favorite armchair. Her spirits
rose briefly, but then she saw that he was different: less friendly,
and somewhat more decrepit. His tweed cap was gone and his
wispy hair stuck out in all directions. His expression was mo-
rose, or worse than that: bewildered and panic-stricken.

She spoke to him, hesitantly. "Hello?"

He raised his head to look at her. "You still see me, I note,"
he said, and his voice sounded smokier than before. "You and
you alone. Perhaps you can help me address a conundrum,
which is this: I am dead, am I not. That being said, why am I
also not dead?"

It was hard to know how to respond. "Maybe it's a sort of error," she said.

"An error," he repeated. "How humiliating. Death itself is a form of humiliation, proof of the pointlessness of life. An error that allows one to live on without a point, unable to act or affect anything, is even worse—a double humiliation. Humiliation is a subject in which I am well versed. Also, an error that allows one to live on pointlessly. I know all about that as well."

She found no words.

"I understand nothing," he added. "I'm in a fog. There is no meaning to be found. How does one construct meaning without life?"

Now she did find a reply and spoke clumsy words. "Newborn people," she said, "are also in a fog, without language, without any concept of the real. Can we see your present state not as an ending but some sort of new beginning in a new reality? Not a death but a birth?"

She saw that she had startled him. "A birth?" That sounded incredulous. And again: "A birth." This time it was dismissive. *No, no, of course not.* And a third time: "A birth." This was judicious. *Hmm. A birth.* The idea was being considered. *Hmm.* And, a moment later, a shake of the head. No, he was not being reborn. That was not his story.

He leaned forward and stared at her through narrowed eyes. "What's your name?"

"Sir, I'm Rosa," she said, her body straightening as if she were on parade, coming to attention. That drew from the Honorary Fellow a mock-military response. "At ease," he told her. "Stand easy." His humor was much improved. She relaxed just a little. "And I am Merlyn, you know," he told her. "Simon Merlyn Arthur." She allowed herself a small smile. "Yes, sir," she said. "S. M. Arthur. Of course I know who you are."

And there we have it. The moment the present author has been waiting for. They have made themselves known to each other, the young woman and the ghost, and so we may, with some relief, abandon the guarded initials we have been using and begin to know them better ourselves.

"Tell me about yourself," he said.

6

It was the end of the Michaelmas term but she was not going home. The flights were too expensive for her to go back and forth during the breaks in the calendar, so she would return home only once a year, at the end of the academic year. It had been arranged for her to remain "up" at the College, in her room, throughout the holidays. The women's building was empty and she would be alone there until the Lent term began, and it would be a solitary Christmas for her.

To make a trunk call to her family back home in the city by the sea on Christmas Day she would have to book a "time call." This would be put through by the international operator and would last exactly three minutes. Near the end of the three minutes she would be asked by the operator if she wanted to extend the call, and if so there would be another three minutes. Beyond that, extensions were not available, and the call was expensive anyway, so she thought three minutes total was probably her limit on her budget. Maybe her parents would also book a "time call" from their end so they could have six minutes more together in that way.

"You see, I will be haunting the deserted corridors in these coming weeks," she said. "So we'll both be ghosts."

This would be her first English winter. She was afraid her overcoat would not be warm enough, and because there was likely to be snow and ice she was worried about the quality of her footwear. But she was doing well academically, she had been congratulated by her supervisors, and that was what mattered. Even with the full scholarship her parents' finances were stretched. Only a good degree would reward them for their sacrifice. She could deal with the isolation and the ice.

England was not what she had expected. She had known quite a lot about it before she arrived, its history, its literature, and her English was fluent (as were her Hindi and Konkani). Yet as soon as she landed she realized that she understood nothing, and that what people knew about where she came from was next to nothing. "India, man," her fellow students said. "Ravi Shankar, man. Beautiful." She learned quickly that in the argot of the moment everything was beautiful except for things that were beautiful. "See you on Tuesday, man. Beautiful." "You like Chinese food? Beautiful." "You want to go demonstrate against the war? Beautiful." But beautiful things, a sunset, a face, music, love, these things were *really nice.*

She was having trouble adapting, fitting in. Go to work on an egg, the bus sides advised her. Drinka pinta milka day. Unzip a banana. That was all foolishness. There was violence in the air. The Angry Brigade bombs, the Irish Troubles; but then there was violence everywhere. The war back home had only just ended and the combatants were burying or burning their dead, in accordance with their different traditions.

"Can I ask," she said hesitantly, "what happened to you? I mean, after . . ."

"After I died." He gave her the honest truth. "I don't know," he said. "Burial or cremation. Nobody told me."

In her own year, her own cohort, there had also been a death and a near death. One first-year male undergraduate found dead in his room. Another, her fellow history scholar, so badly damaged that he could no longer function, and had left the College. She heard he had a job picking up leaves in a public park. These two calamities introduced her to a new word, or an old word used in a new way.

Acid.

The sugar lumps of death. She found herself talking about what had happened, speaking of death to the dead, unable to help herself in spite of the strangeness. "It literally blew their minds," she said. "This is a thing people say now, a piece of music or a movie or an idea will *blow your mind*. But these were actual explosions in the brain. *Bad trips*. I can't use such words after what happened."

This was what she most wanted to say: her generation, or rather its College iteration, scared her. Back home, hanging out with friends near the Bandstand in Bandra, walking in the evening on Marine Drive, going for kulfi near Chowpatty Beach or to weekend jazz "jam sessions," and snapping her fingers to the sounds of Chris Perry, Lorna Cordeiro, and Chic Chocolate, she had not been thought of as a shy, conservative girl. She wore Western skirts and blouses like everyone else; she was outgoing and popular. But at the College she had retreated into her shell.

"I don't know what they expect of me," she said. "I'm not like them."

"Are you punctual?" he asked. "You like to be on time for appointments?"

"I'm always early," she said. "Always the first to arrive. Sometimes I have to go for a walk and come back so that I'm not too early."

"I was the same," said the Honorary Fellow. "But we are both fakes. Timeliness is said to be a sign of being at one with the times. But you are out of step, and I always was myself: timely, but driven by circumstance into a deep alienation. So we are pretending to possess a normality we don't truly have. You in the present tense. I, in the past. We are 'late' people trying to pass as 'timely.'"

"I suppose," she answered doubtfully.

"We're two of a kind," he assured her. "One alive, one dead. But, peas in a pod."

"There's a difference," she replied, while thinking, *There are so many differences. Why is he saying such things?* She offered up only one difference. "My father," she said, "is a sweet man. Good-natured, gentle, honest." Her father was an elected politician representing one of the smaller regional political parties. Many of his colleagues regularly received visits from anonymous men employed by one of the major Mafia dons— Vardhabhai, Haji Mastan, Yusuf Patel—who would leave be-hind suitcases full of high-denomination currency notes. Her father, however, was not corrupt. The crime syndicates did not own him. Therefore he was not rich. "And he's not a brute," she said.

"You've been reading my papers," he said, understanding why she'd mentioned this. "They asked you to. Good. Good. That saves time."

"May I ask," she said carefully, "about the black box file?"

His manner changed, and was no longer friendly. "No," he barked. "No, you may not."

It was near the end of the Tuesday visiting hours. She got up very quickly and began to prepare to close up the rooms before going. "Leave the lights on," he told her, his voice softening again, "and the interior doors and cupboards open."

She hurried through her duties. She had overstepped some mark and his reaction had frightened her. She had no idea what a creature from the spirit world might be capable of if roused to wrath. She needed urgently to leave.

He called after her as she departed. "Come again," he said, and now he sounded apologetic, almost wheedling. "Not just on Tuesdays. Come when you want."

7

Yes, his middle name was Merlyn and his surname Arthur. When he was a younger man there were people who called him by his middle name. Khan Sahib, who never became his lover, and Mr. Shah the accountant, who did. He was Merlyn to them both. And "S. Merlyn Arthur" was of course the reason for Waugh's letter recommending that he take up the Matter of Britain as his second great subject. But long ago, after the deaths of the two men he had loved unsuccessfully and successfully, and after the unspeakable thing, the not yet speakable thing, he gave up the middle name forever. He was no magician. Or, if magic had been his good fortune once, enchanting the pages of his book, that miracle was over. If he had once been a Prospero, he had long since broken his staff. Or, more precisely: it had been broken for him.

But he had used that middle name once more when introducing himself to Rosa. That had taken him by surprise.

After the Waugh letter he asked himself: If he was an Arthur, what was his Grail quest, the thing that all pure knights must search for until it is found, the thing that granted benediction. And he knew the answer but he had no idea of how to seek it. He was not by nature—what was the new word?—an activist. Then four years before his death the Grail was found. The Grail was an act of Parliament that made it legal for two consenting adults of the same sex and over the age of twenty-one to indulge in their preferred homosexual activity in private. There were still severe penalties in place for the public pursuit of such desires. The new freedom existed only in England and Wales. In Scotland and Northern Ireland the homosexual reality continued to be against the law. He would stay away from those parts of the disunited kingdom. But in the rest of the country it was no longer necessary to lie or hide.

It had finally become the love that dared to speak its name. The word *queer* was in general use, but it was almost always pejorative, and the word *gay* was beginning to be used, but to a man of his generation it didn't sit well on his tongue because of its older meanings, merry, lighthearted, happy. He said "homosexual" or even, more archaically, "homosexualist." And sometimes "homoerotic." Those terms suited his old-fashioned vocabulary best.

However, by the time the Grail had been found and had granted its benediction, it was too late for him. His days of "homoerotic" behavior were behind him. That chapter had been brought to a close. And four years later he had woken up dead.

He had now been dead for some months, but at last he began to understand why he was still here, still present within the College grounds. There was something incomplete about his life that needed to be completed before he could rest. Something that might clear away the fog in which, at present, his being was engulfed.

Revenge. Exoneration, and revenge.

And his onliest target was the Provost of the College, Lord Emmemm.

.   .   .

On Christmas Eve in the chapel the Provost in his cardinal fin-
ery presided over a festival service of nine lessons and carols.
The chapel was the chaplain's province and the choir was in the
hands of the choirmaster, but all at the College knew where the
true power lay, whose ring it was necessary to kiss. Emmemm
nodded graciously to left and right, raising a royal hand and offering benevolent gestures to the choir and the congregation
alike, his bald cathedral dome shining as if haloed, and then
sank down into his allotted pew. His scarlet winter cloak settled
around him like a magnificent balloon. *"In dulci jubilo,"* the
choir sang. In quiet joy. All was well with the world tonight. It
was a white Christmas. The luminous Rubens altarpiece, the
Adoration, looked down on the scene. Some years earlier it had
been defaced by a vandal, who'd scratched the letters "IRA" into
the lower right-hand corner, but it had been perfectly restored
and you'd never have known. Restoration was the art of hiding
damage, Lord Emmemm reflected. The College had histori-
cally been good at that.

He saw himself not merely as the head of the College but as
its embodiment, just as the Queen embodied the nation. If the
chapel was stone transformed into music, then the College in
its entirety was made flesh in him. There had often been rumors that he would abandon the Provostship to join the Government but that did not interest him, because here he was
supreme. He had been born with the twentieth century and
had ruled here for thirty years, since the year of Dunkirk. He
had been spared military duty by his fallen arches and so had
walked flat-footed into the life of the mind. Ever since then,
through the war years and beyond, he had been surrounded by
men (and now women) of academic brilliance, and he stood, or
so he told himself, at the very heart of the great philosophical
issues of the time. It was he who had framed and driven the

crucial argument between freedom and goodness. However, this carol service was not the place to consider such things. He sat back and relaxed. *"Adeste fideles"* the choir sang. And come all ye faithless too, he murmured softly to himself. The College was a broad church.

As the carol came to an end, the ghost of the Honorary Fellow S. Merlyn Arthur entered the chapel. Nobody noticed him. The Provost was reading a lesson, the story of the expulsion of Adam and Eve from Eden. The serpent. *It shall bruise thy head, and thou shalt bruise his heel.* The Honorary Fellow stood at the rear of the chapel, his back to the wall, until the choir sang again, about a far-off little town in the Holy Land, but they might just as well have been singing about the place where they stood: *"The hopes and fears of all the years are met in thee tonight."*

The Honorary Fellow began to walk forward. Every seat in the antechapel was occupied. No head turned. This was as he had expected. He passed through the arch in the ornate wooden Renaissance screen that divided the chapel in half and also housed the organ, and then he was with the choir, and alongside and behind the choir were the seats of senior College people and invited dignitaries. Again, every seat was taken. Had he wanted a seat of his own from which he could enjoy the festival service, he would not have found one. But he did not want a seat of his own. Lord Emmemm was in the finest place, and the Honorary Fellow headed in his direction. When he got there he turned around and sat down, and now his phantom self was superimposed upon the Provost, his legs overlapping Emmemm's legs, his posterior within the boundary of Emmemm's more ample rear, their torsos occupying the same space, his head exactly where Emmemm's head was. Nobody saw him, least of all the Provost; but feeling was something else again. Lord Emmemm began to feel cold, then colder, then very cold indeed: deathly cold, it would be accurate to say. He drew his cloak around himself, but it afforded him no relief. He began to shiver, a little at first, then convulsively. His colleagues in the neighboring seats were staring. Now his teeth were chattering. He looked at his hands. His fingertips were blue. Finally the cold became so profound, so painful, that he was unable to restrain himself. He leapt to his feet, to the consternation of one and all, cried out an incomprehensible apology, and fled. The Honorary Fellow did not pursue him. Instead he settled into the vacated pew; and after a moment of utter confusion the choirmaster rallied his singers and the music resumed. The Honorary Fellow sat back to enjoy it. He had not felt this good since the day he died.

Remember that news, back then, could not spread as it does now, technologically. It moved through the world by carrier pigeon, if for "pigeon" we substitute "language." And this old-world, presently extinct bird, "word of mouth," moved almost as fast as our contemporary vehicles do. Within instants of the scandal in the chapel everyone in the College knew that the Provost, Lord Emmemm, had lost his mind and run screaming from the house of God.

Rosa, our Indian Student, heard it from Wyatt, whose parents were French diplomats in Senegal, and who was also staying "up" at the College for the holidays, because Africa was too far away. Wyatt was Black as well as French, and therefore considered by his fellow students to be very glamorous: born to be wild, *chouette*, really nice. His real name was Lionel Septembre, but he admired all the countercultural phenomena of the age that so alarmed Rosa—so he went by Wyatt, which was the name of the Peter Fonda character in the film *Easy Rider*, who also called himself Captain America. He had told her, to make her laugh, that he had seen the film in Paris in a *version originale,* English dialogue with French subtitles, and so the line "Don't bogart that joint" had been translated as *"Passez-moi le cigarette."* She didn't laugh. Joints were alien to her worldview and although she and Lionel Septembre were both what he called *cinéastes*—another new word—her taste in movies was shaped by her movie-obsessed hometown, and those were movies of a different kind. She hadn't wanted to see *Easy Rider,* but she knew the heroes were killed in the end. "So it's about death," she had said. Wyatt had demurred. *"Il s'agit de la liberté."*

They went to the movies a good deal. He was the one who took her to see *Ugetsu* and *The Saragossa Manuscript* at the art-house cinema near the market square. He introduced her to the French New Wave too—*Pierrot le Fou, Breathless, Alphaville*—and she began to see herself in those smoky Godardian heroines, and to imagine Lionel/Wyatt as a kind of Black Belmondo. In the darkness of that little cinema, bathed in the flickering light of the screen, an emotion rose in her that she was for the moment afraid to call by its name.

But she understood what he meant by freedom.

She thought about the Honorary Fellow. Was that what he had wanted in life and never found? Freedom? And was he free now? Could he still become free even if he was no longer alive? She wasn't even sure what she meant. The situation could not be understood rationally.

What was in the black box file?

The Honorary Fellow's rooms had been closed to the public during the holidays, so she hadn't visited, didn't know if he was still manifesting himself there, and didn't see him anywhere else. But she was convinced that the case of the screaming Provost was connected somehow to the ghost story in which she had become embroiled. After all, how many unrelated inexplicable circumstances could one small college contain? The Honorary Fellow was involved in the chapel scandal. And if so, that represented a dramatic change in his comportment. He was no longer passive and melancholy. He had started scaring people.

He had scared her, or at least his anger had, when she had asked him about the black box file. That was the real reason she had stayed away from Staircase A. Also, she had begun to tell herself to turn away from the dead. Turn toward life. Life, that Christmas, was perhaps Wyatt, although he was too beautiful for her, and he wasn't looking for permanence. But maybe she wasn't either. One day she screwed up her courage and told him to let go of the foolish American name. Lionel Septembre was a fine name and he should own it. He talked then about his disenchantment with his parents, with France's colonial history in Africa, with Europe. A few years earlier he had been at school in Paris during *les événements,* the student uprising, the night of the barricades, the general strike, and then de Gaulle's crushing victory in the elections, which ended the revolt. He had been too young to join in the protests. He sat in his parents' apartment on Avenue Foch and watched it on TV. "We lost," he said. "They brutalized us and then defeated us. The status quo triumphed, the revolution failed."

She listened quietly. Then she said, "Those are not reasons to disown your family." A moment later, somehow, they were embracing. But she was a virgin and not ready and he said he understood and then she knew she had lost him. In the era of free love she was not, did not want to be, free. The Honorary Fellow's notes had contained some words about a quarrel between freedom and goodness. However painful it was, even if it separated her from people of her own age, she wanted—at least for now—to be good.

She wasn't scared of the Honorary Fellow anymore. His burst of temper reminded her of one of her uncles, a sweet man who was prone to sudden anger followed by long regret. Often he wrote notes to the targets of his explosions, offering fulsome apologies. He was her favorite uncle and had died young of a heart attack, perhaps the result of too many hot eruptions followed by rapid coolings-off. She began to think of the Honorary Fellow as an uncle, in the Indian sense of the word. An uncle, or *chacha*, didn't have to be a blood relative or an uncle by marriage. It could be any respected elder, any older person toward whom one felt affection. Simon Uncle, was that what she should call him? Merlyn Uncle? Arthur Chacha?

The time in Bombay was five and a half hours later than at the Greenwich meridian. A curious consequence of this was that if you turned your wristwatch upside down in England its hands showed you the time in India. On Christmas morning, feeling melancholy after her three-minute "time call" with her parents in their upside-down zone, she returned to the Honorary Fellow's rooms. There he was in his armchair, still wearing the tweed jacket, and he had evidently found another flat cap. He looked worse than she remembered: more transparent, somehow *more dead*. His skin had lost color, and there was a distinct odor about him, a stink of decomposition. He seemed unaware of the changes and perked up considerably when she came in.

"There you are," he said. His voice was weaker. "I'm glad you came."

"Merry Christmas," she said.

He smiled. His teeth looked discolored. "Think of me," he said, attempting humor, "as the ghost of Christmas Present. Or maybe Past. I'm fairly sure I'm not the Future."

"To tell you the truth," she replied, surprising herself by her boldness, "I'm beginning to think of you as my second-favorite uncle."

He inclined his head, accepting the compliment, and then asked for help. During life, he said, he had been "quite the puzzler," and one of his favorite daily pastimes had been to do the cryptic crossword in *The Times* in nine minutes flat. Now the paper was no longer delivered and he couldn't hold a pencil or turn the pages. However, as his rooms had been frozen in time by his demise, there was an old copy of the newspaper on the table just inside the front door. "Perhaps you would be so good as to turn to the right page and then sit beside me, read out the clues, and pencil in the answers when I tell you what they are."

Fifteen minutes later the crossword had been completed. "How long? Fifteen minutes?" the Honorary Fellow asked.

"Yes, Arthur Chacha. That's very good."

"It's disappointing," he said. "I'm out of practice." Then there was something more important he had to say on this Christmas morning. "I have a sort of gift for you today," he told Rosa. "I think it may be time I stopped being so cryptic myself and answered your question about the contents of the black box file, even though by doing so I will be breaking the law. I am beyond the reach of the law now, but you, my dear, are not. Therefore I leave it to you to answer the following question before I proceed: Are you willing to be given information that it is illegal for you to receive?"

The unexpectedness of these words placed Rosa in a quandary. "I don't know," she said. "Let me think about it?" Her friends back home had often teased her about her cautious disposition, her unwillingness to make snap decisions even about simple things such as whether to see the new movie at the Eros or the Metro (or possibly the Regal or the New Empire or even the Excelsior), and some of them had threatened to make a T-shirt for her bearing the words *Let me think about it.* She couldn't help it. This was who she was.

"Go for a walk," he suggested. "See, it's snowing a little. I always found that cold weather helped me see clearly and think things out."

8

All Christmas Day Lord Emmemm was alone. He had no partner in life, being what was then known as a "confirmed bachelor," and he had sent the staff of the Provost's Lodge home to enjoy the day with their families. They had left him nourishment in the kitchen, on trays and dishes covered with linens, the breakfast fruits and cereals he preferred, and for the day's traditional feast there was smoked salmon with slices of buttered brown bread, and a plenitude of cold turkey and honey-roasted ham with accompanying salads of cucumbers and beets and new potatoes, and, on the side, jars of sweet chutney and horseradish sauce, and finally a Christmas pudding with a bottle of brandy to pour over it at the appropriate moment and set alight. Cutlery glittered, crockery shone, and napkins stood folded into flowers. A good-sized family would have been well fed by these more than ample provisions. There were also celebratory wines set out, decanters of sherry, a fine Burgundy, and vintage port from the College's legendary cellars, each with its appropriate glass standing ready for him whenever he was ready.

He was not ready. His experience in the chapel had chilled him to the bone, both literally and metaphorically. He was aware of having made himself look ridiculous and knew there would be much gossip among the Fellows as well as the students; and no doubt some—perhaps most—of this tittle-tattle would be malicious. As a person much concerned with his standing in the world, defined by his *amour-propre,* this would ordinarily have been uppermost in his thoughts, but today he had darker preoccupations.

He had been terrified by what had happened to him, and doubly so because as the grip of the icy cold had tightened around his body he had received, as though by a supernatural visitation, the meaning and source of the iciness. A spirit was sitting down in his chair, not sitting on top of him but actually inside him, the wraith-body mingling with his own flesh and blood. And at that moment he knew who it was.

The Honorary Fellow. S. M. Arthur. Merlyn. What sorcery was this? What occult black magic, what dire malevolence reaching out for him from the great beyond? For the manifestation was malevolent, he had no doubt of that.

And he knew why.

He left the Christmas banquet untouched, seized the bottle of Napoleon brandy by the neck, picked up a glass balloon, went into the library, and, in a futile gesture that revealed the depth of his discomfiture, locked the door.

A fire was burning low in the fireplace. He had been adding logs to it all day, waiting for warmth to return to his limbs. They had begun to feel better at last, and the cognac helped. He placed the bottle and balloon on a small table by the armchair nearest to the fire, rubbed his hands together, tossed a new log onto the fire, walked to a certain shelf, and took down a certain slim leather-bound folder. Red leather, and on the front of it the legend, in gold print: FREEDOM VS. GOODNESS BY L. L. EMMEMM. Settling himself in his chair, he began to read.

· · ·

Five years had passed since he had been asked to deliver a set of lectures on the radio. It was the most prestigious lecture series in the land. His contribution had created an uproar, which had not displeased him, although the objections of many College Fellows had afforded him some (not much) distress. In this special binding he had preserved his handwritten manuscript. He was proud of his handwriting. It was flamboyant and beautiful, like himself.

These had been his central proposals: *first,* that the concept of "freedom" carried an assortment of other baggage with it, a group of related concepts that might be called individualism, anarchism, carelessness, irresponsibility, selfishness, narcissism, lawlessness, et cetera. If one espoused the cause of liberty, then the question was, Liberty from what? Oppression? Very well, but how was that to be defined? Persecution was plainly undesirable, but *oppression* could also be an "excuse word" to describe opposition to the "free" person's undesirable behavior. —Undesirable to whom? —To the Group. Society. The entity larger than the self. More to be said about this under the argument for "goodness." —Or liberty from the state? Yes, there were groups—women, for example—who held that the state had no right to intervene in the choices they made for their own bodies, and one may well feel that this opinion was just. But extreme libertarians, in the United States for example, used the concept of "liberty from the state" to justify various forms of lawbreaking and even militancy. So could one say that there were extremes of liberty *for the self* that militated against the liberty *of the many*? So that freedom fell into two categories, "good" and "bad." The question next arose, How were good and bad freedoms to be defined, and by whom, and were they universals and eternals, or did the definitions alter as history moved on? He had delved deeply into these questions, offering potential answers that many had found problematic, and his conclusion had been explosive. It may be, he had proposed, that to be "good" one had to abandon the idea of being "free."

And then, *second,* he had examined "goodness." Here it became clearer that his thesis was a "moral" version of or adjunct to the old debate about society versus the individual, and that he came firmly down on the side of "society," which was to say, he believed that in many cases the rights of the group took precedence over the rights of the individual, which in turn was to say that he was a political conservative, and his philosophy derived from his status as a member of the ruling class. Goodness in his argument was communal, a value arrived at by agreement, by shared viewpoints. One could not be good in isolation. To be good was to be seen to be good, to be good in social contexts, *doing good.* He came close to rejecting altogether the idea of *being good.* The good was not an essence of the self; it was a product of social behavior. One could *become* good, however, if one adopted good behavior.

And therefore he *concluded* that freedom and goodness were to be understood as irreconcilable concepts and it was necessary for the moral individual to decide which side he was on. To be good one had to make compromises regarding freedom, and surrender absolute freedom to the common good. To be free was to abandon the idea of being good.

To be free was to abandon the idea of being good. That was the sentence that fueled the fire. Ministers, archbishops, editors, artists rounded upon him. He was called *fantastically wrong-headed,* his thinking was termed *woolly,* his argument *ludicrous.* He had made a *false opposition.* Goodness and freedom were not incompatible. Freedom was a crucial element in the Good, and the arc of goodness bent inevitably toward liberty for all. In the House of Commons he was called, by one of the country's most celebrated radical polemicists, "a disgrace to the College he leads." He dealt with it all with a kind of intellectual shrug. The purpose of serious thought was to encourage society to question itself. That was known. He had merely added a further proposal to that one: that the purpose of serious thought was also to encourage the individual to question him- or herself, and for each, the Good and the Free, to interrogate the other. Democracy was an argument, and he had started an argument that he hoped would be productive.

Within the College it had been the Honorary Fellow whose commentary had been the most cutting. "You lead me to suspect," S. M. Arthur had written in a personal note to Lord Emmemm, "that it is wholly conceivable that a person might be neither free nor good." Emmemm had let that pass. The Honorary Fellow had enough troubles of his own.

Remembering Arthur brought back the terror in the chapel. Was it possible that the Honorary Fellow was pursuing him from beyond the grave? Was he himself losing his mind, or might such a thing be so? And then he remembered what the young Indian woman had said. She had said *also*.

9

Rosa had listened to Lord Emmemm's lectures and had read them when they were printed in *The Times*. She came from a country in which the collective's opinions very often outweighed the rights of the individual, so much of the lectures' content resonated with her. But the spirit of the age, which celebrated freedom, affected her too. She herself was considered a free spirit at home and a conservative here, so she was pulled in both directions. If she had to choose between these two poles in order to be a moral being, as Lord Emmemm had stated, then she must be immoral, because she didn't know how to make the choice.

What she did know, as she walked alone in the evening snow of Christmas Day, was that her encounter with the Honorary Fellow was the most significant event of her life to date, and that she needed to experience it as fully as possible. So, yes, she would agree to hear his illegal words, and if that meant she chose freely rather than obeying the law as a good person would, then she came down, at least for now, on that side of the fence. She had been walking on the path between the river and the Back Lawn. The sky was full of snow, so there were no stars, there was no moon. She turned and walked back toward Staircase A, ready for whatever improprieties the night might reveal. She could keep a secret. Whatever he told her, however scandalous, however shocking, her lips would remain sealed.

She saw Lionel Septembre coming toward her in the last light of day. "To be alone on such a day is a sadness," he said. "May I walk with you?"

Rosa decided that on this day of secrets she would reveal her own secret to this man. "I have something to tell you," she said, "and when you have heard it you will think I am a madwoman and run from me and never talk to me again."

"We celebrate today a virgin birth," he said. "Is it weirder than that?"

So she told him. The first meeting in the students' common room bar. The frequent conversations. Her growing fondness for the dead writer. *Uncle.* Lionel Septembre listened gravely without attempting to interrupt. When she finished she stopped walking and stared at him, waiting for his rejection and ridicule.

"In Senegal, where my parents are stationed," he said, "they have the story of the Ceddo, a phantom from the past who haunts the living. The Ceddo is sometimes understood as heroic, but in other versions he is thought to be brutal. Also, he has an enemy, the Marabout, and chases him across space and time. I hear your story and it reminds me of this other story. Does your Ceddo have an enemy?"

"I believe his enemy is Lord Emmemm," she said. "So you don't think I'm insane?"

"I have been thinking deeply about you, your intelligence, your beauty, and your, let me say, physical reluctance. And I have decided the following: I accept your terms."

She felt her face growing warm. "I am not sure what that means," she told him, "but I suspect that you are lying."

"It means yes, I am for you," he said. "And so what you tell me, I believe. And what you don't want is not necessary."

"Now I know you're lying," she said. He put his arms around her and they stood silently with the snow around them falling softly, softly falling.

"Go to him," Lionel Septembre told her. "Hear what he has to say."

The Honorary Fellow was waiting for her when she returned to his rooms.

"Tell me everything, Uncle," she said.

So he began:

He had always been a dedicated puzzler. Crosswords, chess puzzles, riddles, he attacked them all with enthusiasm and found he had the kind of brain that saw through the puzzle masters' deceptions. In the years after his book was published and he came to live at the College, he found many kindred spirits there, many fellow puzzlers of great skill. Then on September 3, 1939, all such frivolity seemed to become forever irrelevant. The world war, the second in just twenty-one years, had begun. He was twenty-nine years old. Literature felt as irrelevant as crossword puzzles. He felt irrelevant himself. He had been unimpressed to learn that Lord Emmemm's flat feet—his *pes planus* condition, to give it its fancy name, which made it no less absurd—had excused him from military service. But then he found out that his own combination of myopia, astigmatism, and incipient glaucoma disqualified him as well. When he was told this, he felt worthless. He had been convinced that he would have made the very poorest sort of soldier, and had he been sent to the front lines he would have been killed on the first day. Nevertheless his rejection was a disappointment. More than that: a source of genuine shame.

Then he received, without explanation, an order to report immediately to GC&CS. The Government Code & Cypher School, in Buckinghamshire. That name, GC&CS, was not used in any communications. It was called, among other things,

Station X. And that was where the author S. M. Arthur fought his war.

He was told to go to Hut 6. Soon after entering it he heard for the first time the names Enigma and Lorenz, and understood from that moment that these entities, and not Adolf Hitler, were the real enemies he faced. They were machines he had never seen, generating coded messages using techniques about which he knew nothing, and it was his job to break those codes, and to arrange for English translations of the secret German messages for which the code name was *Fish*. He had become a fisherman, far from any river or the sea.

The code breakers: they were chess masters, mathematicians, and crossword puzzle geniuses. But it was information gleaned from their Polish counterparts that gave them their start. After that they broke the Enigma codes and the Lorenz codes, and when variant versions of those machines came into service they broke those codes too, and all this work was done in the deadliest secret. The Germans never knew that their coded messages were being read and passed on by the code breakers to the military high command, and nobody knew the cryptologists' names, or the existence of the pseudonymous HMS *Pembroke V,* also known as Room 47, Foreign Office or as RAF Eastcote—which was to say, Station X, where German fish were caught every day.

"One doesn't like to brag," the Honorary Fellow said, "but the view—and when I say the view I mean the opinion of the official historian of British Intelligence—is that our work shortened the duration of the war by several years, and without our work it's not clear that we would have won."

After the war ended, they all went their separate ways. They never wrote to one another, never spoke on the telephone, never met again. They became strangers to one another, knew nothing of one another's postwar lives, and had no interest in getting acquainted. Their work was never written about, never spoken of, was shrouded in a fog as thick as the fog in which he was now engulfed. That was all right. They were not looking for fame. They had served their country, and each of them carried that memory within him- or herself. That was enough. The Rule that forbade any mention of this great secret was intended to last for fifty years. Then four years ago the law was revised and it became a thirty-year rule.

"Thirty years from the end of the war is four years from now. In four years' time the story can be told," the Honorary Fellow said. "Until then, everything you have just heard is illegal for me to tell you, and it is improper for you to have heard it. The secrecy laws are extremely fierce."

"You have waited so long," she said. "Twenty-six years, you've held your tongue. Would it not have been wiser to leave it four years more, and then gain all the recognition you deserve? Why tell me now?"

"In the first place, my dear," he replied, "because I am deceased, don't you know. I don't believe that any shred of myself will still be here in four years' time. As I'm sure you can see, and as I also know, what's left of me is decaying. It won't be long before what you called an error will be rectified and I will be gone for good. This interregnum in which I find myself turns out not to be a 'forever' type of haven from the ravages of time—not Shangri-La after all but a waiting room. And in the second place, four years from now you too will be gone, done with this College and moving on into whatever future lies in store for you. You will find love, either with this Monsieur Septembre or another monsieur or even, although I suspect not, an arranged marriage back home. You will have your brilliant future and will no longer be concerned with this anecdote from the antique past."

She chose to let this pass. "All of this, everything you have told me, is detailed in the black box file?" she asked.

"No," he answered. "It would have been extremely unwise to write any of this down. This story is by way of a prologue. The file contains another kind of secret entirely."

The war was over. He was back at the College. The part of him that had always been forbidden was still forbidden. Yet his desire for the forbidden had increased. After five years in Hut 6, where, overwhelmed by necessity, he had never thought about the needs of the body, now, in this time of austerity and rationing, he wanted love. People had kissed strangers in the streets on the day peace had returned. He wanted to kiss a stranger too.

"Your country won its freedom," he told Rosa, "although, as Emmemm would no doubt point out, that liberty was at odds with goodness, because of the ensuing massacres, the maybe one million deaths. Maybe two million? We can't know. I confess I wasn't thinking about those religious murders. I was selfishly remembering the two men I had loved. I wondered, if I went back after so long, and in the aftermath of the empire I had detested, might I find again in that land of the newly free what I needed most."

He didn't go back. India came to him instead. In the town's market square he met the man he afterward referred to as "Brown Bobby," a police constable, or bobby, of South Asian origin patrolling his daily beat. In those days there were very few Indian coppers walking English streets, let alone charismatically handsome ones wearing turbans instead of helmets, and the Honorary Fellow engaged PC Jai Singh in friendly conversation and congratulated him on his pioneering civic role. It wasn't long before the constable progressed from Brown Bobby to B.B. to *bibi*, which was to say madam or, alternatively, wife. In point of fact the bobby had a wife, and when the Honorary Fellow first visited his new friend in his home, that was a considerable surprise. But PC Singh reassured him cheerfully. "Not to worry, sir," he said, placing an arm around the Honorary Fellow's shoulders. "It is not a problem. Madam will be happy to share."

And so things proceeded for a while—"almost ten years, actually," the Honorary Fellow said—and all parties seemed to be content with the arrangement. The three bibis, Brown Bobby and his two wives, appeared content with their ménage à trois. They picnicked together, went to the pictures together, holidayed on a chilly English beach together, for all the world "like a tedious little petit-bourgeois family," in the Honorary Fellow's words. "Too good to be true, of course," he added. "And one day the whole kit-cat-caboodle came tumbling down."

PC Jai Singh was summoned into his station captain's office. "Your wife has been in to see me," he was told. "And she alleges that for the past decade you have been performing criminal sodomite activities with a College Fellow. I give you the choice of resigning immediately or being summarily dismissed. After that you will hand in your insignia of office and your uniform and then fuck off out of these premises, never to return, while we consider what action we wish to take against you. Now get out."

Soon enough the news reached the Provost's Lodge at the College. There was an unusual local bylaw according to which the College could not be entered by officers of the law without the agreement of the Provost. Lord Emmemm declined permission "for the moment" and arrived at the Honorary Fellow's door.

"A bad business," he said.

"Bad for the College," he additionally said.

"The College has been good to you," he added. "Too good, some might say."

"All we expected from you was discretion," he next remarked.

"A pretty pickle," he concluded. "Let me consider the best course of action."

"I was at a loss," the Honorary Fellow told Rosa. "The idea of being imprisoned horrified me. I was haunted by Wilde's words. The 'man who looked / With such a wistful eye / Upon that little tent of blue / Which prisoners call the sky.' And also: 'I know not whether laws be right, / Or whether laws be wrong; / All that we know who lie in gaol / Is that the wall is strong; / And that each day is like a year, / A year whose days are long.' It was unbearable for me to contemplate. I knew I could not survive there. I feared my life was at an end.

"Then Emmemm came back with a 'solution.' That's what he called it, even, if memory serves, 'an elegant solution.' He had already discussed it with the authorities, he said, and if I accepted it there would be no arrest, no scandal for myself or the College, and no prison time. Well! My heart leapt, I can tell you. But what could this miraculous solution possibly be?

"This was the day on which I first heard the name of the drug DES, which is to say, diethylstilbestrol. This drug, Emmemm told me, was in use as a treatment for prostate cancer, and that would be our cover story. I had been diagnosed with this cancer, was undergoing treatment, and the prognosis was excellent. Nobody would know anything about anything else. PC Singh and his wife had been given one-way economy tickets to Delhi. They had already left, and would never trouble anyone again.

"But the drug had another use. It had the effect of stopping the production of sex hormones. The drug was what was called an androgen synthesis inhibitor. It made it impossible for the body to produce testosterone.

"The common name for its prescription and use being *chemical castration*. That was what I was being asked to accept. Medically induced eunuchdom. The benefit being the preservation of my reputation and the avoidance of a long jail term.

"I accepted. The alternative was unthinkable—and so I took the drugs. I took them until the day before I died. The bottle of pills was found on my bedside table when I was discovered dead in bed. Even after the legalization four years ago, I was obliged to continue with the treatment, or I would lose my College accommodation. That was the deal. Until today nobody knew the truth except some anonymous figures of high authority, Emmemm, and myself. And now you know as well."

10

Suddenly Emmemm was standing in the doorway of the Honorary Fellow's rooms. There was an unusual look about him: one of fear. He tried to cover it up by blustering. "I've been looking for you, young lady," he boomed. "What are you doing in here?"

"You yourself asked me to look after these rooms, sir," Rosa replied. "I'm just making sure all is in good order."

"The rooms are closed for the Christmas break," Emmemm said. "There's no reason for you to be snooping about."

"Excuse me," she said. "I apologize. I'll go immediately."

"Stay," he said. "I need to talk to you."

"To me, sir?"

"Yes, damn it, you. You recall our last conversation?"

"I'm not sure, sir."

"Yes, yes. I said, speaking metaphorically, 'His ghost would approve of you.' And you responded, apparently not metaphorically, 'He appeared to you also?' *Also,* you see. Meaning he had appeared to you. So now I ask you, young lady: Is that so?"

She didn't know what to say, and stood before the Provost, mute, stupid.

The Honorary Fellow spoke to her: "Tell him yes."

"Are you sure?" she asked.

"Yes," the Honorary Fellow said.

"To whom are you speaking?" Lord Emmemm demanded. "There's nobody else here." Then his eyes widened. "Is he? Is he in this room?"

"Tell him yes," the Honorary Fellow said.

"Yes," she said. "Yes, my lord. He's here."

"And you can see him?"

"Tell him yes."

"Yes, sir. I see him and hear him. I don't know why, but I do."

"Extraordinary," Emmemm exclaimed, and then demanded, "What does he want? He must want something. What the devil is it? He should be at peace. You understand, Simon Merlyn? Can you hear me? At peace."

"Tell him I want the truth."

"Sir, he says he wants the truth."

"What truth? What the dickens is he on about?"

"Tell him he knows very well what I'm talking about and it's time to stop lying."

"Excuse me, sir, but he says you know very well, and should stop lying."

Lord Emmemm was silent.

"Tell him if he doesn't, I'll crawl inside him and give him the deathly cold treatment every night until it kills him too."

"I can't say that." Here were two gladiators, she thought, one vengeful, the other finally at his mercy, and she stood between them as a kind of translator, bewildered, terrified, and out of place. The arena was no place for an intermediary.

"What can't you say? Young lady? Are you playing games with me?"

"No, sir. Of course not."

"Tell the bastard."

"This is very difficult."

"What's very difficult? Out with it. Come on."

"Sir, he says if the truth is not revealed, he will—he will continue to torment you until it kills you. Excuse me, sir. I can't do this anymore."

Lord Emmemm clutched at his brow. "This is a nightmare."

"Tell him I want a detailed description of the way I was treated. I want it on the front pages of the newspapers. And I want a public apology. A groveling public apology."

Trembling, she repeated the Honorary Fellow's words. Then he spoke again.

"Tell him he removed an essential part of my freedom, but there was nothing good about it. He himself is the living disproof of his own preposterous theory."

She told him. Emmemm staggered slightly, then lurched toward the leather armchair.

"Sir, don't sit there," she cried.

"Damn it. Why not?"

"Because he's there, sir. That's where he is right now."

With a loud inarticulate howl, Lord Emmemm fled the room.

"Now, that was satisfying," the Honorary Fellow said. "That was actually fun."

The confession of Lord Emmemm on national television began with a claim that it was timely, because social attitudes had changed: the attitudes that had caused homosexuality to be outlawed had been replaced by a far more liberal consensus, and the law had followed where public opinion had led. Back then in the old days the world was different. It had been his desire to save a great literary talent from what William Wordsworth had called the "shades of the prison-house," which were beginning to close around him. He now recognized, he said, that an unjust law had led him to commit a grave injustice, to place the author in a prison-house whose walls and bars were made not of stone or steel but of chemicals, fogging his brain and therefore no doubt depriving the entire culture of the further fruits of his genius. He wished, he said, to express the most profound regret at his actions, coupling that regret with a great relief that the time had come when persons of S. M. Arthur's private preferences could live openly and without fear. The confession ended, oddly, by contradicting its opening. "This explanation, this apology, this expression of bitter regret from myself and the whole of the College I serve, comes late, many may say too late, but, perhaps, better late than never."

The severe criticisms of Emmemm that followed his statement included, most damagingly, anonymous letters to the press outing him as a closet adherent of the same practices that had led to the Honorary Fellow's "castration." (It should be said that the terms *outing* and *closet* were not then in common use, and are used here because they are widely understood today.) The charge of "traitor to his own kind" finished him off. He resigned from the Provostship, retired to a small cottage in the West Country, withdrew from both public and academic life, and passed away in obscurity some years later, meriting only a small obituary in *The Times.*

Rosa watched the apology on television alongside the Honorary Fellow, who nodded his head vigorously at the end.

"Here is the difference between real life and books," he said. "In books it is necessary to bring things to a satisfying resolution. In real life things are not so neat. In my own case, the second secret will only be revealed when I am long gone. I fear it will soon be my time to die again. One thing is done not 'better late than never,' which sounds just a little self-congratulatory, but, let us say, 'just in time'; the other thing is late. Too late for me, and I am too late myself. The fog that wrapped itself around me is clearing, and I see my way. It's time to go."

"Surely you can stay awhile yet," she said, a pleading note in her voice. "Uncle, you can't want to leave . . ." And here she stopped herself from saying what she was thinking.

To leave me.

"My dear," he said, "to weep over a first death is understandable. To mourn a second death, the death of a dead man, is faintly ludicrous."

She dried her eyes.

"Besides," he said, "I have planned quite the exit for myself. Come to the bridge over the river tomorrow evening at six. Bring your Monsieur Septembre if you wish. He probably won't see anything, but you can hold his hand."

11

I t was New Year's Eve. The snow stopped, the sky cleared, the stars came out in force. Rosa and her Lionel, well wrapped up against the cold, stood on the little bridge across the thin river and waited. The Honorary Fellow arrived punctually—on time, not late, the way he had been in life—dressed in his habitual tweeds. He walked across the Back Lawn to the riverbank, looked toward them, and raised a hand. Then Rosa saw the punt approaching.

Standing on the platform at the rear of the punt, wielding the pole, was an Indian gentleman in elegant attire—cream suit, floral waistcoat, burgundy cravat, and cream-and-chocolate two-tone shoes. Sitting down in the punt, but coming to his feet now, was a dhoti-clad man wearing a simple black-and-white checked Nehru-collared jacket, a far less aristocratic figure, but similarly clean and neat. Khan Sahib, for it was he, steered the punt slowly and deftly in along the river's edge. Mr. Shah, for it was undoubtedly he, stood up in the craft and stretched out his hand. The Honorary Fellow had become almost completely transparent, and the other two—Rosa now saw—also allowed the flat landscape, the thin river, the punt itself to be visible through their shade forms. She remembered all of a sudden some lines of Kipling that spoke of the magic of England.

She is not any common Earth, / Water or wood or air, / But Merlin's Isle of Gramarye, / Where you and I will fare.

But today there would be an end to magic and then a return to the everyday.

The Honorary Fellow was in the punt, and it was moving toward the bridge. "Where are you going, Arthur Chacha?" she called to him. Lionel, seeing nothing, squeezed her hand. She allowed her body to lean against his. That felt comforting.

"Where else?" the Honorary Fellow called back to her. "Avalon." Then the punt passed under the bridge but did not emerge on the other side.

A FOOTNOTE

Four years later, when the thirty-year embargo was lifted, the invaluable work of Station X during World War II became widely known and the code breakers were celebrated at last. Those who had survived received high honors of state, and those who were dead were awarded the same honors posthumously. There was a set of stamps commemorating the half dozen leaders of the Hut 6 team, and one of the stamps bore the image of Simon Merlyn Arthur.

One of the survivors told the press that the code breakers of Buckinghamshire had had a private nickname for themselves.

They were "the Round Table."

Oklahoma

Foreword

The text that follows is the last work of a writer whom we sadly lost too early, Mamouli Ajeeb, who preferred to be known by his *initiales de plume,* "M.A." The manuscript was mailed to the publishing house the day before he left us, accompanied by a note asking that it be published (contradicting an indication in the text itself that it should not be published) and that it be considered as a wholly fictional work, in spite of its "autofictional" form. He described it as "a narrative that is untrue and therefore true, as fiction is." It is given here exactly as he sent it, without editorial interventions. The inexact chronology and deliberately imprecise location of parts of the tale, which may be an obstacle to some readers, are essential to its dreamlike quality, and in the author's absence it would be improper to adjust these aspects of his work. Inevitably they may also be seen as an indication of the author's troubled mental state. It remains only to indicate that some explanatory notes have been placed at the end, and the title *Oklahoma* has been added. The work as received was untitled, but the selected title felt inevitable.

Oklahoma

by
M.A.

"Kafka was about your age when he wrote the first novel," Uncle K. said to me that first weekend on Long Island, "and he never called it *Amerika*. That was the title his friend and executor Brod put on the unfinished manuscript after his death. Have you read it?"

"No," I confessed, twenty-seven years old, and embarrassed. I was half Uncle K.'s age but that felt like no excuse. We are supposed to have read everything, aren't we, if we want writing to be our calling. We must carry whole libraries in our heads, like Peter Kien, the hero of Canetti's *Auto-da-Fé*. I had friends who could recite reams of poetry from memory. "Shelley," I could say, and they would do twenty minutes, verbatim. "Byron." Another twenty minutes. I don't have that kind of mind. Or, if it's Bob Dylan, maybe I do.

"He thought about calling it *The Man Who Disappeared*," Uncle K. reflected, "but he abandoned it in the middle of the last chapter and never went back to it."

Uncle K. was obsessed with disappearance. His novels and stories were full of vanishings. He wrote ghost stories about missing persons who reappeared as specters, and stories in which human beings were kidnapped by spaceships, never to return. He wrote about what happened to those who remained when those who did not remain went away, either to a war or another woman or for reasons that were never explained. Death was a form of disappearance, of course, so it interested him as a subject too, especially as he grew older. He wrote a lot about death. The best known of these books had a title borrowed from an English playwright: *The Absence of Presence.*

He made lists of true-life absences as well as fictional ones. The holes in the Beatles left behind by John Lennon's murder and George Harrison's fatal illness. The thirteen works of art stolen from the Isabella Stewart Gardner Museum in Boston and never recovered, in spite of the museum's offer of a ten million dollar reward. Amelia Earhart. The Lindbergh baby. The dingo baby.

And mythological disappearances. Wounded King Arthur spirited away to Avalon, and Barbarossa asleep somewhere in a cave. The giant Finn MacCool asleep under an Irish ridge, sucking his thumb. The Greek gods, after attending the marriage of Cadmus and Harmony, withdrawing forever from human affairs. It was a long list. And he had faith, too, in reappearances, in unlikely returns. "All Finnegans," Uncle K. liked to say, especially after he had whiskey taken, "eventually wake."

This afternoon he had Kafka's first anti-hero, the unfinished Karl Rossmann, on his mind. "He's only sixteen in the story, just off the boat from Europe," Uncle K. said. "And he's in a smoke-filled railway carriage on his way to Oklahoma to join something called the Nature Theater. It's a long journey and it makes him understand how big America is. He passes high mountains and dark ravines and there are bridges over rolling rivers. The geography seems more or less arbitrary. But he is a hopeful fellow and hopes that in Oklahoma he will find—this is not how Kafka puts it—some sort of personal fulfillment, a realization of the American dream. Perhaps even happiness. But he doesn't get there. Kafka just stops writing him. It's almost cruel. He's lost forever in that railway carriage, wreathed in smoke and frozen in time, eternally. The boy who disappeared. And I really want to know what happened to him."

"Why don't you finish the story?" I dared to suggest. Uncle K. frowned. "Don't imagine I don't think about it."

I think I understand now why he never did try to write that ending. In the first place I think he saw Karl Rossmann as another Kafka—lost too young but also eternal—and to "finish" him would be a kind of lèse-majesté, an act of treason, a stepping into boots none of us could fill, boots none of us were worthy to wear, even if our foot sizes were the same. And in the second place, could any of us truly imagine what that Oklahoma would be like, that Kafkaesque discovery of happiness, that New Jerusalem à la Franz? A happy ending to a Kafka story would—perhaps inevitably—just feel *wrong*. Uncle K. was not a Utopian thinker. Oklahoma would have to remain undescribed, at least by him.

And in the third place, he thought of his country—"Amerika" or, as I grew up calling it in my mother tongue, "Amríka"—as somehow unfinished too, somehow lost in the middle of its own story, its future unknown; so the unfinishedness of the novel felt appropriate. In its incompleteness its meaning was complete.

We sat in silence for a while. Then he asked me for the thing I found hard to do. "Tell me a bit of poetry you like," he said. "So I can get a sense of who you are."

I'm bad at that, I wanted to say, but there was one poem that for some reason was stuck in my head, by the great Polish poet, Zbigniew Herbert. So I recited it. I won't repeat it all here, but here are some fragments of it.

Go where those others went to the dark boundary
for the golden fleece of nothingness your last prize

and

and let your helpless Anger be like the sea
whenever you hear the voice of the insulted and beaten

"What is that," he asked.

I told him it was called *The Envoi of Mr Cogito* and Mr Cogito was an imaginary alter ego of the poet.

"So," he said, "you want to take on the public subject, the big stuff. Democracy, fascism, history, ethics, revolution, God, mythology, ethics, the grand questions. You'll probably fail. Most public writers do. Me, I wrote my war novel, but these days I'm increasingly interested in the private subject. You have your Cogito . . . me, I pay attention nowadays to Mr Palomar, who is the alter ego of Calvino of course, and who only cares about the patterns of birdsong in the trees in his garden, the calls and responses, and the rhythm of waves arriving at the nearby beach, which also, so to speak, call and respond. And of course I'm failing too. Now you must take a glass of whiskey and then maybe we can get along. In that cabinet over there is my collection of more or less antique tumblers and wine- and shot-glasses. Choose the one you want."

There was a large Sunday brunch prepared by the lady I'll just call Auntie K., a fine writer herself, a brilliant and important essayist who was quietly furious that her essays were more admired than her fictions, comparing herself to the Argentinian genius Jorge Luis Borges, who always thought his real achievement lay in his poetry, and not the strange little stories he occasionally dashed off, which had made him immortal. "Admit it," she challenged me when I made the mistake of complimenting her on her nonfiction, "you've never read a word of my fiction in your life!" I made some sheepish reply, but what I didn't admit was that I had read those experimental novels, and that was why I hadn't mentioned them.

On the brunch table alongside the waffles, the maple syrup, the scrambled eggs, the bagels with lox and cream cheese, the hash browns, the juices, were two bowls of store-bought candy—chocolates both commercial and artisanal, macaroons, and sweet sugary mass-market things wrapped in plastic. Uncle K. had a sweet tooth that was, he admitted, bad for his actual teeth, which were in terrible shape. "If I hadn't gotten myself into this writing game," he said, "I'd have been happy running a candy store on a street corner somewhere in the middle of nowhere."

After brunch I caught the bus back into the city, and I admit that what was on my mind was something other than Franz Kafka and his Oklahoma. As we sat talking on Uncle K.'s back porch that sunny afternoon on the East End of Long Island he was dressed in a light blue polo shirt and loose khaki shorts and, ahem, as I could not fail to observe, no underpants. He was nursing his second or perhaps even third whiskey of the morning, looking out at Auntie K.'s garden through tortoiseshell-frame sunglasses, seated in a white cane outdoor chair with his legs splayed wide apart, displaying to the innocent young visiting author much more of himself than the young author expected to become acquainted with.

I asked myself, on that excited and confused bus ride back into New York City, if the display might have been intentional. I decided, out of respect, to believe that it was not. Uncle K., I reminded myself, dealt in unexpected appearances as well as vanishings.

Everything was new to me then. Six years after graduating from Cambridge I was enjoying my first success as a writer and visiting New York for my début book's very positive American publication. The doors of the literary world were opening and here I was almost magically as the weekend guest of a writer I had long admired, and who had randomly and generously decided to invite me to visit. After that first weekend, for a while, he occasionally sent me short handwritten postcards containing words of advice and he would sign them "Uncle K." It seemed I had a gift for acquiring uncles. At an Indian literary congress I met the eminent and prolific novelist Mulk Raj Anand, a socialist and Gandhian, friend of E. M. Forster and other Bloomsbury Groupers, author of *Untouchable* and *Coolie,* admired portraits of the lives of the poor; he, too, started sending me messages—aerograms—and signing them "Uncle Mulk." Thus well-Uncled I sallied forth into the writing life.

(Uncle Mulk lived on until he was ninety-eight years old but as he faded he proved to be incapable of completing the seven-volume autobiographical novel he had decided to write. The fourth volume was published twenty years before he died but there was no fifth book. I began to think of him as an elder version of Kafka's Karl. He, too, was unfinished, frozen in time four-sevenths of the way through the story of himself. He, too, had disappeared into a blank page.)

After the surprise attack on Pearl Harbor and the United States' consequent formal entry into World War II, a number of American airmen (and more Canadians) volunteered to join the Royal Air Force. The young Uncle K., who was nobody's uncle at the time, was one of these, and became a part of the Pathfinders force whose task it was to fly ahead of British bomber squadrons and drop flares to light the bombers' way to their targets. This system, fully operational by early 1943, greatly increased the efficiency of the bombing raids, but placed the

Pathfinder crews in danger, because they had to fly home across brightly illuminated skies and were therefore vulnerable to German anti-aircraft fire. Many Pathfinder pilots who survived the war afterward suffered from psychological problems which were then known as battle fatigue, combat fatigue, combat neurosis, or, more dramatically, as shell shock, and which would now be grouped under the heading of post-traumatic stress disorder, PTSD. When Uncle K. returned to America after the war, he got married almost at once to his formidable beloved, and made his name as a writer with the novel *The Illuminators,* based on his wartime experiences. He made light of the subject of mental troubles when it cropped up. "Nothing a glass of good whiskey can't fix," he would say. But as he grew older the damage became increasingly apparent. His mood swings and depressions grew deeper and more frequent. I was fortunate that my introductory weekend with him on Long Island coincided with one of his better spells. Much worse was to follow.

I was living in London back then but I stayed in intermittent touch with Uncle K. and visited the house on Long Island once or twice, when I could, although I noticed that Auntie K. was beginning to think of me as something of an interloper, probably because, as a writer of Indian origin based in the United Kingdom, I came from far outside her circle. But I admired them both and felt privileged by my small connection with them and hoped to win her over. And on one of my last visits she told me some details of her husband's slow decline. The booze got hold of him early, I saw that on our first meeting, but he was a happy drunk, a sweet drunk, not an angry or scary drunk, and so nobody seemed to mind his whiskey consumption too much. But the depressions were bad. And sometimes he couldn't tell the real from the unreal. He watched *The Wizard of Oz* on Christmas Day television and (according to Auntie K.) when Dorothy, at the end, cried out that Oz was a real, live place, and why didn't anyone believe her?, Uncle K. shouted at the top of his voice, "Yeah!" After which he passed out in his armchair by the fire and the gathering of worried family and alarmed friends tried with some difficulty to recapture the Christmas spirit.

I moved to New York fifteen years after my first visit. I was in my early forties but by then Uncle and Auntie K. were lost to me. Paradoxically now that I was closer our lives moved further apart. I regretted it but told myself that changes like that sometimes happen in people's lives, and without any apparent estrangement our contacts ended, the postcards stopped arriving. To console myself I tried to imitate his handwriting on postcards I bought myself—I know, pathetic, right?—and in my opinion I got pretty good. (He wrote in a distinctive, large, looping script, very unlike my own natural scrawl.)

And then, one day, without warning, he disappeared.

I saw the news in the *Times*. I called Auntie K. who sounded surprised to hear from me. (We hadn't spoken in a long while.) I had to ask her twice for a little information, and at length she told me what I already knew. "He walked into the sea sometime last night and didn't come back." She wasn't crying but it was the voice of a woman who had wept, perhaps too much, for too long, and no longer had it in her to weep.

"I'll come," I said, although she hadn't asked me to, and she answered, pretty stiffly, I thought, "There's really no need." So, not wishing to be where I wasn't wanted, I didn't get on the bus.

But I followed the news. Uncle K.'s clothes had been found on the beach, neatly folded, just above the high tide line. Khaki pants, a surprisingly pink polo shirt, his favorite pair of sandals, the signature tortoiseshell sunglasses, a gray baseball hat without the markings of any ball club, even though he was known to be a committed Mets fan who loathed the hated Yankees. No underpants. An early morning beach walker had recognized the clothes, which were pretty much Uncle K.'s uniform, and had run to alert Auntie K. at their house, which wasn't far, only a half-mile up the road from the beach entrance. A search on land and sea found nothing. He wasn't floating out there and no body washed up on the shore. He had simply performed the act that had always obsessed him.

Disappearance.

A large plane once crashed in the waters off Long Island. All that summer the beaches felt ominous. At a literary party in New York I tried to avoid a woman was shocked to hear that I had gone for a sunset walk on a beach "out there." "Aren't you afraid," she asked me, "that you might *encounter* some *severed body parts?*" But none were encountered. The *New York Times* published a photograph of a paper cup bearing the airline's logo. That was all. Otherwise . . . disappearance. The newspaper used peculiar euphemisms to explain why the drowned bodies were hard to identify. They had suffered "marine life intervention." In many cases, "radical marine life intervention."

In plain English, the fish ate their faces.

And now Uncle K.'s clothes had been discarded by the shore of that same sea and I couldn't avoid thinking about the fish. But I didn't mention them to anyone.

I remembered my Herbert poem. *"And let your helpless Anger be like the sea."*

Because I had lived in England for a long time, I also inevitably thought of Virginia Woolf who, fearing the return of madness, wrote a loving last letter to her husband Leonard, placed a large stone in her pocket, and walked into the rapid flow of the River Ouse near her home, Monk's House in Rodmell, East Sussex. Uncle K. left no such note for his wife or anyone else although I believed that he, too, was suffering from mental troubles, and it was suggested by more than one commentator that he might have been thinking about Woolf. He left in silence, without explanation.

I also thought of two less exalted "water disappearances," one real, one fictional. In the mid-Seventies the BBC television comedy series *The Fall and Rise of Reginald Perrin* told the story of a sales executive who, bored with his life, faked his death by leaving his clothes and other personal items on a beach and then assumed a series of false identities. This series aired two years after a disgraced British politician, John Stonehouse, had tried to fake his death in the same way, and had attempted to start a new life in Australia, where he was discovered a few months later and arrested. He was found guilty of several charges of financial fraud and forgery and sent to jail.

So: which case fitted Uncle K.'s exit? Was it, like Woolf's, a sad true thing? Or was it a Perrinic/Stonehousian comic/fraudulent deception? Real or unreal? The question remained open for two years. Then there was a sort of answer.

All Finnegans eventually wake.

2

The last time I saw Uncle K. was several years earlier at his favorite Manhattan restaurant, a high-end French spot that no longer exists. I was in New York at the beginning of a book tour and I invited him to dinner to celebrate the new publication with me. "I'm an envious bastard," he told me, "and on the whole I avoid applauding my fellow writers, but on the condition that you let me choose the place, and agree that it should be as expensive as possible, I accept." I already knew the place he would pick, and told him that was fine. "See if you can get one of those tables in their little back yard," he instructed me, and to my surprise such a table proved to be available. When we arrived for dinner I understood why. There was a sudden heat wave and the back yard was too hot for comfort even though the restaurant had installed electric fans by the tables out there. That evening taught me that Uncle K. had a mean streak. Maybe he really was an "envious bastard." To make me pay for a pricey meal and make it as uncomfortable as possible was his idea of a good joke. When we had been seated he ordered eight bottles of Badoit water and when they arrived he opened them all and poured most of the fizzy liquid over his sandaled feet to cool off. "That's better," he declared, and ordered a bottle of whiskey "and," he instructed the waiter, wagging his index finger, "one glass."

I never forgot the incident and told the story more than once to entertain friends, and the pouring of the water was always the punchline. But when I received the package and read what it contained I realized that Uncle K. had a very different memory of the occasion. At some point during dinner I had talked excitedly and probably for too long about my recent visit to the Prado Museum in Madrid during a visit to promote the Spanish translation of my début novel. In particular I had talked about my love for the "three greatest rooms in any gallery anywhere in the world," the room containing the "black Goyas" with their occult imagery, the room dominated by Velázquez's *Las Meninas* with its tricky sight-lines, and the Bosch room. During the Hieronymus part of my soliloquy I had mentioned that, as well as *The Garden of Earthly Delights,* my interest had been piqued by a much smaller Bosch canvas depicting what looked like a torture scene. Its title was *The Extraction of the Stone of Madness,* I told Uncle K., and what an idea it was, I had probably gone on to say, to imagine that madness was an actual stone in the brain, and that if you had a pair of pincers and some assistants to hold the mad person down, you could take the stone out and cure him.

"Yeah," Uncle K. replied thoughtfully, "that'd probably work."

The thick manila envelope that was left for me at my apartment bore no stamp or postmark and my address had been printed on a white sticky label and stuck onto the thing. There was no return address in the upper left-hand corner, and no trace of handwriting anywhere. The doorman had no memory of the person who had delivered it. "It wasn't the regular guy," was the best he could offer. Young? Old? Black? White? Gender? Distinguishing marks? The doorman shook his head. "Just a delivery," he said.

The envelope contained two typescripts, each held together by a rubber band. The title page of the first typescript read *Stone: Insertion, c. 1819* and the title page on the second typescript read *Stone: Extraction* (undated). Both typescripts were anonymous, but there was a note scrawled on the first title-page and there could be no mistaking that flamboyant, looping hand.

This is your fault, the note said.

3

Stone: Insertion, c. 1819

That was the year the great painter turned seventy-three and bought the house on the hill just outside of Madrid. The Villa of the Deaf Guy, it was called. He himself had been deaf for twenty-seven years on account of lead poisoning but he wasn't the deaf guy after whom the villa had been named. He was the deaf guy who bought the deaf guy's house. He built a new wing for a kitchen and lived there for five years, until after his seventy-eighth birthday.

Not many people lived so long in his times and the ones who did were probably as angry as he was at the way life had turned out and how it was ending and at the stupidity and cruelty of the human race. Maybe, Francisco mused, maybe all people in all times felt something like this as the curtain began to fall. But no, there were fools who were moronically serene as the light dimmed and were grateful for "beauty" and "love." He had been told that a stone-deaf German composer had chosen to set to choral music another German (Schiller)'s ode to Joy, even though he couldn't hear the music he had composed, his choir might as well have been opening and shutting their mouths without letting out any sound at all, and where was the Joy in that? He had also been told that deaf musicians, particularly percussionists, often went barefoot because they had learned to hear rhythms through their feet. Francisco was furious with such persons also. His feet heard absolutely nothing. And he had heard no music for close to thirty years.

He had needed to get away from the royal court. He had spent much of his professional life there, making the works he was commissioned to make, painting *majas* naked and clothed, and creating the portraits of wars whose violent images of executions and other deaths haunted him. For a long time he had been well respected in those palace corridors but now there was a new kind of king in town, Fernando VII, a despot who wanted to be *desired,* to be called *the Desired One.* He had twenty-seven given names—perhaps one should say "Christian" names, although there was little that was Christian about his behavior. The twenty-seven names allowed him to claim that most of the men born during his reign were named after him, that's how "desired" he was. But after his death he became known as *el Rey Felón,* the Criminal King. That was a few years after Francisco disappeared, so the artist was denied the satisfaction of hearing how history intended to remember that totalitarian bastard. It might even have improved his mood.

King Twenty-Seven Names the Seventh ascended to the throne, got overthrown, climbed back up onto it five years later, overthrew the liberal constitution, assumed absolute power, faced down a revolution, re-assumed absolute power, jailed liberal leaders, journalists and writers, ran a police state, did many terrible things you don't want to know about, lost all of Spain's American territories, clung to power, left a civil war behind him when finally, phew, he died.

When Francisco bought the villa the court was filling up with clowns and fools. There were frauds pretending to be members of wealthy families who actually owned no more than a few haulage wagons and crept around the palace trying to steal expensive clothes from other courtiers' wardrobes so they could look the part. There were women seducing distant members of the royal family in the hope of preferment. There were women fawning on the king who allowed them to fawn, and more than fawn, but gave them nothing for it and discarded them like used nose-rags. There were murderers looking for the right people to murder, people whose deaths would gain the approval of the king. There were jesters-in-reverse whose job was not to make the king laugh or to tell him uncomfortable truths but to laugh uncontrollably at the king's humorless witticisms and listen to and applaud his barefaced lies. There were members of criminal gangs whom the king had placed in charge of the police force. There were crooked lawyers, crooked judges, crooked legal clerks, all there to make sure that the laws of the land would crumble and fail beneath the stamping foot of the king who had placed himself above the law. There were grandees bearing sacks of gold with which to bribe the king's inner circle, and bigger sacks of gold to bribe the king himself. There were, above all the other courtiers, powerful choruses of reality twisters, mirrors and clones of the king who had lost all understanding of what was real and what was not, whose job it was to praise the monarch for his triumphs even though the news from the Americas was only of defeats, to accuse liberals of the crimes committed by the servants of the One with Twenty-Seven Names, the Desired One, to accuse the few remaining stalwarts who pointed to the corrupt sacks of gold of being themselves the recipients of ill-gotten gains, and to change the meanings of words, so that when the king married not one but two of his nieces, the word *incest* was simply expunged from the lexicon and made illegal to use; and after that it became necessary to make other changes to the dictionary, to redescribe rape as love, horror as patriotism, bullying as good governance, war as peace, freedom as slavery, and ignorance as strength, so as to ensure that the absolute monarch had absolute power over the language itself, over vocabulary and syntax and metaphor and fable, and to turn the world upside down, so that it would only mean what the monarch wished it to mean.

Francisco, a man of liberal inclinations, needed to put distance between himself and this paranoid and vengeful crew, to escape this cowardly crowned head for fear of losing his own elderly noggin, and that was why he was in the deaf man's house, seething, resentful, and entering a darkness of his own, lost in despair, subject to hysterical panic attacks, in an old man's creaking physical pain—*everything hurts,* he thought every day—and fearing the onset of madness. He was gripped by occult visions which he began to portray in black scenes which he painted over all the villa's walls.

One day a young man, a fledgling painter, came to the house. Francisco refused to let him through the door. The young man managed to get in anyway.

Don't look at them. Don't come in here and tell me what you think. These aren't for you to look at. They are for nobody to look at. They are mine. I spent half my life painting what people paid me to paint, what people approved of. Now I paint only for myself. Close your eyes. Don't tell me you don't understand how I can live with images like these. I don't care what you think. I'm painting my rage. I live with my rage day and night. It's not only on the walls. It's within me. The screaming, it's in me. And don't you dare call me crazy even if I fear that word myself. It is not I who am insane. It is the world. To be sane in an insane world is to feel insane every day.

You're young. Go away. Leocadia, where are you. Show this young man the door. I'm tired of young men. They are greedy for me and I don't even have enough of me to feed myself. I don't want admirers or students or protégés. Leave me alone. I have drink and Leocadia and that's enough for me. You want to know how I'm facing the end? With fear, wine, and sex. And these last paintings. More than enough. Go away.

—*There are two doors leading out of the deaf man's house, Leocadia told the young painter. One takes you to a better place, the other opens onto Hell. Choose your exit route.* —*The young man chose the front door.* —*He chose the door to Hell, Leocadia told Francisco.*

He had never felt so alienated from his world and time. He was disappointed in the young. They should have understood the danger of a dictatorial ruler and made it their generation's calling to fight him until he was overthrown, and some of them did, he was prepared to mention the name of Rafa del Riego, who conspired with the Masons against the king, but damn it!, he failed!, all his conspiracies came to nothing!, and Francisco was too old and angry to celebrate honorable failures, losing was losing, and there wasn't time for defeats. And most of the younger generation were preoccupied by other squabbles, the young men, fearing and wanting to crush the independence of young women, turned out to like the "manliness" of the king, and young women had their own preoccupations. In short the young were engaged in their own little squabbles so that the big squabble, the crucial squabble against the tyrant, went un-squabbled, and Francisco threw up his hands and wrote off the young, as it was an old man's privilege to do, as it was also the right of the young to ignore the old man's irrelevant gesture, his message from yesterday when they were looking towards tomorrow. They would, maybe they should, proceed down their (in his opinion) wrongheaded paths. The future wasn't his business anymore.

And so, the fourteen paintings on the walls. In an earlier mo-ment of bleak depression he had painted his small *Yard with Lu-*

natics that now came back to him, except that the yard had grown into the whole world and the lunatics were the entire human race. As for beauty, he wasn't interested, and love, what was that at his age, there was Leocadia Weiss who looked after the house and sometimes occupied his bed, and that was a comfort, he supposed, but she had a husband, that had to be accepted, and *love* felt like one of those words that had fallen out of use, like *incest*. Certainly he no longer felt like creating art that might be called romantic. At his decrepit age romance or even romanticism would have felt absurd.

He didn't name the paintings and he never explained them to anyone but maybe they explained themselves. His hatred of his own old age is present in the paintings of the aged. An old man looking reasonably calm had a crazy old man screaming into his ear, as if death were screaming at life, *here I am, old fool*. The two old creatures eating soup were caricatures of old age, one wild-eyed and clown-smiling, the other stooped and almost like a skull. And Saturn devouring his son, the wide-mouthed giant with the insane eyes clutching the bloodied headless body of the child expressed a hatred of youth so deep that Francisco didn't realize how deep it ran in him until he painted it. Judith beheading Holofernes contained all the artist's feelings about the impossibility of anything between men and women except violence. Next to that, the portrait of Leocadia at least hinted at some softness towards his subject even though her dress was funereal and her expression was sad. Two young men fought brutally and senselessly with cudgels. Six men huddled together reading an anonymous paper that could be political or pornographic or even demonic. He had at first given the central figure horns sprouting out of its head but then he painted over them. When he looked at the painting, however, he still saw the horns. On the opposite wall he painted women laughing and it was obvious he meant the women to be laughing at the men. Two large portraits of pilgrimages looked like long marches of the dying, the frightened, and the dead. Two visions of flying figures, a demon queen in the first and, in the second, the Fates led by the goddess of death herself, holding scissors that had the power of cutting through the Thread of Life. And the two greatest and most terrifying paintings, one large, one small. The large one was a black sabbath. Devil worship had seized the world and the devil, a great goat painted in silhouette, ruled over all. That was reality as Francisco saw it. It wasn't just a matter of a cruel king. Satan had taken charge of the human spirit. He saw that wherever he looked.

And then there was the dog. He had never had a dog. He didn't even like the idea of a dog. Human life was bad enough without making oneself subservient to the requirements of canine life. And yet here was this dog that appeared from nowhere, its head above an unspecified sloping darkness with an unspecified ocher lightness above it. What was happening to the dog? He didn't know. He thought it might be falling into the Pit, it might be saying its farewells before it sank into eternal nothingness or doggy hellfire. It looked like a sad little dog. Why would it not. Its creator was a sad human being.

It was on the night after he finished work on the final painting, the portrait of Leocadia, that he dreamed up the Dutchman's ghost.

Can you understand me. My Spanish not so good but I think your Dutch is worse.

What are you. I have lived here five years now and it has never been a haunted house. My hauntedness comes from within.

I am the shade of Joen van Aken. Jerome or Jéronimo of Aachen. Sometimes I signed my paintings Jheronimus. Or Hieronymus. I am from the town of 's-Hertogenbosch, commonly called Den Bosch. I took the town's name for my own. Ik ben Bosch. I am Bosch.

Dead for three hundred years. When you lived you never visited Spain, in fact you hardly ever left your unpronounceable town. Yet here you are, halfway across Europe. Now I know I have gone mad.

No, you are not mad. But I have come to warn you of impending madness and to urge you to seek refuge from it.

Look who's talking. A dead man who specialized in madness, who painted the most insane visions ever set down by a human hand. Scenes of wild abandon. A broken egg with legs. A naked man captured in a clam shell. Many Adams eating apples from a tree with naked Eves lying on the grass around them. A Black woman carrying a peacock on her head. A hellscape panel with long beams of intruding, oppressive light. An arrow through a pair of ears which are being parted by a knife. A bird-headed prince of the underworld with the head of a naked man in its beak and the rest of the man waiting to be devoured. Things that make no sense.

On the contrary. You can see and hear me even though you are as deaf as a post because you are the one—these walls reveal it to me—who knows that what I painted was the truth. That the flight of reason brings forth monsters. And that my garden, which you describe, was and continues to be the real world.

Go away. You are disturbing my sleep. I already sleep badly. Leocadia says I often shout belligerently in my sleep, for unknown reasons. No, the reasons are known, they are obvious. I shout belligerently in my sleep because there is much to shout belligerently about. Enough. Please depart.

Madness is coming. You must leave. There is a worm. It enters through the ear and lodges in the front of the brain and then hardens until it becomes a stone and when it is thus petrified the brain is deranged by it and remains so unless and until the stone is removed.

I have never heard of such a worm.

The wormstone of madness. It is traveling from Cathay to the Americas and will pass through Europe too. It will be everywhere and years will go by and you are already old.

Then there are no safe places.

Go north into France and look for Eaux-l'Homme. Unusually, the x is pronounced as a k.

What is that? Where is it?

That is the message. There is no more. If you ask me to guess I would surmise it lies in the direction of Bordeaux. But I am bad at geography and there are no maps.

Why should I go there? If what you say is true then the madness stone will come there as well. If madness is everywhere then it doesn't matter where one is.

Go there. You will be safe there. You will find calm and ease in your old age.

There must be a reason.

There is no reason. If you want me to make up a reason I'll say that the red claret wine made there provides immunity from the wormstone and perhaps in time that wine will be sent everywhere and it will save the world.

You want me to leave my home and disappear in a northward direction looking for a place that may not even exist, because the instruction comes from a phantom who doesn't exist either, who is a figment, at whom I am at this moment shouting belligerently in my sleep. I see that your air is one of serenity and calm which I am thinking is probably a state one can achieve after three hundred years of death. I am neither calm nor serene but you offer me a fantasy of ease, an enchanted space. It sounds fishy to me.

Then stay here in the deaf man's villa and the stone of madness will surely come. And yes, death brings serenity. Death is another kind of Eaux-l'Homme. Nothing can hurt you there.

The first typescript broke off here. There was one additional handwritten page on which the writer had copied out some scraps of lines from near the end of Kafka's *Amerika,* the unfinished ending of the last chapter entitled "The Nature Theater of Oklahoma." "The first day they traveled through a high range of mountains . . . narrow, gloomy, jagged valleys opened out . . . the direction in which they lost themselves."

Two added notes. "Was I the artist? Or the felon king?" And, "He'd have to get around those Alps. So, left towards the Bay of Biscay? Or right, to the Balearic Sea? Border crossing near Hendaye or Narbonne? Did those towns even exist at that time?" And two final sentences. "Maybe this is a story that says, Art lives on but artists are vulnerable. Maybe it says goodbye, life, and hello, forever, eternity, immortality." And lastly, a question that threw back at me a question I had asked him, that first time on Long Island. "Why don't you finish the story?"

Of Velázquez, the third artist I had praised, there was no mention. Such was the perfection of *Las Meninas,* I thought, that there was nothing to add. It was necessary only to admire, and bow one's head.

4

Stone: Extraction

(scrawled in the upper right-hand corner: *This is your fault also.*)

Second message from a dead man, or at least dead-ish. No storytelling this time. A little straight talking and some of what passes in my whiskeyed brain for thought. An attempt, let me put it ambitiously, at sanity.

Me? I was always a prose guy. I published precisely one (1) poem in my life and we don't need to say more about it than that. When I looked at poetry I often thought, wow, see what you made language do there, how much you made it mean. Alternatively I just as often thought, what the fuck are you talking about, I really have no clue. In the days when I was an interesting writer I would go to my bookshelves in the morning, before I went to my desk, and pick out a volume of poetry at random and open it anywhere just to see if it had anything to say to me today. And what it always said was, pay attention. There is no reason why the language of prose must be *less* than that of poetry. No reason not to be *equal*. If it takes longer to write the book, so what? If it takes years or your whole life or you die leaving it unfinished, who cares? Nobody's waiting. Ask Kafka. You're on your own in that room, turning into a big bug. An *Ungeheueren Ungeziefer*. A monstrous vermin. Do your work.

You once recited urgent Mr Cogito at me (with all his Anger and Scorn) and I threw meditative Palomar back at you (with his rhythmic birds and the sea) and your Prado soliloquy led me to the poet Alejandra Pizarnik, Argentinian, dead like me (?), killed herself like me (?), but before that also inspired by Joen van Aken a.k.a. Bosch. Author of the poems collected in *Extracting the Stone of Madness,* dreaming constantly of death, and of finding a small place of her own that was all hers and, perhaps, safe. *Some small spot where she could go to sing or cry in peace.* Maybe she was looking for Oklahoma too and died because she never found it. Or maybe death was her Oklahoma. She had an alter ego too. It was named Shadow. So let's start there. *Faith, hope, and love,* we find in #1 Corinthians, *but the greatest of these is love.* So now Herbert/Cogito, Calvino/Palomar, Pizarnik/Shadow, these three. And the greatest of these is . . . stop. There is no need to choose. I am not writing a bible here, or a Top Ten list.

I am trying to come back to life.

I love Palomar because he rejoices in small loveliness. The times are filled with large ugliness so we turn to the microcosm to save ourselves. Once in a science museum in Toronto I saw a film that began with an overhead shot of a woman sunbathing on a roof terrace. Then the "camera" pulled back and further back and further back until we saw the city, the country, the continent, the planet, the solar system, the galaxy, the universe. The universe was a work of abstract art that also embodied everything not-abstract. Real. Then the camera reversed direction and dived back from the universe to the galaxy, the solar system, the planet, the continent, the country, the city, the sunbather on the roof, but it didn't stop, it went inside, into the interior of the body, into the blood, the molecule, the cell, the sub-atomic minuteness of life. And not only was it the smallest of microcosms, not only beautiful, not only real, but it was *the same as the universe*. Or enough the same to make the point it was making.

We are the universe. Singly and plurally. We contain the stars.

This helps me.

And Kafka, unlikely optimist, he has something to say also. He makes "an appeal to youth not to be sad, for after all, there is nature, freedom, Goethe, Schiller, Shakespeare, flowers, insects, etc." Maybe this can also be read as an appeal to old age. Pizarnik/Shadow quotes it in her poem about a garden. She hopes for a place of earthly delights. And she has advice for me. *You shouldn't play the ghost, lest you become one.*

I am hoping I can unghost myself.

I am near Mr Cogito's dark boundary. But I'm not sure about what he recommends. *The golden fleece of nothingness.*

I am wondering if somethingness—beingness—is a golden fleece also. If life can be as precious as not-life.

I'd settle for a silver fleece. I don't want to be greedy.

That's enough for today.

i'm going to hide behind language (this is Pizarnik speaking)
   and why is that
   i'm afraid

And if one decides to stop hiding, and if one's chosen hiding place is not language but an imaginary world, Otherland, Elsewhere, that *Decameron* villa outside Florence where talkative folk went to escape the Black Death? Or, yes, Oklahoma? I'm trying to find a way out of fantasy and back into reality. Or, let's be clear: out of insanity and back into what we might agree is sanity. A man leaves all his clothes on a beach to do what, to go where, if not actually to drown. Madness is a kind of drowning, the actual self swallowed by the ocean of the Other. She who knew me best knew I was losing it. I lost it. Now I am thinking, how to find it again.

What are the requirements for a resurrection? (Always assuming lack of support from the Almighty. I am trying to define the elements necessary for rebirth.)

I read somewhere that Calvino's last words, after his stroke in 1985, were "Giovanni di Marsalia, fenomenologo," *Giovanni of Marsalia, phenomenologist,* and nobody understood them until his wife, looking through a box containing some of his earliest writings, published in the Piedmontese edition of the left-wing newspaper *l'Unità,* found that he had invented a socialist paradise, *Marxalia,* which soon enough became *Marsalia.* So at his very end he reached back to his beginning, maybe hoping, futilely hoping with the last hope of his dying brain, to restart himself and begin again.

There was an old man named Michael Finnegan / he grew whiskers on his chinnegan / the wind came up and blew them innegan / poor old Michael Finnegan / beginnegan . . . and so on around and around.

T. S. Eliot, somewhere, can't remember where, said "In my beginning is my end." Well, Tom, agree to disagree. At my end I want to reach back to my beginning. And beginnegan.

September 4th, 1942. The raid against Bremen. The Pathfinders flew in three waves, *illuminators* dropping white flares to mark the route, *visual markers* dropping colored flares to indicate the targets, *firestarters* emphasizing the location and burning longer than the visual markers' flares. We were among the third wave, the firestarters, and as our bombers did their work (major successes against aircraft factories shipyards hundreds maybe thousands of other structures) we flew back over brightly illuminated German territory with long lethal streams of ack-ack fire coming to get us. Often I think I never left that flight home. I'm still on it. I did my work but now the ack-ack is coming for me. The only reason I know I left it is that I did it again over one hundred times.

Ack-ack-ack! Ack-ack-ack! Ack-ack! Ack!

My wife will tell you how often I woke up shouting belligerently into the night.

I wrote about it. That helped. It didn't go away. Slowly it came back. I need to send it away again.

I'm beginning to like your Mr Cogito. He orders me about. Do this, don't do that. That's what I need right now. I need what Mr Bellow called *reality instructors*. (Nobody reads Mr Bellow anymore I think. This is sad and wrong. Never mind. Not my point today.)

Go upright

Easy for you to say. With my back? Not a straightforward matter. Nothing straightforward about this spine. The best I can do is, stooped outside, but upright within.

You must give testimony

I take it this is a political instruction. I must speak of war and tyrants and the corruptions of (but not only of) the soul. I had come to feel that my political days were done. I, like Pizarnik, had begun to desire only a small private place: a tree, a stream, a book in my hand and a glass by my side. Silence and water. Maybe a little music. Must I abandon that precious (and, I would argue, hard-earned) spot and dive back into the ugliness?

Be courageous

I guess that's a Yes.

Anger

When I was young I was angry. I would get into loud arguments with friends. Now I'm afraid the anger will be directed at me. Look what I did, the grief I caused people who didn't deserve it, the attention-seeking vanity of the act, I got to read my own obituaries, which were less lavish than I might have hoped. So I'll rewrite the instruction. I must accept the anger of others. I must bow my head and feel ashamed and say yes, you are right, and I was wrong, and I won't do it again.

Scorn

See under: Anger.

Do not forgive

But instead, hope to be forgiven.

your clown's face in the mirror

Well, no argument about *that*.

Be faithful Go

I'm trying. I'm trying.

No, I can't (won't) tell you where I am. I already pointed out: it's not a real place. Could Alice tell you the location of Wonderland, or even find the rabbit-hole again? I'll say this: I had a choice of two doors facing me when I stood naked on the beach. One led to the place I wanted, the other led to Hell. I actually don't know which world I ended up in. Maybe there was only one world behind both the doors. Maybe the place I wanted to arrive at was a place I would never be permitted to reach. After all, Kafka's Land Surveyor, who was only playing at being a Land Surveyor, whose true identity we never learned, was never allowed to reach the Castle. The Castle wasn't playing.

I know. I still sound crazy. I'm working on it. Trying to extract the stone.

That was the end of the second text, which I also took to be incomplete, as "extraction" would mean a full return to sanity, or at least that's how I understood the metaphor, and the text as I received it openly stated that its author's state of mind was still troubled.

After I finished reading it I felt that the unstated message of the pages in the manila envelope was, *Find me.* The disappeared man asking for my help to reappear. For a long time I had no idea how to begin to do that. Maybe his mental state was so poor that he himself didn't know exactly where he was. As Kafka writes in the last pages of *Amerika,* when his character begins his long railway journey from New York City to Oklahoma, *Only now did Karl understand how huge Amerika was.* Uncle K. was the needle in that enormous haystack.

When I looked up the statistics on disappearances, on people who just stepped out of their lives, the picture became even bleaker. Six hundred thousand people went missing every year, so the sudden absence of a mentally disturbed writer was hardly big news. And this huge number was in America alone—a country that had little or no history of political or, to use the preferred euphemism, "enforced" disappearances. Latin America and Africa had experienced such atrocities for long periods, and Mexico still "lost" 30,000 people a year. The current list of vanished people included not only Syria (no surprise), but also . . .

depressingly, India. The self-styled "world's largest democracy." My country of origin. That depressed me for a week.

And the ordinary disappearances of everyday life had to be added to the list. Parents, grandparents, aunties, uncles, parents' friends, aunties' friends, until the day came, as it had come for me, when the entire generations of those who went before had taken their leave and there was nobody standing between my own generation and the yawning patient grave. And then distressing numbers of this generation, too, took the dark dive into the earth. I had become painfully aware of the holes left in the world by all these disappeared, and of my own mortality too. Uncle K.'s disappearance felt willful in the face of so much sadness and for a time I didn't think it was any of my business to intervene. I hadn't asked to be sent the two *Stones*. I needed to think about what to do with them, but I was no private eye. I couldn't see myself sleuthing across America to search for him.

He had put the subject of America into the forefront of my mind, that was certainly true. America with a c as well as Amerika with a k. Uncle K. had a dubious opinion of America with a c, and even of the actually existing Oklahoma one might find there. On one whiskey-fuelled evening he had lectured me on the Osage County murders of Native Americans by white folks wanting to steal their oil, and on the Oklahoma City bombings. The Oklahoma he was interested in, he declared, was the place in the musical—*Oklahoma!* with the exclamation mark being a part of the name—where the wavin' wheat can sure smell sweet and where my honey lamb and I sit alone and talk and watch a hawk makin' lazy circles in the sky. "I sure hope young Karl Rossmann found himself a honey lamb in Oklahoma," he once said to me, "a honey lamb and happiness, or that he might if he could just get unstuck from that unfinished

paragraph, if the train would just arrive in the damn station."
Amerika with a k, the Amerika of dreams, Uncle K. said, was
the country with which he had always been in love. America
with a c, actually existing America, was problematic. "USA," he
told me, paraphrasing Joyce's Stephen Dedalus's remark about
History, "is the nightmare from which I'm trying to awake."

I should have guessed then that a man who preferred the
nonexistent to the existing was on the edge of crazy. But I just
told myself, oh, he's a novelist, and then thought no more about
it, until the vanishing.

In the end, of course, I got in touch with Auntie K.

5

Whehen I got off the bus that morning after a three-hour ride East from the city nobody was there to greet me and drive me the mile or so from the disembarkation point by the village church to the K. residence. This surprised me, but it was a beautiful day and I only had a small backpack with me so I was happy to walk. With luck I'd be offered lunch, but in any event I'd be back in the city by nightfall.

She was sitting in a rocking-chair on the front porch. There was a small table on which she had placed a jug and two glasses. Age, I thought, had made her look grimmer than I remembered. That, and the tragedy of her marriage too, of course. She didn't get up, but gestured towards the second (non-rocking) chair on the porch.

"You got old," she said uncharitably, as if reading my mind and batting its contents back at me. "Want some lemonade?"

I accepted the glass she poured out for me, put down my backpack, and took my appointed seat. Then a longish, awkwardish silence followed, and I wasn't sure how to break it. Finally she spoke.

"We stopped seeing you," she said flatly, "because I thought you had fixated on him in a way that felt *ungood*. It was kind of obsessive. You weren't living in America at the time or I'd maybe have pegged you as a stalker. Then you did start living in America and I thought it was time to break things off between us."

I hadn't expected to be greeted by something so wounding. "And he?" I asked weakly. "Did he think that too?"

"Oh, yes," she said. "He was kinder about it than me but it was pretty obvious."

"I'm sorry," was all I could think to say.

"Also," she added, rubbing salt in the wound, "there was a quality in your writing that confirmed my suspicions. You stole real people and put them in your books. *Try fiction, why don't you,* I almost said to you more than once. Madame Bovary wasn't a real person, you know. Nor was Raskolnikov. Or, because you both talked about Kafka, nor were Gregor Samsa or the Land Surveyor or Karl Rossmann. They were *made up.* Anyhoo. I didn't want you to steal us."

"And did he think that too?"

"I told you. He was kinder than me. All he said was, *a little lacking in imagination.*"

"He said that?"

"He said that."

After that there didn't seem to be anything left to talk about. In that devastated moment I had completely forgotten why I was there. The envelope in the backpack had ceased to exist. I should go, I was thinking. I should just get up and leave.

She was the one who brought the envelope up, pulling me out of my shocked trance. "You called to tell me about the two typescripts," she said. "As I'm sure you can imagine, that got my attention. Posthumous material by a significant writer who also happened to be my husband doesn't materialize every day. You brought the pages?" She stretched out her hand and beckoned imperiously.

"The thing is," I forced myself to say, "I'm not sure it is post-humous."

The rocking-chair stopped rocking. She became absolutely still. It was as if a motion picture had turned into a photograph.

"Give," she finally said. And when she had the envelope in her outstretched hand she added, "Now go for a walk. Come back in two hours."

The neighborhood had changed. Where there had been fields of corn or sunflowers there now were houses. Villages in the countryside had turned into suburbs by the sea. Jeeps had turned into Porsches and the back roads now had traffic jams. On certain streets high hedgerows concealed large mansions. I cared about none of it. I walked aimlessly with Auntie K.'s words ringing in my ears. I felt like an outcast, from their world, maybe from the whole great world as well. I found a beach entrance and went out through the dunes onto the sand. There was a young woman with a dog some way away and the tracks of a sand buggy. None of it mattered. I wondered if I too should just take off my clothes and walk into the sea. I never did learn to swim. How far out would I have to go before I was in danger. I knew nothing about currents or riptides. I imagined the young woman leaving her dog and swimming out to rescue me. This was all foolishness.

How slowly the time was passing. I no longer wore a wrist-watch. The time was on my phone and seemed to be standing still. How long would it take her to read the pages. Would she read them more than once.

I realized that I was scared of her. I didn't want to go back. I wanted to go and wait for the bus back to the city. This was the last time we would meet. I should have known better. It would have been better to mail the envelope to her with a brief covering note. This was not my business. I was not a part of this story. I never had been. I had deluded myself.

In exactly two hours I was standing in front of her. She was still in the rocking-chair. The envelope was on the table next to the lemonade. There was something long lying across her lap. As I approached the house I thought it might be a walking stick.

It was a shotgun.

"I'm an old woman living alone," she said. "I keep this close in case of unwanted guests."

I just stood there, uncertain of what was happening, or what would be best for me to do. Should I just turn and run?

"Sit," she commanded and so, on the edge of the chair, tension stiffening me, my hands closing into fists, I sat.

"Since you have taken so much trouble, that long bus ride et cetera," she said, her voice heavy with what sounded very much like sarcasm, "let me tell you that I agree, this is not posthumous work."

I was startled. "Did you already know that he was still alive," I managed to ask.

"Yes," she said, and her voice was harsh. "In the twenty-first century it's not easy for anyone to disappear. Cellphones, credit cards. If you're alive, you leave traces. He was never declared dead, as perhaps you know. Officially he's missing."

"Have you always known," I said. A long silence followed.

"I'll tell you what I have always known," she said, "and also what I have just now found out, and after that you will leave and never speak of any of it to anyone again. And you must never return here or contact me in any way."

"I knew that our marriage was ending. He had withdrawn. We were under the same roof but not together except that I made the meals and ran the household and washed the clothes and looked after the garden and he didn't help. What he did do, was make artisanal chocolates. That sweet tooth he had, you saw that. He taught himself with the help of his phone and he turned out to be good at it. Truffles, all of that. I don't like chocolates or candy which didn't improve matters between us. And he got in my way in the kitchen. When I threw him out he sat quietly in his den and if there was football on TV he watched that and at other times baseball. He formed the opinion that he needed to get away from all aspects of the life he had lived and I was an aspect like any other. So he needed to get away from me, from our children, from our friends. From his work also. No more books. He wanted to be *not a writer.* He needed to be somebody else."

"Neither of you ever spoke about your children."

"Not to you, no. There were many things we didn't talk about with you. But there are children. There are also grandchildren, siblings, nephews, nieces, great-nephews, grandnieces. It's a reasonably big family."

"I didn't know."

"As I say, the list of what you didn't know is long. You didn't know, for example, that he was not losing his mind. He suffered from severe depression but he was sane. He knew in from out and up from down. He was afraid of madness but he was never mad. The idea that there was a mental decline is yours."

"You told me once he was sometimes unsure what was real and what unreal. Like Dorothy at the end of *The Wizard of Oz.*"

"It was a figure of speech. These days being confused about truth and untruth has become the human condition. Or at least the American condition. I won't speak for the world."

"So he staged his exit. The clothes neatly on the beach."

"The timing took me by surprise. And there are parts of it I'm not sure about. How he left the beach without being seen.

How he left the village. But I knew he had made preparations. These were careful preparations. Money moved into a different bank under an alias, a dummy corporation registered in Delaware behind which he could hide. He left our doctor of many years who he used to say looked like an Ewok for another primary care provider in a galaxy far far away. He went away from big places to small places. In small places in America writers don't move the fame slash celebrity barometer so anonymity is not just possible, it's normal."

"You know where he is."

"At first I was angry and thought, let him go. Then I changed my mind. I'm still angry, however."

"You're not going to tell me."

"Don't be ridiculous."

"I understand."

"You understand nothing. I said I would tell you more than what I used to know. I still have to tell you what I have just found out."

"About him?"

"No. About you."

"I don't know," she said reflectively after a while, "if I should shoot you for being stupid or shoot you for being vain or shoot you for thinking me stupid. That's three strikes."

Yes, I was afraid of what this clearly crazy old lady might be capable of. "Maybe don't shoot me?" I said. "That might be a fourth option?"

"Did you really think you would get away with this? Were you that stupid, that vain, or did you think I was that stupid?" Suddenly she was shouting at me.

"I don't know what you mean," I said. But I did know.

"You clearly practiced forging his handwriting," she said, more calmly. "And it's not a terrible forgery, I'll give you that. It might even fool some people. But did you really think it would fool me?"

I said nothing.

"And these texts. Again, you imagined I would believe they were written by him, and so again, I ask the three questions. Are you that dumb? Are you that full of yourself, to think you could write his stuff? Or do you think I'm so dumb that I wouldn't work it out?"

I had nothing to say.

"You realize that these pages only half sound like him. Kinda sorta. But guess who they actually do sound like?"

I would probably never have anything to say to anyone ever again, I thought.

"They sound," she said, "like you. Like a writer who steals real people. They sound like a dialogue between your younger self and your older self. And you're merging your older self with him."

I bowed my head.

"Now I see that you're the insane one," she said. "You didn't just want to know him, to obsess about him, to get as close to him as you could—much closer than he wanted you. You actually want to be him. I should shoot you for that.

"They say the faker, the plagiarist, the forger actually wants, in some dark corner of his mind, to be found out. The art forger Elmyr de Hory actually showed his phoney Blue Period Picasso to Picasso himself. But Elmyr was a kind of minor genius. You are not.

"I'm seriously thinking of pulling this trigger. The way I see it, you're an intruder on my property and I have to defend myself and my home. You're a scary stranger unknown to anyone around here and I'm an old white lady that's well regarded in the neighborhood. How do you think that would play?"

She lifted the shotgun and pointed it at me, considering her position.

"Don't shoot," I said.

"I'm going to count to three," she said, "and before I get to three, you're going to start talking. To stay alive you need to confess."

I looked at her face, her eyes, and I believed her. So there was no escape.

I confessed.

I am calmer now so I can set down these words that probably nobody will ever read. This is just for me now in the way that the paintings in the House of the Deaf Guy were only for the painter's eyes. I have to confess to myself and also to you, my probably nonexistent reader. I deceived you. I deluded myself. And now that everything is known there is still a little more. There is still what I have to do. That decision has to be made.

Everything you said is true. I was trembling when I finished talking and when she lowered the shotgun I thought I might throw up or, worse, wet myself. Either would make my humiliation, my loss of self-esteem, complete. I asked her if I could use her bathroom before I left and she began to laugh, too hard, too uproariously, and I saw that her own high tension was being released as well as mine. Her body was shaking too.

"You really are a piece of work," she said. "Go on. You know where it is."

I went indoors, through the living room and then the kitchen.

I passed the antique pine Welsh dresser that had always been there with fine china standing on its shelves and some books and magazines too, and there was a rustic wooden bowl containing cards with useful phone numbers, a plumber, an electrician, a handyman, some friends. I noticed a brightly colored card sticking out from beneath the card of her favorite local restaurant: a card that drew me to it, that forced my hand to reach out to pick it up so that I could look at it properly, and when I did look, I knew I had to steal it, and I did. After that I used the toilet and then fled that house, never to return. She stood on the porch and watched me go. It felt like the end of a whole segment of my life.

This is what it said on the card:

OK KITCHEN
Candy—Chocolates—Ice Cream

K. Rossmann—Prop.

And below that, an address, a phone number, a website URL. These confirmed the location as a town in the north-eastern United States.

But OK?

That had to be *Oklahoma*. Oklahoma, where Karl Rossmann would perhaps have found peace if Kafka had finished his story instead of abandoning him on the train.

Oklahoma, in the wrong place.

6

*I*t was completely dark when I arrived in the outskirts of the lakeside town of O. in my rented Mitsubishi truck, in search of something or someone I could not properly name. I had driven a great distance that day, traveling through interstellar space, or so I thought, passing bright galaxies and burning nebulas and black holes that swallowed time and space and I marveled at the great size of it all and felt my own insignificance deeply. Once I saw the lights of the town twinkling in the night my spirits lightened. It looked like a welcoming place and I hoped it would open its arms to this weary traveler and help him in his quest. As I entered the town limits I experienced a severe bump in the road that jarred my body and made my back hurt. People in sweet little country towns, I thought, should do a better job of maintaining their access roads.

Of the nature of the quest I myself was unsure. You could call it a manhunt but a manhunt correctly defined was a hunt for a wanted man and this man was not wanted. Maybe his wife still wanted him, maybe not. Maybe she had let him go. Maybe I wanted him but who cared about that? Not the law, that was for sure. Not the wife or children, the unknown children. Not enough here for a Wanted poster. There had been no crime committed. At most a deception. There was no search in progress, no pursuit. He was The Man Who Disappeared, and that appeared to be okay. And yet here I was, driving, driven, hunting for "Rossmann."

As well as great Franz K. I thought about Godard, about Lemmy Caution entering les faubourgs d'Alphaville in his Ford Galaxie, also searching for someone lost, finding himself in a place of dead heroes (—Et Batman? —Il est mort), a world ruled by a totalitarian and a machine, in which love was illegal, a "ville" not unlike our own Omegaville. And I thought of the narrator of Mary Shelley's Frankenstein, also entering a town, Geneva, when it was completely dark, on his way to the place of monstrosity. And on my oldies radio channel a singer feeling "about half past dead." Maybe I had passed through some membrane separating the living from the dead and had entered a half past dead world. Maybe I could never return.

I shrugged off such mental wanderings. They were ways of making myself feel more significant than I was. I remembered the message of the universe. I was nobody on a journey to nowhere for a purpose of no importance. A string that had connected me to the world had broken and I was floating in space, lost to the mother ship. The present had dissolved and I was either in the past or the future or both, or somewhere else entirely. The twinkling lights offered no clarity. I was here. That was all there was to know.

I had booked a small resting place using the information technology of our time and the guidance system on my phone brought me without trouble to its door. A third technology, the code-operated key box, granted me entry and so without any human contact I found myself in the presence of a bed, a purple sofa, an empty refrigerator, a kettle. It was enough. I had brought a sandwich and a beer with me but I had lost all appetite. My faceless landlord had left a bottle of Poland Spring water for me on the counter of the kitchenette and I drank that. I had only booked the space for this night and the following. I didn't expect to be here for long. If "K. Rossmann"'s opinion of me was as poor as Auntie K. had said it was, then our meeting would be brief and unpleasant. I knew this but I needed to hear the words to be free of him. This was as close as I could come to the meaning of my journey, although I knew there was more to it, there were things which in my fatigued state I could not access. I lay down and tried to sleep. At dawn the clock-radio on the nightstand clicked on, following the uncanceled instructions of an earlier human being, and out of it came the voice of the poet Ginsberg reading his poem Howl. Evidently he had just died. I listened for a few minutes and then turned the machine off. Today of all days I didn't need machines to interfere with my mind.

The morning was bright, crisp, clear. "No birds were flying overhead" (Lewis Carroll showed up unbidden in my head) / "There were no birds to fly." I attended swiftly to my toilette, shit shower shave, the solitary trinity of the morn. Then for a long stretch I sat on the purple sofa, upright, on the edge, mimicking my pose on Auntie K.'s shotgun porch. It felt impossible to move.

There was a question in my head: when it was my time, who would come looking for me?

Bagel, coffee. A walk along the lakeshore. The tactics of delay. Procrastination driven by fear. A man in a hat and coat, hands in his pockets, tapdancing on the boardwalk to his own inner music, I thought, but then I saw the earbuds and understood once more that we were in thrall to our technology. We danced to its secret beat. The tapdancer, noticing me, unleashed upon me all of a sudden an enormous, dazzling smile, a rictus filled with teeth, glittering, dangerous. Then a woman on a bench, middle-aged, white, talking loudly to empty air. This time I didn't need to look for the cord, the small speaker hanging by her scarlet lips, to know that she too was plugged in. She too bestowed upon me the same glittering toothy mouth, this time the teeth stained with red. These smiles were disconcerting. What was this township of the terrifying mouths?

I turned away from human beings to consider the movement of the water. The lake stretched away into misty distance. The surface looked

*still out there, sunbathing in early morning light, but here at the edge
there were small waves. In from the left, in from the right, and now
from straight ahead. Then in reverse, from straight ahead again, then
the right, then the left. A liquid dance pattern for a three-footed water-
sprite, a tripod Lady of the Lake.*

*The candy store might not be open yet. It was still early. I ate my
bagel and sipped my coffee on a bench some way away from the woman
on her cell. It was okay to wait. I didn't want to be standing at the
door like a hungry fool. It was okay to allow the strangeness of the
place, its unfamiliarity, its teeth, to enfold me. A young dark-haired
woman in long dark coat, beret, big shades took up a position on the
boardwalk, clasped her hands together and began to recite, attracting
no attention. Everybody had their own morning rituals and this was
hers. She did not smile at me.*

*She spoke quietly, casually, in a deep throaty voice, the voice of a
French film star. The lines she spoke to everyone and no-one were fragments, broken utterances, unfinished sentences, incomplete thoughts.*
In disaster and lies, *she began, and then paused.* A butterfly
changes history because. I see you in the middle distance coming. Tenderness, harshness, fictions. When I learn the word love
I. Listen the bombs are about to. Music rains down and rescues
us from. *From what? She didn't say. I listened to her string of non
sequiturs, entranced. I understood what she was telling us. There was
no coherence. Nothing led to anything else. There were only jagged moments of half comprehension. Nothing could be known. We were all
incomplete, unfinished. That was life until completed by death. And
none of us could complete our own story because we would no longer
be present. We were all frozen in our railway carriages waiting for
another to finish our tale, to complete us, if anyone cared to do so.
Otherwise, unfinishedness was our inescapable fate.*

*A second stanza was made up of what seemed to be statements of
the obvious.* It is what it is. The rain is like heavy rain. Fear is like

fear, love is like love. *The similes that weren't similes also had a lesson for me. The world was what it was. The tricks of the trade, simile, metaphor, irony, just got in the way and obscured the truth. It was necessary, even imperative, at this moment in history to speak plainly, to rebuild our polluted language from the ground up.* War is war. Horror is horror. A caterpillar becomes a butterfly. The end comes at the end.

When she finished she walked away without any tooth-baring. A little way down the boardwalk she entered a shimmering ray of light and was gone. I understood that this apparition, this sci-fi incarnation of beauty, was not real, she was a phantom I had brought into being to express my need for love. The lake was like the liquid surface of the planet Solaris in Tarkovsky's great film, a planet-sized consciousness that could bring into being the secret fantasies of the circling cosmonauts, could reincarnate their lost loves as ghosts and drive them mad. Maybe this was what I had come so far to learn: Forget Rossmann. Forget everything that rejects you. Find what comes towards you and accepts you. Find love, before its ghosts drive you out of your mind.

I stood across the street from the bright pink storefront for a long time. OK KITCHEN in a rainbow arc of drop-shadowed lettering on the window. A hanging shingle reading CANDY CHOCOLATES ICE-CREAM. A pink awning and a pink door. I watched the security grilles rising at 10 a.m. sharp. Somebody must have parked in the lot behind the store and come in through the back door. A hand flipped over the sign in the glassed doorway. CLOSED became OPEN. I didn't move.

Bright lights illuminated the interior of the store. I saw a cold bin of ice-cream to the right of the main door, a display of chocolate boxes in the window itself, more shelves of candy to the left. And behind the store area an impression of booths where adults and children could eat their delights in peace. People began to go in and out. When they emerged they all wore that terrifying smile. They didn't need to do that to scare me, I thought. I'm afraid already.

I didn't know how to go inside when the store was populated by strangers. I needed to be in there by myself, just myself and the Proprietor. I remained standing on the sidewalk across from the store. In there it was Oklahoma. I didn't know its laws.

The day lengthened into afternoon. The store reached a certain peak of population, then began to empty. Finally I saw the interior lights being turned off and I made my move. As I reached the glass door a hand emerged from the now-shadowed interior to flip the sign from OPEN to CLOSED. Before it could complete the action I knocked on the glass. Then for a long moment nothing; after which the door was opened and I went inside.

When one entered the store one was greeted by a merry tune. I was familiar with it but couldn't remember the name. Standing there just inside the doorway in the dark I said my name. The man in the store, the Proprietor I presumed, did not turn the lights back on.

"You're expected," he said. (His voice sounded different, but then it was a long time since we last met, and we were both older.) I guessed that Auntie K. had noted the missing business card and called to warn him I might be on my way. I wondered if he had a gun behind the counter. I had guns on the brain. Auntie K.'s shotgun had spooked me. You never knew who had a firearm these days. You never knew who might be trigger-happy. I didn't know if I was safe.

"I had to come," I said.

"The way I see it," the man in the shadows commented, "there are three possible reasons for that. There's forgiveness, which is a transaction between human beings. There's absolution, which is a transaction between a man and his god. And then there's revenge."

"It's true," I conceded, "that a part of me wanted to see for myself that you're really here, and then blow your cover, destroy this quaint little slice of happiness, undo what you did when you left your clothes folded on the beach, and force you out of your hidey-hole to be miserable in the real world like the rest of us." This surprising anger burst out of me and caught me unawares. I understood how deeply I had felt his rejection of me. He had mattered to me. I hadn't mattered to him.

"What makes you believe that there is happiness here?" he asked me. "Pinocchio made it to Pleasure Island but what he found there was pain."

"What is this place then," I asked him, "that looks like an idyll but is actually a purgatory?"

"You have left the real world behind," the other replied. "You must have felt the bump in the road at the point of entry."

"Yes," I concurred. "What of it?"

"That was where it happened," he said.

I didn't understand what he was talking about, so I chose to leave it there and return to the earlier subject of my motives. "In the end I decided that exposing you would be an irrelevance. What would be gained? Nothing. So I gave up that idea. Also, absolution is not for me, I know of no god to whom I would beg, father, absolve me." After this substantial statement I felt my heart pounding and wanted to sit down. But the booths were some distance away and there were no chairs or stools in this part of the enterprise.

"So it's forgiveness," he said.

I said nothing.

"That's easy," came the voice from the darkness. "There isn't even anything to forgive."

"All right" was my hesitant reply. "Good, I suppose."

"But that isn't why you came," the other said. "You came to put yourself face to face with the one who troubles you most."

What was he talking about? I asked myself. Also, why did his words arouse such a renewed pounding in my chest—my heart hammering inside me as if it would burst out through my skin, as if my body understood what my mind did not?

He turned on the lights. I staggered and came close to fainting. The man in the candy store—"K. Rossmann, Prop."—was bald and gray-bearded, whereas I had dark hair and was clean shaven. He was also at least thirty years older than me. I placed him in his mid- to late seventies. He had lost weight and, because age can shorten the body, he was perhaps an inch shorter than I was.

But I was looking at myself.

Afterword

The manuscript ends there, quite suddenly, at a major dramatic moment. We cannot know if the author was unable to complete it for artistic reasons, or if he intended to finish but was prevented from doing so by the deepening depression that led him to bring upon himself a premature ending.

The following notes are intended to offer some clarifications about the nature and intent of the work, in particular to examine and illuminate the author's insistence that it be considered a wholly fictional piece.

1. *The Narrator.* The unnamed and quasi-autobiographical character in the story, only marginally likable, disliked by the other characters, and revealed as dishonest, bears little relationship to the author, a gregarious, hard-drinking man with many friends, talkative, full of amusing anecdotes, and as honest as the next man—a courageous person who concealed the darkness growing within him that eventually claimed him. (The theme of depression in *Oklahoma* clearly reveals to the reader what the author worked hard to conceal.)

2. *Uncle and Auntie K.* Although there are faint echoes of well-known American literary personalities in the portrayal of

both these figures, it is plain that they are not intended to be portraits of actually existing individuals but are figments of the author's fancy. In other words, what we are given is invention masquerading as memoir, an appropriate choice for a tale in which truth and lies are not without importance.

3. *Possibly Related Fragment No. 1.* Certain passages have been discovered among the author's papers that may have been drafts or sketches for inclusion in this story. One such fragment describes the meeting of a father with his long-lost son, and the consequent arrival of both characters at a place of joy—in short, that *rara avis* in M.A.'s work, a happy ending. He imagines them in a rowboat out on a long lake not unlike the lake on whose shore the town of O. is said to stand, fishing, catching nothing, but talking incessantly. One may speculate that this was an earlier version of the meeting between the narrator's younger and older selves in the candy store.

4. *Possibly Related Fragment No. 2.* A fantastical account of a journey into the future by a narrator (once again, a writer) eager to know what life has in store for him. Again, an encounter with an older (wiser?) male figure. The older man does not disclose what must not be known by those to whom it has not yet happened, but encourages the narrator not to give up, telling him that while his work might be presently out of favor, the wheel would turn, and his situation would improve. "There is fashion in literature as in all things," the older man says, "and finally you may become fashionable again, a development which, like any true artist, you should despise." (The poor reception of M.A.'s later work no doubt contributed to his decision to end his life.)

5. *Regarding the Town of O.* The reader's attention is drawn to the "bump in the road" as the narrator approaches the town at night. It should be understood that this point marks a radical departure in the text, which leaves behind any pretense of naturalism and transforms into full-fledged fantasy. We must assume that the town does not exist, and nor do its inhabitants. Neither does the candy store or its proprietor. We are in a ghost town, one that may be compared to the town of Comala in *Pedro Páramo* by the great Mexican writer Juan Rulfo or other haunted locations. The author indicates in his manuscript that the entire passage should be set in italics to make this departure clear, and this has been done. The "town of O." is to be thought of as an illusion or a delusion, created by necessity or hope. Or despair.

6. *Possibly Related Fragment No. 3.* A sheet of paper on which appeared the following lines of unattributed dialogue. One may speculate that this was intended to be a conversation between the narrator's two ghost selves, younger and older, and may have been discarded or, possibly, preserved for later inclusion:

"How must a man face the last days of his life? Serenely, or with rage?"

"On Mondays, Wednesdays and Fridays I am furious, with life, with the world and what's going on in it, about the passing of friends, the weaknesses of the body, the entire human race, and the approach of the end of the railway line. On Tuesdays, Thursdays and Saturdays I am perfectly peaceful and choose, often, to listen to Doris Day singing *Que Sera Sera*. On Sundays I am confused and resort to drink, preferably either a Manhattan cocktail on the rocks or an Old Fashioned, made with bourbon rather than rye."

It must be added that on account of the premature ending of the author's life, his older self never came into being, and therefore could not have met his younger self even in a ghost story. Alas, perhaps this passage was excluded from the text because the author already knew he would never make old bones.

7. *Mamouli Ajeeb.* Curiously, in his mother tongue, *ajeeb* means unusual or strange, while *mamouli* translates as ordinary or commonplace. So he was Mr. Ordinary Strange. Mr. Humdrum Peculiar. Mr. Everyday Weird. His choice not to share this oxymoronic name with his readers, to conceal it behind the anonymity of initials, indicates, one may suppose, a degree of embarrassment about it. But he was always drawn both to the strange business of life on earth and also its ordinary dailiness. So one could truthfully say he lived up to his name.

He must remain, sadly, a man who disappeared too young, who left his clothes folded neatly on a beach and walked into the water. An unfinished man, hoping for happiness but unable to reach it, forever frozen in time before the train arrived at its destination. A man searching for, but never finding, his Oklahoma.

The Old Man
in the Piazza

E very day, at about four o'clock in the afternoon, when the sun's heat has begun to diminish, the old man comes into the piazza. He walks slowly, shuffling his feet, which are encased in dusty brown loafers. He is wearing, most days, a dark blue jacket buttoned all the way up to the neck and navy pants that fasten with a drawstring at the waist. His hair is white and there is a beret on his head. He goes to the only café in the piazza, the Café of the Fountain, and sits on a wooden chair at a wooden table and orders a small, strong coffee. At six P.M. he orders a small beer and a sandwich. At eight P.M. he rises, wipes his lips, and shuffles away, presumably to go home. We do not need to know where he lives. Everything of any significance in his life has happened, and will happen, right here in this little piazza.

He takes his seat. He is the audience, an audience of one. The show is about to begin.

It is a piazza into which seven narrow roads debouch, one at each corner and one each at the midpoint of three of the piazza's four sides; only the side with the church is uninterrupted by a cobbled street. It should be a quiet place, a sleepy provincial square, but it is not. All around the piazza you can hear the loud sounds of people quarreling, six days a week. On most of these days there are more people in the piazza than live in the locality.

It's as if people come here, to this peaceful little square in this peaceful little town, to get into fights. They drive fifteen kilometers from the big city to express their bad moods. They raise their voices, they pound their right fists into the palms of their left hands, they stamp their feet (doesn't matter which foot— both are stamped equally). If they sit astride motorcycles they sound their horns in frustration or to silence their adversaries. If they are arguing while seated in adjacent motorcars with the windows down, they toot like the motorcyclists but they also rev their engines and, when irritated beyond the point of their endurance, they roll their windows up.

There is no end to their disagreements. They quarrel about the likelihood of hurricanes, about the scandal of bribery behind the contentious award of the Summer Olympic Games to a city in the Arctic Circle, about the impossibility of love and the futility of politics and the secret illegal affections of eminent Catholic priests. They dispute the flatness of the earth and the efficacy of the measles, mumps, and rubella vaccine. They disagree about the best flavors of ice cream, and have strong and irreconcilable opinions concerning the beauty of film actresses. If they have read novels by writers who are also, or were at one time, married couples, then they vehemently take the side of one author or the other and will not be persuaded to change their minds. It appears there is nothing that unites our people except their love of the quarrel itself, the quarrel understood as a public art form, as the defining heart of our culture. The noise is terrible, grows louder as the days darken into evenings, and continues late into the nights. By midnight the populace has had a fair amount to drink, and that makes their discussions even more heated. It is not unknown for punches to be thrown.

The old man sits at the Café of the Fountain and listens.

However, because he leaves at eight P.M., he avoids the later phase of the day, when alcohol has had its effect and fists start flying.

Sundays are quiet. On Sunday everyone stays home and eats, or goes to church, begs for forgiveness, then returns home and eats.

On Sundays the old man does not come to the piazza.

This is how it has been in the square ever since the end of the so-called time of the "yes." That dark age began forty years or so ago, a time when for a period of half a decade it was made illegal to argue. We all were obliged to agree, at all times. Whatever proposition was made, no matter how risible—the transubstantiation of bread and wine into flesh and blood, the nocturnal metamorphosis of the immigrant population into drooling sex monsters, the benefits of raising the taxes paid by the poor, the transmigration of souls, or the necessity of war—it was forbidden to debunk it, even though immigrants ran the best bakery in the town and our favorite wine store also, and even though most of us are poor, and none of us remembers any earlier lives as tortoises, or foreigners, or eels, and only a small minority of us are warlike by nature. It was necessary at all times to assent.

Even our language—the language in which such great poetry has been written!—was altered. She was no longer permitted the word "no." There was only "yes" and variations on "yes": "of course," "certainly," "for sure," "absolutely," "totally," "no question about it," and "agreed." When someone, some rash radical, remembered the word "no," it felt worse than shocking, worse than sinful. It felt archaic. A broken word from an ancient ruined time, like the remnant of a temple built to honor a god in whom nobody believed any longer, in whom nobody had believed for thousands of years. The god of "no."

What a laughable god that must have been! At any rate, that was how it felt to many of us.

Our language, however, sulked. She came to sit by herself in a corner of the piazza and often shook her head, mournfully. She became pedestrian. She informed us that she was unwilling for the moment to fly or soar, or even to travel by train or bicycle or bus. She said she felt leaden-footed and preferred to sit quietly and contemplate the things languages contemplate when they are by themselves and feel maltreated. If she needed to move, she told us, she would plod.

Her attitude was forbidding. She wore tight clothing that must have constrained her movements, and uncomfortable shoes. We did not approach.

Our language did not join the old man at his table in the Café of the Fountain. She sat alone in her corner. They did not speak.

In the time of the universal "yes," the piazza was quiet. You could hear the songbirds, the larks, whose numbers had not yet been decimated by weekend shooting parties. In the center of the piazza there is a small fountain—the fountain, obviously, from which the café takes its name—and back in the old days the silence allowed you to listen to the peacefulness of the water and soothe your aching heart. The old man was younger then, and his heart ached a lot, thanks to the repeated rejections of its sincerely offered emotions by young women with hair of different colors.

Even in those days when the word "no" was forbidden, the women were able to inform him that his feelings for them were not requited. "You are so kind," the women with variously colored hair said, "but on that evening we are having our yellow (or brown, or red, or black) hair done." What about another evening, then, he dared to ask, and they replied, "We are deeply moved by your generosity, but we will be having our black (or red, or brown, or yellow) hair done every evening for the foreseeable future, except on Sundays, when we will stay home and eat, or, in some cases, some of us will first go to church and ask for forgiveness, and then go home and eat."

After a while the old man, who was younger then, stopped asking. He continued to come and sit, most afternoons, on his upright wooden chair at the Café of the Fountain and listen to the water flowing. He grew old before his time, distressed, like faux-antique furniture, by his discovery that even the time of "yes" contained an unspoken "no." His hair grew white and he sat on his wooden chair and watched the world going by.

Five years passed. In the end it was our language herself who rebelled against the "yes." She got up from the corner of the piazza where she had been meditating silently for half a decade and let out a long, piercing shriek that drove into our ears like a stiletto. It traveled everywhere as fast as lightning travels. It contained no words. However, no sooner had it been uttered than all our words were unleashed. Words simply burst out of people and would not be held back. People felt great globs of vocabulary rising up in their throats and pushing against their teeth. The more cautious among us pressed our lips tightly together to stop the words from getting out, but the insistence of the word torrents forced our mouths to burst open and out they came, like children released from single-sex boarding schools at the end of a long, dour semester. The words tumbled pell-mell into the piazza like girls and boys in search of happy reunions. It was a sight to see.

These were rough words, these first utterances—"Crap!" for example, or "Get lost!" or even the excessively emphatic "Go fuck yourself!"—and this crudeness was perhaps regrettable, but these workmanlike, hard-edged words were certainly effective, that has to be said, they were like bludgeons or explosives, and as they hammered down around us they swiftly brought the reign of the "yes" to an unsavory conclusion. The "yes" and its fellow travelers (the aforementioned "of course," "certainly," "for sure," "absolutely," "totally," "no question about it," and "agreed") were hung up on meat hooks in the piazza, and that was an end to that.

That's when the age of argumentation began. "But!" "Rubbish!" "Tripe!" "Nonsense!" "Bullshit!" "Liar!" "Idiot!" "Don't you dare!" "You must be crazy!" "That is such ignorant bigoted shit!" "Just go away! Nobody wants to listen to you!" Who would have guessed that these unlovely words would take center stage in that moment—these, and not our language's beautiful and justly celebrated poetry, to which we previously referred? Odes and sonnets, lyric and epic poetry stood ignored, striking attitudes and gesticulating impotently.

Our language remained in her corner of the piazza, watching, but she had cast off her corset and her disfiguring clogs, and her long hair and her long skirt flowed loosely around her. The skirt came all the way down to the ground, so we could not see her shoes, although we sensed that she was tapping her feet to the beat of some private music.

The old man also felt the pressure of words struggling to emerge from within him. He tried to contain them, for he was not sure what they might be or do or make possible or engender or destroy, but out they came, like vomit, words he hardly recognized as his own pushing through his lips, angry, contemptuous, blaming. Fortunately everyone else was experiencing his or her own version of the same phenomenon, so nobody was paying attention, and he himself soon forgot what those first words had been, and settled back into his wooden chair to observe the life of the piazza as it now was.

Once the "yes" time had ended, and the quarrels had started up, they drowned out the songs of the larks and the soothing plash of the fountain, which cared nothing for changes in society and kept itself busy, in its insouciant way, with its fountaining. The old man—the man made old by sadness—no longer asked women questions of the heart, questions to which he already knew the answers, which could now be stated plainly without beatings about the bush or pretenses about appointments at the hair salon.

At first, for a little while, he missed the silence of the five "yes" years. There had been something heartening about being in a constant state of affirmation, eschewing negativity, accentuating the positive. There had been something—what was the word?—something *modest* about declining to be judgmental, no matter how great the temptation. And something infinitely relaxing about being excused from a life of objection, of critique, even of protest. It had required a certain remodeling of the brain, that was true. He had had to restrain his natural impulse toward dissent, toward sentences that began "But on the other hand . . ." or "But isn't it true that . . ." or "How can you possibly . . ." Save your breath—that was the instruction of the age. Keep your unattractive words to yourself. For a time he found a measure of comfort in accepting the "yes." In saying the unutterable "no" to "no."

All this happened quite a long time ago. Today, the old man— old now in years as well as sadness—still sits at the Café of the Fountain, but he is calm, no longer afraid of the rush of forgotten words from his mouth. He watches our disputatious citizenry as one might watch a soap opera on television, or a three-ring circus, or a professional football game.

Our language is still there, in the corner of the piazza farthest

from the old man's chair. These days she often has companions, and these companions are invariably much younger than
her, young men of a physical beauty that is almost obscene.
These Byronic creatures plainly worship her, and perhaps, the
old man thinks, she even allows them to ravish her in private,
on those occasions when she leaves the piazza for a while. The
companions change all the time. It is possible that our language
is promiscuous. It is possible that her morals are exceedingly
loose. When this thought comes to the old man it is as if a devil
were whispering in his ear. But the thought doesn't appear to
have occurred to anyone else, or if the devil has whispered it
into other ears, the owners of those ears think nothing of it and
react with a dismissive shrug. Let her be whatever she wants!
Let her do as she pleases! That is the general attitude nowadays.
The old man sees that he is in a minority, and holds his tongue.

In all these years they have never exchanged even the most
perfunctory of greetings, the old man and our language. There
they sit, across the piazza from each other, he on his wooden
chair and she on a little cushioned stool that was a gift from one
of the obscenely attractive young men, who fell into disfavor
with her not long afterward, and was erased from her consciousness. Nothing of him remains except this stool. Recently,
however, it seemed to the old man that she, our language,
might have nodded in his direction once or twice. But that may
have been a trick of the light.

The architectural elegance of the piazza cannot be denied. The
Baroque façade of the old church is splendid, and many of the
other buildings on the piazza—buildings of mixed use, with
little stores at street level and apartments above—are handsome
structures made of golden stone, with burgundy shutters at the

windows. They are mostly old, the golden houses, and in some cases are not in the best state of repair, but there they stand, solid, attractive, with red barrel-tiled roofs, giving the piazza an air of faded grandeur, like an impoverished nobleman who has squandered the family fortune. To tell the truth, the piazza looks as if it belongs in a loftier environment than this little town. It feels as if it has been imported wholesale from one of our beautiful cities, perhaps even our capital city, just fifteen kilometers away.

Facing the church across the piazza, on either side of the little cobbled lane that feeds into the piazza over there, are two structures that, if we were in Italy, we would call loggias—covered outdoor galleries with delicate pillarwork and arches—and in these loggias the municipality has housed marble statues that imitate far more famous statues elsewhere, that copy those other, absent statues to the extent that their makers' skills permitted. We enjoy these mimic figures as profoundly as if they were the real thing. In the absence of genius, imitation is an acceptable substitute. Through these copies we pay homage to the masterpieces that we will never see. Some of us go so far as to assert that the originals do not exist and never did exist, so that these alleged replicas are in fact the great works themselves, and should be paid the respect due to their greatness. This is one of the popular subjects debated daily in the piazza. The question remains unresolved.

Now that he has stopped missing the peace and quiet of the "yes" years, the old man has actually begun to enjoy the quarrelsomeness of his fellow citizens. In his old age he has unexpectedly attained a kind of serenity. The disputatious instincts of his youth have been replaced by a spirit of acceptance, coupled with an amused enjoyment of his fellow citizens' lack of a similar calm. The vanity of certainty, which gives each finger-wagging debater in the piazza his or her reason for her or his insistence on that or this dispute, strikes the old man as the very *fons et origo* of comedy. As does the fervor with which many people in the piazza hold opinions that are demonstrably untrue: The sun, madam, does not rise in the west, however vehemently you may argue that it does, and, sir, the moon is not made of Gorgonzola cheese, and to deny that is not to agree with your opponent, who describes it as an elaborate papier-mâché fake, nailed to the sky to make us believe that we live in a three-dimensional universe of stars, planets, and satellites rather than upon a dish with a great lid over it, a lid like an inverted colander, with many holes through which, at night, shines the bright thing we are deceived into calling starlight. The piazza is full of passionate nonsense such as this, and the old man thinks, *Oh, let them go on, there's no harm in it, after all.*

This, too, is a subject of many spirited discussions: Are mistaken notions harmful to the brain, to the community, to the health of the body politic, or are they simply errors to be tolerated as the product of simple minds? The fact that all those involved in discussing this question have heads full of tosh and piffle does not make for productive debates. The old man has the impression that at the end of each day people go home, drunk on wine and niggles, knowing less than they knew in the morning. And yet, he tells himself, the tongue set free is an excellent thing. Our language, sitting on her cushioned stool in the far corner of the piazza with the divine young men at her feet, is clearly happier than she was in the subservient, acquiescent days of the "yes."

A day comes, however, when a certain argumentative twosome descends upon the old man seated on his wooden chair;

and the two of them—it turns out they are husband and wife, happily married for thirty years—shout at him in unison, "We can't stand it! You decide for us!" Their disagreement, as it happens, is a small thing. Where should they go for their summer vacation? To the sun-kissed island of A., which isn't very far away, or the distant country of B., which would be a far more adventurous choice but less restful. "We just can't seem to agree," they chorus. "So we'll do whatever you say."

"Very well," he says, and with those two words he abandons the neutrality of a lifetime, and the little wooden chair upon which he has spent half a lifetime being no more than a contented observer of the passing cavalcade is transformed—just like that!—into a judgment seat. "Very well," he repeats. "In these times of strife and stress, I recommend a good rest. Go and sunbathe on the sun-kissed island of A."

The husband and wife stand very still. Then they turn to look at each other. "Nonsense!" they cry with one voice. "It's a life of adventure for us!" And off they go to that distant country of B. Some weeks later they return and thank the old man for his judgment. They have seen enormous crocodiles, which carry off several children a year and munch on them in the swamps, and giraffes that have grown to record heights, and giant axolotls. They have heard languages they'd never heard before and witnessed the most vivid of spectacles, an avalanche that buried an entire village and a military coup that littered the streets with corpses. For a few days while on safari they were both transformed into hippopotamuses, but that soon wore off and they were told that they should have read the instructions to travelers and had the inoculation against the local mosquitoes, insects notorious for spreading numerous virulent strains of metamorphism, but they said, "Never mind, it was quite an experience, so worth it! So unique! And rolling in mud—we could

get used to that!" In sum, they have had the holiday of a lifetime.

"Thank you, thank you," they cry, and their gratitude is genuine. The old man replies mildly that he had proposed they go
elsewhere for a quiet time, and they laugh prettily. "But that's
how we fly!" they exclaim. "Always! We're contrary! We ask
people what they think and then we do the opposite thing. Call
us perverse! But it has worked for us, and given us thirty years
of happy married life."

Word spreads across the piazza that the old man sitting on
the wooden chair at the Café of the Fountain is a judge with the
wisdom of Solomon. A crowd rushes across the square to ask
him to judge them too. The old man has never been in such
demand at any point in a long uneventful life. It is, he concedes,
flattering. He has read about cultures far away on the other side
of the world where the elderly are granted the authority of
their years, where age is believed to be the consequence of a life
spent accumulating experience, and wisdom deriving from experience, and where the final act of life is the one in which even
the least of us are granted the respect that their youth denied
them, so they can end their days feeling a little like kings. In his
own culture the old are often considered irrelevant and discarded. This crowd of supplicants is as unexpected as it is grati-
fying. He gives in to its demands.

He asks his petitioners to form an orderly line, and after that,
every afternoon between four and six P.M., when the heat of the
day has passed, he hands down judgments, declaring in tones of
growing authority that no, the earth is not flat, and no, most
immigrants are not sex monsters any more than you or I, and
yes, one hundred percent, God exists, and so do heaven and
hell.

Word spreads farther. The nearby city hears that this little piazza in this little town contains a sage of such profundity that he can resolve all your disagreements on the spot. The crowd in the piazza grows larger every day. The police are needed to maintain order. There are television cameras. The old man extends his hours until seven P.M. so that he can adjudicate more disputes every day (except Sunday). After seven he adjourns his court and refuses to answer any more questions, insisting on being allowed to enjoy a quiet hour by himself, with his beer and his sandwich. And promptly at eight he leaves the Café of the Fountain and shuffles off to who knows where.

It is rumored that leading members of the government and the opposition are discussing a visit to the old man, to see if he can resolve their differences. However, it is hard for these persons, both on the left and on the right, to accept that they may be told they are wrong. The visit of the politicians remains theoretical. It does not happen.

The old man in the piazza is experiencing something utterly alien to him: renown. Among the growing group of children and adults sitting at his feet, surrounding his little wooden chair, he notices some familiar faces, and identifies them as belonging to some of the golden young men who until recently were our language's most ardent disciples. Our language, suddenly left almost alone in her corner of the square while her acolytes rush over to the Café of the Fountain, is not pleased by this development. She warns the two disciples who have remained loyal to her that this will not end well. They listen respectfully, but her pronouncement comes across as envy. Times have changed. Our people care less for our beautiful and complex language than for the great, crude questions of what is correct and what incorrect. We have ceased to be the poetry lovers we once were, the aficionados of ambiguity and devotees of doubt, and we have become bar-room moralists. Does the thumb point upward? Does it turn down? The old man in the piazza is our arbiter, and his thumbs have become matters of national interest. We are all now gladiators in the Colosseum of the Thumb.

Our language is uninterested in the verdicts of the old man's thumbs. She cares only for words of many-layered beauty, for fineness of expression, for the subtlety of what is spoken and the resonance of what is better left unspoken, for the meanings between the words, and the illumination of those meanings that only her greatest disciples can provide. She finds the old man's cheap dictums disgusting, and even more disgraceful is his growing pleasure in being accepted as the judge of what is right and what is wrong, what is so and what is not so. He was the one who used to laugh at the vanity of certainty, the obstinacies of the foolish, and the emphatic assertions of the wrongheaded. Now he is the dispenser of nuance-free certitudes, and becomes more vain with every passing day.

Frontiers have long been a vexatious subject around here. In our recent history the drawing of borderlines through our territory by ignoramuses from elsewhere has caused much heartache and loss of life. In our minds the words "borderline" and "ignoramus" are inextricably connected. On those rare occasions when we have tried to cross the frontier at one of the few border checkpoints that now exist upon that blood-soaked frontier, either we have been rebuffed or, if allowed to pass, we have been sold counterfeit currency by hawkers on the far side, who knew we would be unable to distinguish the fake currency from the real thing. In our minds the words "land border" and "fake currency" are inextricably connected.

There are, of course, many frontiers other than those that separate us from our neighbors and make them our enemies.

There is the invisible frontier between what we, as individuals or as a group, deem acceptable and what lies beyond that unseen line, in the realm of the unacceptable. That frontier is a place of dangerous land mines, and most of us don't like to go anywhere near it. There is also the invisible frontier between action and observation. There are those who do, and then there are those who see them do it. The audience sits over here; the stage is over there. The fourth wall is a powerful force.

The old man in the piazza has enjoyed his visits to the theater, but it has never occurred to him to climb up onto the stage, and in those avant-garde moments when actors have descended into the audience he has felt deliciously shocked in an old-fashioned way. Long ago when he was young he saw a show in which an actor, pretending to be an audience member, sat in the front row throughout the first act. In the intermission a telephone onstage began to ring, and finally the actor lost patience and went up onto the stage to answer it. (It was his wife.) While he was onstage, on the phone, the second act began, and he was trapped in the play. The old man found this to be a delightful conceit. Utterly implausible, but a joy to watch. It never occurred to him that one day he would be the person answering the phone during the intermission. He has never imagined that he would become the audience member trapped in the play.

But now that he has crossed that border, he has taken to his new role with relish. He is not, however, an adversary of frontiers per se. On the contrary, he has begun to see it as his duty to define the new zones of propriety, winnowing out unacceptable attitudes and corralling them under the heading of Forbidden Things, while those whose attitudes are permissible remain here, among us, in the freedom of our undoubtedly free country. No longer willing simply to answer yes-or-no questions, he seeks to establish which of the disputing parties is the more virtuous, and to hand the palm of his judgment to those who have led better lives. It is even suspected that on many occasions he judges in favor of a plaintiff who is undeniably in the wrong because his rival has been shown to have led a less wholesome existence. In short, he is making himself a judge not only of rightness but of rectitude. This worries some of us, but we are unwilling to express our worries, because of the old man's popularity.

Our language, languishing in her corner, is perturbed. She tries to argue that the old man may be returning us to a new version of the time of the "yes," one in which even more words than simple expressions of negation may be placed off-limits, the words deemed to express Forbidden Things. That's frontier justice, she warns. Stay away.

She also has worries, she reveals, about herself. For as long as we have known her she has been sprightly, energetic, vivid, the very best of languages, but she has to admit that of late she has begun to feel unhealthy. On some days she is feverish; on others there are aches and pains. She hopes it isn't anything serious. It may just be a consequence of her advancing years, for while she may look youthful and beautiful—she thanks us for our compliments on her appearance! she is always grateful for our approval!—she is, in fact, a very old language, one of the oldest and richest, even though she prefers not to flaunt her wealth, requires no throne to sit upon, and is content with her simple cushioned stool. But she is our language, after all, and so she feels it is her duty to inform us of her condition. She fears she may be decaying. It's even possible—though it's hard for her to admit this, even to herself—that she may die.

Nobody's listening.

Nobody cares.

And finally she rises to her feet, as she has risen just once before, and shrieks.

It is a shriek of an even higher pitch than the earlier one. It rises and rises until it passes beyond the capacity of human ears to hear it. At that point all the windows in the houses looking onto the piazza shatter and a rain of glass falls and there are many injuries in the crowded square, injuries that cause other, reciprocal shrieks. These shrieks are of a lower order than the shriek of anguish uttered by our language, and they don't break anything.

We see our language standing upright and open-mouthed but we cannot hear the shriek, which has reached such an intensity that it begins to crack the red barrel tiles on the roofs and even the stone from which the buildings are made. One of the statues in one of the loggias, an elaborate copy of the one in a Vatican museum depicting the Trojan priest Laocoön wreathed in angry serpents, explodes into a hundred thousand fragments.

Do the golden buildings of mixed use fall? Do the loggias collapse entirely? Is the piazza demolished? No, that doesn't happen. In spite of our many failings, we are not creatures of melodrama. We prefer drama, pure and simple.

So, the piazza stands. But the cracks are there. We can all see them. The buildings are cracked from roof to street. The fallen tiles, the burgundy shutters hanging askew. That is the truth. The piazza is broken, and so, perhaps, are we.

In the meanwhile, she's still standing there, our language, her mouth wide open, screaming her silent scream. And over at the Café of the Fountain, the old man feels something happening to his words. They are drying up. His words are scrambling farther and farther back in his mouth and diving down his throat, to be dissolved by various digestive fluids. There is a crowd waiting to hear what he has to say, but he is lost for words.

The people thronging the piazza are displeased. They want what they came for—to be judged—and they open their mouths wide to protest the judge's failure to deliver his verdicts. But there are no words to protest with. They look over at the corner that our language has occupied for so long, our language, whom they have so totally ignored of late, and they see her gather up her skirts and walk out of the piazza, forever leaving behind the corner she made her own for more years than anyone can recall. She holds her head high, our language, and then she is gone. And after her departure nobody in the piazza can talk. The people make sounds, but the sounds are shapeless, devoid of meaning. The old man rises helplessly from his wooden chair with his beer in one hand and his sandwich in the other. He stretches out his arms to the people, as if he's offering them the sandwich and the beer. They turn their backs on him and walk away. He has become once again what he always was: nothing more than an insignificant old man.

It is unclear what we must do now. What will become of us? We are at a loss to know how things will proceed.

Our words fail us.

Credits

The following stories were originally published in *The New Yorker*: "In the South" (May 11, 2009) and "The Old Man in the Piazza" (November 16, 2020).